"The Piper Pays"

"The Piper Pays"

TABLE
OF
CONTENTS

INTRO – PAGES 1-3
PART I
PRELUDE TO TERROR

PART IV
THE RETIREMENT

PART V
"DOIN' TIME"

PART VI
TRIAL BEGINS

PART VII
THE DEFENSE

PART VIII
TRIAL #2

INTRODUCTION

This story begins on Thursday, July 27th, 1972, and continues today, 35 years later. Will it ever end? For some, maybe, for others, no!

Although a true story, sometimes it may sound like fiction. The unbelievable happenings will open your eyes to what our legal system is all about.

This tale is based on actual events, which occurred in the "Kidnap for Ransom" of the beautiful socialite, Virginia Piper, wife of Harry C. Piper Jr., CEO, and President of Piper/Jaffray/Hopwood, Minnesota's largest investment firm.

This crime would change the lives of hundreds of individuals, and would directly or indirectly cause the death of at least seven. There are those who would disappear, never to be heard from again. There are many who would spend most of their lives in jails and prisons. Lives would be ruined, families torn apart, never to be re-united.

This story will show what depths our FBI and its leaders are willing to sink to in order to claim that they have solved a crime. It will show on numerous occasions, that in reality, the FBI was/is more interested in "publicity," to assure the American people will focus on the agency with "favor" rather than what the true picture is.

Two individuals, Donald Floyd Larson and his lifelong friend, Kenny Callahan will go through an un-ending "living hell," trying to prove their innocence of the crime for which they were "framed." They would become famous-infamous for this "crime of the century." It is up to the reader to decide which.

This "true" tale is dedicated to all of those who have been arrested, tried and or convicted of crimes they did not commit. Lord knows, there are plenty! It's estimated that throughout the "good ole" USA, of those convicted, there are about 30 % who are wrongfully incarcerated! Our prison system is over-flowing, the cost of confinement has risen dramatically, and our taxpayers are "royally getting screwed!" Yet, nobody is getting kissed, and no one seems to care!

People escaping tyranny, wrongful imprisonment and dictatorship, founded our nation! Now, we, the descendants of those very same people, are doing the same things our "fathers" escaped from! It must really be true, "The apple never falls far from the tree!"

Seamus "D" McGee

PART I

PRELUDE

TO TERROR

I
CALM BEFORE THE STORM

It is a beautiful, warm morning, in the small town of Orono Minnesota, a suburb of Minneapolis. Orono has the distinction, and honor of being one of the wealthiest towns in the state. Doctors, Lawyers, Business Executives, and retirees make up the largely affluent population. Homes will cost up to and over a million dollars. (A million dollar house was considered high in the year of 1972. Houses in other communities were selling for less than fifty thousand.)

Orono is a quiet town, where crime is extremely rare. About the only excitement were a few firecrackers going off on the 4th of July, or a rumor of someone's wife or husband thought to be cheating. No one was ready for what was about to occur on the morning of July 27th, 1972. This date would alter the lives of hundreds of people. It will remain etched in the minds of everyone involved, and in the minds of many who were not involved. This date will show no mercy to anyone. It will bring fortune to some, death to others, and pain, dishonor, and anguish to still more. This date will pile shame upon what was believed to be one of our countries biggest protectors, the FBI. Not only will the FBI lie, and withhold evidence, they will get caught red-handed manufacturing a fingerprint, in order to "frame two innocent individuals!"

Thirty five years later, they will still be trying to cover up evidence. Mysteriously, thousands of pages of evidence will disappear from their custody. The Piper sons, looking into the abduction of their mother, would be forced to get a Judge's order to force the FBI to release information. The papers they received were not legible. They had been "blacked out!"

Virginia Piper, beautiful wife of Harry Piper Jr. is working in her garden, located near the pool of their prestigious home. The garden, like the pool, like Mrs. Piper, is in perfect condition. Everything is where it is supposed to be. The lawn is well manicured.

The rakes, shovels and mowers are as they are supposed to be. Nothing is out of place.

Virginia's mind marvels at the beauty of the comfortable July weather, yet she knows that in a couple of months, the flowers will disappear, the green from the leaves will be gone, and the trees will turn to browns, yellows and gold. The Minnesota chill will set in shortly thereafter, and snow will start to fall.

Although Mrs. Piper enjoys working in her garden, she also likes cavorting in the snow, sledding, skiing and snow-mobiling. The pastimes winter shall bring are very important in her life also, and are cause for her anticipation.

Harry C. Piper sits behind his antique desk at his office. His mind is on the daily duties, which he must perform as CEO, President and Chief Stock-holder of his wealthy investment firm. Sometimes he wonders if it is all worth it, but then, he will snap back to reality and think, "Good God, it is worth it!" Without his company, he would be lost, unable to live the lifestyle he and his wife so much enjoy. They have the best of everything. They travel at will, and buy at will. He then smiles, as he thinks of his beautiful, platinum haired wife. His thoughts are interrupted as his phone starts ringing.

II
THE ABDUCTION

Inside the Piper home, two maids laze over their morning duties, laughter mixed with their idle banter. Both are originally from Germany, and share a very close relationship with each other. There is a large beef roast slowly cooking to perfection in the oven. Everything seems to be going as usual, calm, quiet and every day. Their tranquility will soon turn to horror!

Approaching the house, are two masked men, furtively nearing the unlocked kitchen door. They rush inside, and the surprised maids scream in fear, then, as they see the pistols, freeze in terror. One of the individuals, in a grating, gruff voice, demanded to know where Mr. Piper is. The two maids answer in unison.

"He's at work!"

The surly man, glancing at his partner said, "That fucking Chino gave us the wrong information again."

The other man answered, "This time, the son of a bitch is gonna get his ass kicked!"

Suddenly, one of the intruders asked where Mrs. Piper was.

One of the maids answered in a quavering voice, "She's working in her garden."

"Then go get her ya dumb broad!" The surly man said.

The scared maid immediately ran from the kitchen, out the back door, and confronted Mrs. Piper. With stuttering sounds, she told her that someone in the kitchen wanted to see her.

Perplexed by the behavior of the maid, Mrs. Piper placed the rake she was using in its proper place, and followed the maid back inside.

When the 45-year-old Mrs. Piper entered the kitchen, she was immediately sorry that she had done so. In fact, she was so surprised she could not speak! She quickly complied when she was ordered to put her hands behind her back. She was then immediately handcuffed!

Terror in her eyes, she watched as the maids were placed in chairs, and then securely tied to them. Next, a pillowcase was roughly placed over her head, and she was forced to walk outside, forced into the back seat of an automobile, and told to lie down.

(This automobile would later be identified as one that was stolen from Larson Chevrolet, located in Minneapolis approximately a week earlier. It was a green 1972 Chevrolet Monte Carlo.)

The car slowly left the area with the frightened Mrs. Piper lying on the back seat, face down. She was trembling and bewildered, not knowing what they were going to do with her.

Mrs. Piper had no inclination, that what was happening to her would set off one of the largest investigations in U.S. history. It would ignite a chain of events, which would cause the deaths of many people, while other individuals would simply disappear.

Over two hundred and fifty FBI Agents and various state, and local law enforcement agencies would embark on a five-year effort to solve the crime. Not since the "Ma Barker/Karpis" kidnapping of St. Paul banker Edward Bremmer, would so many agents be used. This investigation would last until there were but two days remaining in regards to the "statute of limitations." Finally, with smiles on their faces, agents would make an arrest.

Pete Neuman, head of the investigation would say, "No two bit punks are gonna make fools out of the FBI!"

To make these words come true, he and his army of followers would use every underhanded tactic, trick, ruse, illegal or not to have Donald Floyd Larson and Kenny Callahan charged as the perpetrators of the "Virginia Piper" abduction. To this day, the FBI carries the stain, which will forever remain on their reputation. Their shoddy work, illegal transactions, including the manufacture of evidence, can never be erased.

They would be directly at fault in the deaths of at least six people. They would make deals with "Prison," and "Jailhouse Snitches," so corrupt they would sell out their own mothers for the price of a bottle of cheap whiskey!

After they manufactured a fingerprint, they testified that they did no such thing, even though one of their own teachers, "Leon MacDonell," would testify that they indeed did manufacture it. The FBI even denied knowing the man, and denied having an office in Corning New York where he taught! Forensic and fingerprint expert MacDonell would later testify in Federal court, making liars of the FBI.

There was irrefutable evidence that the FBI misused their authority and ignored blatant evidence, which could have solved the crime.

After Mrs. Piper was placed in the back seat of the Monte Carlo, her memory, though usually sharp as could be, suddenly and inexplicably began wavering.

She told various renditions as to what route was taken to where she would be held.

In one remembrance, she states that from her home in Orono, the kidnappers traveled north out of Minneapolis on highway 35, towards Duluth.

She said they continued north to Carlton Minnesota, approximately 125 miles. She stated they then proceeded to Jay Cook State Park where she was chained to a tree in a remote area.

In another remembrance of her journey, she would say that she was taken on a route that took her into the state of Wisconsin. She said that just before arriving at Jay Cook Park, the car slowed and proceeded cautiously over a double set of railroad tracks. Supposedly, these tracks were located in Sandstone Minnesota, and a short distance from the Park. It is very important as to what route was actually taken. If indeed, the kidnappers entered into Wisconsin, the crime would be a Federal Case. If they did not enter Wisconsin, it would remain a Minnesota case. It is possible to enter Jay Cook Park from both states.

In one of Mrs. Piper's statements, the route she gives would actually put them approximately 200 feet inside of the state of Wisconsin. This is the route the FBI needed to enable them to take charge of the investigation and the criminal prosecution. This is the route they used in the re-enactment of the crime. They would place a pillowcase over the head of Mrs. Piper, and then try to retrace the route taken by the kidnappers. This was at least four months after the actual kidnapping took place.

III
$ MILLION DOLLAR $
$ DEMAND $

A half hour after Mrs. Piper was abducted, the two maids were struggling feverishly, trying to loose their bonds. The kidnappers had done a good job of tying them up. The bound pair was about to give up and just wait for someone to show up. That would probably be quite some time though, as Mr. Piper would not be home for at least a couple hours.

Suddenly one of the maids had an idea. She had watched a Western movie where a couple got tied to chairs. They freed themselves by bouncing their chairs around so that they were back to back. It was not difficult for one to untie the other that way.

It took a while but the maids were finally able to pull it off, and a few minutes later were free from their bonds.

After ridding themselves of their ties, the maids proved beyond anyone's imagination that they were indeed worthy of the wages paid them.

One of them finished with the housecleaning, while the other took the roast from the oven, wrapped it in a damp towel, turned the oven off, and replaced the roast in the oven so that it would cool slowly, thereby retaining its moisture and assuring tenderness.

When they had finished with their duties, they decided they should notify someone as to what had occurred earlier.

They were told by one of the gunmen, "Do not use any of the phones in the house!"

Obeying the order, they walked to Virginia Piper's brother-in-law's house, which was a half-mile away. Upon arriving there they called the police and Mr. Piper.

Harry Piper had picked up the phone, expecting one of his business associates. When he heard the person on the other end of the call say, "Mr. Piper, your wife just left with two men," he immediately hung the phone up.

Piper's secretary saw the angered look on his face, and when she questioned him about anything being wrong, he replied, "Just some prankster."

He no more than spoke the words, when the phone rang again. This time he recognized the voice as belonging to one of his maids.

After hearing, then digesting what the maid told him, he realized that something was dreadfully wrong! He immediately rushed outside and sped home.

Upon his arrival, he ran into the house, and was handed a "ransom note" which one of the abductors gave to the maids. It stated that they wanted "one million" dollars in twenty-dollar bills. The note went on to read, "The safe return of your wife depends on complying exactly to the instructions given you."

Harry Piper did not blink an eye. He picked up the phone, dialed his personal banker, and informed him that he needed a million dollars. When he was asked when he needed it, Mr. Piper curtly replied, "Now!"

He then told the banker that the money needed to be in twenty-dollar bills, and placed in four separate packages. The banker did not ask at any time why the money was needed. He simply asked, "Where do you want it delivered?" The answer was, "At my office in twenty minutes!"

Piper left his Orono home, and then drove directly to his office, where he was given the million dollars in twenties. *(It was almost as if the money had already been counted at the time the phone call was made. To count a million dollars in twenty dollar bills would take some time. There would be 50,000 twenty dollar bills to count!)*

(It seems as though the money was counted, and already packaged. How many banks at that time would have a million dollars in twenties just lying around? In addition, how many banks at that time would have an electronically capable machine that could count the money?)

After Mr. Piper received the million dollars in ransom money, FBI Agents counted out the money to make sure the "count" was correct. Everyone then proceeded to the Piper home.

The ransom note gave specific instructions as to how the money was to be delivered. No one but Mr. Piper was to deliver it, and the method of delivery was spelled out in a very exact manner.

V

THE RANSOM DELIVERY

When the million dollars was placed in Piper's automobile at his Orono home, the FBI insisted that a two-way radio also be placed in the car. A tracking device was also used.

The message left by the kidnappers, instructed Piper to take the money, place it in the trunk of his car, then to proceed to highway 12 and Louisiana Avenue. There, he was instructed to go to a small shopping center where, in the back he would find a telephone pole. At the base of the pole he would find another note with further instructions.

These instructions directed Piper to look around the shopping center until he found a green, 1972 Chevrolet Monte Carlo. The keys would be in it, and he was told to take the money from his car, and place it in the trunk of the Monte Carlo.

In yet another message, Mr. Piper was instructed to drive to Broadway Avenue in Minneapolis, and then proceed to Lyndale Avenue, where he was ordered to take a right turn. He was to go to the first telephone booth he came to. There, he found another note. This third note instructed him to drive to the "Sportsman's Bar" on Broadway Street.

At the "Sportsman's Bar," Piper made a phone call, as instructed, to the same phone booth he had just left. The number was busy so Piper drove to a large Holiday Store on 90th and Lyndale Avenue, located in Bloomington. This was not far from the "Sportsman's Bar."

(Records become mixed up here. Did Piper somehow have a message that told him this?)

After arriving at the Holiday Store, Piper parked the Monte Carlo, and according to him, got a taxi, and proceeded back to his home. (***This proved to be false!***)

Shortly after parking the Monte Carlo, Piper's brother-in-law showed up. He and Piper were seen driving around the Holiday parking lot. In fact, the FBI Agents asked them, "What the hell are you doing?"

Piper's answer was, "keeping an eye on the Monte Carlo!"

The FBI put a stakeout on the Monte Carlo, and Piper was told to, "Go home!"

All of this happened on Friday evening. No one went near the green car! Finally, on Saturday, agents opened the trunk. "What the fuck," one of them exclaimed, "The fuckin money's gone!" Later, when Harry Jr. was asked where the money went, he just raised his arms, shrugged his shoulders, and said, "It simply disappeared!"

(Where does the brother in law fit in? Did Piper call him from the "Sportsman's?" Does the fact that the brother in law habituated the

Sportsman's have anything to do with anything? Does the fact that one night while drinking in the Sportsman's he drunkenly mentioned the kidnapping of someone for ransom mean anything? What would have happened if the FBI had searched the brother-in-laws car when they saw it at the Holiday store? Would or could it be that at that precise moment, the FBI, in reality, was closer than they knew to solving the case. In fact, what if there was "no case" to begin with?)

Two days after the money disappeared, four men entered a restaurant on Louisiana Street. The owner recognized one of the men as a person he saw putting something next to a telephone pole across the street from his restaurant. It was at the same spot where Mr. Piper supposedly picked up one of the ransom notes from the kidnappers!

The description of the person at the telephone was, "black hair, dark complexion, muscular build, with a short stocky neck." *(This description was the same as the man who came into the restaurant and would again come up on numerous other occasions during the investigation.)*

V
CHAINED TO A TREE

Virginia Piper, riding in the back seat of the Monte Carlo was desperate to find out where her captors were taking her. She did not know if they were going to kill her, rape her, or what they were going to do with her. Her mind was totally confused about what was happening.

Suddenly she asked, "Where are you taking me?"

The answer she received was brief and to the point. "Don't worry, we're almost there."

This was of little comfort to the bewildered, fear filled socialite.

Without warning, the car slowed, and Mrs. Piper realized that it was leaving the Interstate. It was only a few minutes before the car came to a stop and she was taken out of the back seat. The pillowcase was removed from her head, and she immediately realized that she was in a remote, wooded area.

She was led to a small tree, and a chain was fastened to her, and then to the tree. According to her, she remained chained to that tree until Saturday, *July 29th at approximately three PM in the afternoon!*

After being secured to the tree, Mrs. Piper was informed by one of her captors that she should not worry, that someone would be staying with her and would be attending to all of her needs. This did little to add to her well-being. She still did not know what was going to happen to her, or how long she would be tied to the tree. The words, "attending to her needs," in fact scared her a little. She may very well be there for a long period of time.

Minutes turned to hours, and soon Mrs. Piper lost track of time. Sometimes her mind would tell her that she would be killed. Then it would tell her that if this was to be, there was nothing she could do about it.

The person left to stay with her, seemed pleasant enough, and offered her 7-up to drink, and also gave her menthol cigarettes.

(Later, these cigarettes would cause much controversy in and during the investigation.)

The person who gave her these items seemed to be quite talkative, and they both carried on lengthy conversations. Mrs. Piper would later remember that she felt that he was genuinely concerned about her welfare. She said he tried to make her as comfortable as possible, and on numerous occasions was told, "Don't worry; you'll be released very soon." As time slowly inched by, Mrs. Piper was beginning to doubt those words.

Besides the Menthol Cigarettes and the 7-Up, Mrs. Piper also received crackers and cheese from her caretaker. Pretty soon she became more at ease and began sharing some of her childhood memories. This also caused her captor to become more at ease. He gave her tid-bits of information about himself. During one of these conversations, it was learned that he was sometimes called "Tom." She said he also told her that some of his friends called him "Alabama." These conversations would take place until her release. At one point, Mrs. Piper complained that she was starting to get chilled. She was immediately given a pair of men's pants and a sweater to put on.

Minutes turned to hours; hours seemed to turn to days. Then, unexpectedly, according to Mrs. Piper, her companion said that it was time to go. He disappeared into the darkness. Now she felt totally alone. Would anyone ever find her? Would bears get her, or wolves, or other North Woods creatures? Would she just be left there, chained to a tree, to be devoured by wild, hungry animals? Many thoughts raced through her already beleaguered mind.

Finally, realizing that the tree she was chained to was quite small; she began frantically digging at its roots in an effort to free herself. No matter how hard she tried to dig, success was not to be accomplished. According to her, at that point she almost gave up, and was ready to leave her life in the hands of God and to fate. She would relate later that the only thing that kept her going was the fact that she could hear cars traveling on a highway. It seemed as though they were fairly close! This would later coincide with the area where she was found, secured to the tree. She was actually located about a hundred feet from the service road, which led into Jay Cook Park. Highway 23 was also very close.

Mrs. Piper, scared, alone, tired, and frustrated, was sure that her captors had left her to die. Hope all but gone, sobbing uncontrollably, she thought she was starting to hallucinate when she heard voices calling her name!! It was approximately three PM on Saturday, July 29th, 1972!

VI
THE RESCUE

Around eight AM, on Saturday, the FBI was notified that Virginia Piper was chained to a tree in Jay Cook State Park, 120 miles North of Minneapolis.

The Reverend Kenneth Hendrickson, a Lutheran Minister, from St. Louis Park, Minnesota, called the FBI. He notified them where Mrs. Piper would be found. He told the agents that a male person had called, and instructed him that Mrs. Piper was chained to a tree in the park. He also told agents that the caller gave specific directions on where she was. He stated that the caller said she was safe, and to thank Mr. Piper for being so precise in the following of their instructions on the delivery of the money.

Upon receiving this important message, the FBI did exactly the opposite of what one would think they would or should have done. For, instead of calling the authorities near Jay Cook Park, and thereby securing Mrs. Piper's safety, and immediate release, and also being much closer to the kidnappers in time, they went on a media hunt!

Agents began calling the "news media" in and around Minneapolis and St. Paul. They said they had located Mrs. Piper, and were on their way to rescue her! By the time the FBI had notified the News Media, rounded up their numerous agents, and formatted the excursion to the park, hours had elapsed! They left Minneapolis in a caravan of vehicles, which gave the whole group a carnival or circus appearance.

Meantime, Mrs. Piper, still secured to the tree was feverishly trying to free herself.

At approximately noon, the kidnappers made another phone call! This one was to the House of Charity, located on Broadway and Washington Avenues, in Minneapolis, just two blocks from the *Sportsman's Bar!*

A secretary at the House of Charity took the call, and was told in no uncertain terms that Mrs. Piper was chained to a tree in Jay Cook Park, and that someone better go get her right away. The caller, in a rough, gravelly voice said, "Call the fuckin FBI, tell the bastards that the wife of Harry Piper is alone, and may be in danger!" Again, specific instructions were given as to her exact location.

(Could it be that the abductors were genuinely worried about the safety of Mrs. Piper? What was going through their minds? They called, and told where Mrs. Piper was being held; yet four hours later she was not yet rescued? Does this mean the abductors were "holed up" fairly close to the park? They were evidently close enough to where she was if they knew she was not yet rescued. Is it possible that one of the abductors or a relative of one of the abductors lived close to

the park, so that it would be known the minute she was saved?)

The individuals involved with the abduction of Mrs. Piper, were certainly not aware of the well-planned procession of FBI agents, and News Media, which had embarked on the rescue. They did not know that the FBI was more interested in its fame and glory, rather than the importance of a fast and speedy rescue!

The spectacular show, which FBI Coordinator Richard Heldt had planned for the news media, would show what a wonderful job the FBI was doing. There may even be promotions involved.

"Hell," Mr. Heldt muttered to himself, "The big guy might even give me a commendation!"

Along with twenty-five other agents, and dozens of reporters, the caravan finally reached its destination. It was now three PM in the afternoon. It took seven hours to get there from Minneapolis! It is a proven fact that had agent Heldt informed agents, and authorities closest to the park, Mrs. Piper would have been rescued in less than fifteen minutes!

The Agents, followed closely by the various news agencies, went straight to where they were instructed to go. They began calling Mrs. Piper's name, and soon heard the excited voice of her yelling, "Here I am, here I am!"

The rescue party soon reached her, and was amazed at the condition she was in. Slightly disheveled, and looking a little tired, Mrs. Piper looked in wonderful shape. Her platinum blond hair, which she was so proud of, was barely out of place. She actually looked quite composed after going through such a harrowing experience. She had been tied to a tree for two days where there were bugs, mosquitoes, and had rained. She had been digging in the dirt, yet her fingernails were not even broken. She indeed was a remarkable woman!

With a smile on her face, she turned to face the media cameras and reporters. It looked as though she was about to give an interview, but agent Heldt quickly arrived at her side, and firmly led her away. He had actually moved faster then, than he had all day long.

Within minutes of her rescue, Mrs. Piper was flown back to Minneapolis, and reunited with her husband. She was in excellent condition, and after a cursory exam by her doctor, Harry and Virginia Piper took a limo to Stillwater, Minnesota, where they dined at the "Lowell Inn!" *(The Lowell Inn is known to serve the finest food in all of Minnesota, and is ranked as one of the top eating establishments in the States.)*

The FBI and the News Media interviewed Mrs. Piper. She fared quite well with both. Her ordeal had not put a damper on her enthusiasm when it came to cameras and interviews.

VII
THE FBI IN CONTROL

On Monday morning, July 31, 1972, two days after Virginia Piper was rescued at Jay Cook Park, a deluge of FBI Agents invaded Minnesota. Most congregated in the Minneapolis area where they would begin one of, if not, the largest investigations in the City's and agency's history.

Led by Pete Neuman, the agents would sweep every nook, and cranny, ferreting out every ex-con, and nee'r do well they could locate. A desperate and fevered search was undertaken in an effort to solve the Piper kidnapping as soon as possible. All of the known stool pigeons, winos, alcoholics, parolees, bums, small time hoods, and snitches, along with all of the other malfunctioning individuals were questioned, and requestioned. Promises were made, favors offered, yet very little, if any information was gleaned. If anyone knew anything about the case, they were indeed keeping their mouths shut.

Agent Neuman stated, "This was definitely perpetrated by professionals. It had to be someone other than the ordinary run of the mill thug! There was too much planning, and preparation put into this caper. No small time, local crook could have done it."

That same day, the FBI received a phone call from an individual by the name of *Paul Harris*. This same person would later become known as a 'notorious snitch', which worked with the FBI and other law enforcement agencies on a regular basis.

Mr. Harris talked to an agent by the name of Francis Grady. No one knows exactly what Harris told Grady, but whatever it was, caused the beginning of a life of ruination for many people. Death, dishonor, and treachery would ensue for years to come as a result of the undisclosed message Harris gave Grady.

Shortly after the phone call to Grady, Harris made another call. This one was to Donald Floyd Larson.

The forty six year old Larson worked with his best friend, Kenny Callahan, at the "Custom Cabinet Shop." It was located at 38 Glenwood Avenue North, in Minneapolis. Besides Larson and Callahan, Harold Combs also worked in the cabinet shop.

Harris told Larson that an FBI agent by the name of Francis Grady would like to talk to him immediately. Harris, acting in a secretive manner, would not tell Larson why the agent wanted to talk to him.

All he would say was, "It would be to your advantage to talk to Grady, cause he can help you out, and you can trust him!"

This statement left Larson bewildered. First of all, he had never heard of agent Grady, and second, he knew of no reason why Grady would want to talk to him. *(At this time, no-one knew Harris was a snitch and trouble maker.)*

Mr. Larson no more than hung up the phone when Francis Grady walked in the shop. Accompanying him was another agent. Without hesitation, they began questioning Mr. Larson about the kidnap for ransom of Virginia Piper.

Grady had a very long list of questions for Larson. Donald recalls that there were at least fifty questions on that list. He would later find out that all of the agents involved in the case had the same set of questions.

Donald answered all of the questions without hesitation, being straightforward in his answers, and having nothing to fear by his answers. He told the agents he had no reason to lie, and that he knew absolutely nothing about the Piper Kidnapping case.

Mr. Larson was quite relieved when the questioning was over. You see, Mr. Larson, and his friends were not what one could call "honest Joe citizens." Throughout their lives, the three had managed to get into some pretty serious trouble, on a fairly regular basis.

When Larson was told that Grady wanted to talk to him, he actually had some cause to worry. He thought it was about an entirely different subject, than the Piper case. He sighed a "sigh of relief" when all he was questioned about was Mrs. Piper. *(However, even after the two agents left, Larson still wondered if there hadn't been an ulterior motive for Grady and his partner showing up at the shop.)*

A few days later, Grady again showed up, this time at Larson's home! When Donald answered the door, he was shocked to see Grady standing there. Grady had a crooked grin on his face.

Donald thought, "Aha, now for the real reason he wants to talk to me!"

When agent Grady informed Larson that he had checked out all of the answers he had given on the questionnaire, and that he had told the truth, Larson was still perplexed.

"Larson was thinking if he checked out all of my answers, and I was telling the truth, then why the hell was he at my house?"

Grady apologized, then said, "good bye," and left.

Donald was glad that the agent was gone, but something was telling him, he would be hearing from him again. He was still concerned about his, and his partner's endeavors in other areas of earning an honest living.

It is really surprising how the human mind operates. In many instances the longer amount of time that passes the stronger the effect on a person. It has a tendency to enhance, rather than cause loss of memory! It seems that most of the people questioned in 1972 and 1973 had better memories five years later! Of course, many of those questioned earlier, were now in trouble with the law or doing time.

Many hundreds of hours were put into the investigation, and agents had no more information than what they originally had at the beginning. They were willing to do anything to get something, anything which would lead to the arrest of the perpetrators of the crime.

A fifty thousand dollar reward was posted for anyone who could, or would come forward with information or assistance in identifying the culprits responsible for the kidnapping of Mrs. Piper. This was like giving a "get out of jail free card" to anyone in trouble with the law, or doing time.

Besides the interview with Larson, the FBI also questioned Kenny Callahan, Harold Combs, and numerous other friends of Donald Larson. Basically, all of his associates, and friends told the same story, and that was, they knew nothing about the Piper case, nor anyone connected with it. This left everything literally at a standstill!

Pete Neuman, the agent in charge of the case, worked for five years, intent upon solving the case. He was getting seriously worried. The "statute of limitations" would soon run out, and the FBI was about to get "egg on their face!"

Neuman did what any law-abiding FBI Agent would do. First, he would find someone who had a lifetime of scrapes with the law, someone whom would be "no loss to society", some one with whom society would automatically blame for the crime. And once they were blamed, and their past was put on public display, no more egg!

This person or "these" people would have to be suspected of other crimes or illegal activities. This person would have to have a tendency to be a "loner," without a lot of money, but at the same time seemed to be living "above his or their" means.

He needed suspects who could be paraded in front of the public, so that the FBI, and mainly himself, would gain back some of their credence. They had failed for five years in the game of "cops and robbers," and it was time to win the final chapter. The agency of J. Edgar Hoover and his dictatorship could not allow anyone to beat them, nor allow anyone to think for a minute that his agency could fail. Therefore, the case must, and would be solved before the time limit expired.

Soon after the investigation came to a "standstill," FBI Agents began handing out false information to the "news agencies," which were willing to accept anything the FBI chose to tell them.

The "News Media" was eager to satisfy the cravings of the zealous FBI. One such stated example was, "We've all but got the Piper Kidnapping case solved, and are ready to make arrests!" Stated also was, "We have a 'star witness' willing to testify against the thugs who perpetrated this terrible crime."

VIII
STAR WITNESS FOUND

(The star witness turned out to be Robert Earl Barne a Federally convicted prisoner whose prison number is 33321. Mr. Barnes was known in both the Federal System and the Minnesota Prison System. To Convicts in both arenas, he was known as a snitch!)

It seems that Barnes had been busted for some burglaries, and managed to receive a parole within a couple years of the "Piper Kidnapping." He was paroled to Minneapolis, where he was supposedly ordered to find employment and to lead a "crime free" life.

Barnes, for reasons known only to him, rushed to "Occies's Bar" which was owned by Occie Fleetman, a very close friend of Donald Larson, Kenny Callahan, and Harold Combs! The bar was located on 29th Street and Lyndale Avenue.

Barnes approached Occie, and told him his story. He said he had just been released from the Federal Pen, and had to do some parole time. He said that unless he found a job, they had promised to revoke his parole, and then send him back to prison. Barnes said he was willing to wash tables, clean floors, bounce, and bartend; anything that would keep him from going back to prison.

Being a very kind, and sympathetic person, Occie hired him immediately as a bartender and bouncer. He started work that very same day, and seemed to be adept as a bartender. He made friends quickly, and it seemed the patrons liked him.

IX
THE HEART ATTACK

In October of 1974, Donald Larson suffered a major heart attack. Doctors said that the only thing that saved his life was his age, and that he was physically in good shape.

Just forty-eight years old, Larson hovered between life and death for days. He was kept in the hospital in Des Moines, Iowa.

At the time of the attack, Donald was working for Arthur Stillman. He owned a number of stores, called "Flower City," located throughout the United States. Mr. Stillman put Donald to work as a truck driver.

Stillman, a believer that everyone deserves a second chance, hired Larson after his release from the Minnesota State Prison in Stillwater. Mr. Stillman was a member of the parole board. It turned out to be a good decision by Stillman. Larson proved to be a valued and trusted employee. He was trusted with large sums of money and proved to be very honest.

When Donald went to work for Stillman, it was the first legitimate job he had ever had. It was also the first time that anyone had ever really trusted him. In return for that trust, Donald vowed to never give cause for Stillman to distrust him. He was so thankful that he actually swore to "give up crime!" This may not sound like a big thing, but Mr. Larson had been afoul of the law for over thirty-five years!

Donald would spend over two weeks in the Des Moines hospital. Finally, the doctors decided to release him, only after promising to take it easy, that he would not work, would keep from getting excited, and would not worry about anything. Donald made all of these promises, and was willing to keep them. His heart attack literally "scared the hell out of him."

Donald left the hospital, and came back to Minnesota to recuperate further.

While "on the mend" Donald met a woman by the name of Ruth. She had two sons. Their names were Cye and Scott. Down the road, Ruth and Donald would become parents of a son, whom they called Mark.

After their marriage, Donald purchased eighty acres of land, eleven miles West of Willow River, Minnesota. Considered to be in the "North Country," it was the ideal place to raise a family, and for Larson to rest, recuperate and retire.

Donald was an excellent wood-worker, and ended up totally remodeling the home on his land. The finished product was something that he was very proud of. Everything was "rustic," and attuned to the area where it was located. There were numerous lakes, hundreds of thousands of wooded acres, forestland, and scenery that was breathtaking. His property was teeming with wild life. There were deer, wild turkey, an occasional moose, and every once in a while wolves would be heard, and seen.

The land consisted of forty acres of wooded land, and forty acres open. It was quiet, peaceful, and just what the doctors ordered! He had grown tired of the city life, and in fact, never was known to be a partier. About the only time he would have a drink was at mealtime. Once in a great while he would drink a beer. He preferred the relaxed, serene life which nature offered.

Most of Donald's friends were the opposite. When it came to partying, drinking, and chasing women, they were all for it. On numerous occasions they tried to get him to participate in their revelry, but he would always refuse. He would sometimes go with them, but instead of drinking, he would sit sipping a coke, or some other soda.

When it came to food, it was a whole new ballgame! Donald liked food! He liked it in the morning, noon, afternoon, evening, or whenever. Food was one of his greatest delights. His eyes sparkle as he recalls the fine "eating establishments" he has habituated during his lifetime. From Minnesota, to Chicago, to New York, to Miami, to Atlanta, to New Orleans, to Dallas, Houston, Los Angeles, San Francisco, Reno, Las Vegas, and Canada, Mr. Larson has consumed vast quantities of delicious foods. He never forgets the names of the fine eateries he has been in. Not only does he remember the name of them, he can tell you what he ate there.

At one time, his over six-foot frame supported three hundred pounds!

While lazing around on "the farm," Donald would do a little fishing, some gardening, or take leisurely strolls through, and around his property. He was totally at ease with himself, his family, his surroundings, and his life. He had no big worries.

X
DIRTY DEEDS/ SMILING FACES

Donald was required to visit his heart doctor on a regular basis. His name was Doctor Belzer, and his practice was in Methodist Hospital, located in St. Louis Park, a suburb of Minneapolis. He would visit Dr. Belzer at least once a month, and his visits were always on a Friday.

On these Doctor visits, Donald would always take the time to visit his old friends. He would stop at Occies's Bar, and visit with Occie, talking over how things were going.

Occie and Donald were lifelong friends, and each knew the other's habits and friends.

During one of these visits, he noticed there was a new face in the establishment. Occie introduced Donald to Paul Harris! Had Donald known then what he knows now, he would have made a beeline for the door! He would have jumped in his car, sped off, and never returned!

Harris was now a regular at Occie's. Larson did not know it then, but Harris and Donald had been neighbors years ago. Tommy Grey, Donald, and Harris all lived close together. There was another person with Harris. His name was Robert Barnes!

Donald recalls that it was a Friday night, about eight in the evening. He also recalls that it was chilly outside. Fall had started, and leaves were already turning to their fall colors.

When Donald recalls that introduction, he actually shivers! He says that when he shook the hand of Paul Harris, the feelings, which raced through him, were very foreboding! Donald states that he has never felt hands like Harris' before. He says they were as cold as the weather outside, and his mind told him they felt like death itself.

Harris had nothing but praise for his friend Barnes, and did not hesitate to tell Larson that Barnes was a wonderful person and 'stand up convict!' He told Donald that he could trust his life with this guy. This statement would come back to haunt Donald. Not only should he not have trusted anything about Barnes, he should never have trusted him with anything. This introduction would alter Donald's life to such degrees that it would never be the same.

Donald says, "I can still feel that handshake." As he says this, his right hand clenches automatically, for from that handshake, Donald's life would become a living nightmare!

Robert Barnes would try desperately to become Donald Larson's closest friend. He tried on numerous occasions to get Donald to "party" with him. Every time Donald saw him, he seemed to have his pockets full of money, and would repeatedly offer to "buy" Larson all of the "women, booze, and song" that Donald could handle.

Donald recalls telling Barnes, "I'm just an old country boy from the farm, and don't believe I could handle any of them things."

He also told him that he was a married man, and that his wife, and family was enough to keep him happy.

Barnes was not wanting to take no for an answer. He tried to get Donald to change his mind every time he saw him. He tried desperately to ingratiate himself to his newfound "best friend!"

One time Barnes told Donald that he liked to fish. He added that he would like to visit Larson's farm because he knew every name of every lake, which was closest to the farm, and could say what fish was in each of the lakes. Donald thought this was very strange. He knew that Barnes was not from Minnesota, and wondered how and why he knew so much about the area in which Donald's farm was located.

Barnes had told Larson that he had lived most of his life in St. Louis, Missouri, Kansas, Washington DC, Baltimore, and Las Vegas.

Approximately three months after Donald became acquainted with Barnes, Mr. Barnes disappeared. It turned out that he had been arrested for the burglaries of three homes in the Lake Calhoun area, a very wealthy suburb of Minneapolis. Many of the Twin Cities' most affluent people lived there. Somehow, Barnes got all three charges dropped and disappeared from the scene.

Suddenly the mysterious actions of Mr. Barnes and of Mr. Harris began fitting together.

First of all, when Donald had suffered his heart attack in Des Moines, Iowa, who showed up? Harris! He had driven all the way from Minneapolis to visit him. This seemed very peculiar to Donald because at no time were Harris, and Larson ever considered to be good friends. They actually did not know each other very well!

The Piper kidnapping took place in 1972. Harris had talked to the FBI very soon after, exactly what was discussed, no-one knows, except that after he talked to them, the FBI talked to Donald Larson.

It turned out that Barnes was a full time "snitch" for the FBI! It would also come to;pass that Harris would, in 1977, falsify evidence against Donald Floyd Larson, and Kenneth Callahan. This phony evidence would be in reference to the Piper Kidnapping.

Harris had managed to get himself arrested by the ATF in 1975. He received a 45 year sentence, which should have kept him locked up for a considerable amount of time. However, after numerous meetings with Agent Peter Neuman, concerning the Piper case, Harris was suddenly released, short of his required stay with the Federal Prison System. He was supposed to serve fifteen years. He only served two!

The information gleaned from Mr. Harris was evidently quite powerful. A short time after Harris was released from Federal custody, the FBI began to "home in" on Donald Floyd Larson, Kenneth Callahan, and Thomas Grey, the life long friend of both Larson, and Callahan.

The "statute of limitations" was getting short and Neuman had to do something soon, even if it meant having a "life-long career criminal and snitch" released from prison.

Neuman must have gone straight to the "big man" to do this.

XI
PAUL HARRIS

Tommy Grey, a friend, a confidant, a life-long cohort, and a pal of Donald Larson, and Kenny Callahan, sat in his house, wondering what he should do for a pass-time. Lately, he had been getting a little bored. Donald was married, Kenny was busy, and everyone else that he knew seemed to have something to do, or were doing time.

As Tommy half-hazardly watched the ten o'clock news on WCCO, he was thinking of much more exciting times. His memories of exploits with old friends brought a smile to his face. He was starting to "nod off," when suddenly his reverie was interrupted by his doorbell. His mind was in the area between wakefulness and sleep, and he really did not want to get up to answer the bell, and wondered out loud, "Who the hell can that be at this hour of the night?"

Tommy opened the door, and there stood Paul Harris. Draped over his shoulder and arm, was a beautiful "Mink Coat!" *(This coat would later be valued at over $ 9,000! It would also come to pass that it had been stolen in a burglary from Bartholomew Furriers, located in Alexandria, Minnesota, about three hours West of Minneapolis. A total of 42 expensive minks were stolen during the heist!)*

"Hey Tommy, how ya doin," asked Harris. "What ya think of this gem?" He handed Tommy the coat.

Tommy examined the coat, and was about to ask Harris where he got it, but decided it was none of his business where it came from. Instead, he asked, "What's it worth?"

Harris, smiling at Tommy did not hesitate. "For you buddy, I'll take a 'fifty' for it!"

Tommy, not known for turning down a deal such as this, hurriedly reached in his pocket, retrieved fifty dollars, and handed the money to Harris.

Tommy couldn't believe it! "Maybe the day wasn't so boring or worthless after all," he muttered to himself.

This deal seemed to be "too good to be true!" Usually when something seems as such, it is exactly that!

Tommy thanked Harris for the coat, put it in the closet, bid Harris "good night," and then went to bed. He went to sleep with a big smile on his face.

Bright and early, the next morning, Tommy was rudely awakened by loud, hard banging on his door. Having heard this sound on other occasions, Tommy knew instantly that it had to be the "cops!" The first thing that flashed before him was, "that fucking coat!" He resignedly got out of bed, yelled, "ok, ok!" He got dressed and opened the door.

Tommy was suddenly confronted by at least a dozen cops, all from various agencies. The cops consisted of the Minnesota Bureau of Criminal Apprehension, the Douglas County Sheriff's Department, the Minneapolis City Police Department, and some "plain clothes" cops that Tommy couldn't recognize.

The first one through the door handed Tommy a "search warrant!" On the warrant was listed "forty two mink coats!"

Immediately, and without hesitation, two policemen went directly to the closet. One opened the door, and the other, with camera in hand, snapped a picture, then reached inside, and took the coat out. Everyone examined it, and then the one who took it out, placed it back in the closet, and closed the door. This left Tommy speechless. Expecting to be arrested, Tommy was standing with hands clasped together. Expecting to have cuffs placed on his wrists, he was even more surprised when; the small Army of cops turned, and marched out of his apartment, closing the door behind them.

As soon as they were gone, Tommy went to the closet, grabbed the "hot" mink, and went straight to Paul Harris' house, located only three blocks away.

"Pissed off" does not even begin to describe how Tommy felt. He was mad to the core, ready to rip Harris' head clean off his shoulders!

Grey walked to the front door, flung it open, and barged in. Harris was sitting at the table, with a cup of coffee in front of him. Tommy threw the mink coat in Harris' face, picked up the cup of coffee, and also threw that in his face.

He said, "Give me one good reason why I shouldn't kill you right now you son of a bitch, what the fuck are you trying to pull?!"

Tommy had his fist drawn back as if to hit Harris. Harris, thinking quickly, reached inside his pocket, pulled out the fifty he had sold the coat to Tommy for, then quickly handed the money to the red faced, angered Tommy.

Harris began making excuses, but Tommy wouldn't hear it. He simply said, "Just shut the fuck up, and don't say another word!" he then turned and walked out.

Paul Harris was really a piece of art! Instead of "Thanking God" for Tommy Grey not killing him, he calmly got up, grabbed the coat, and went out to his car. He drove straight to an old ex-con's house. This person's name was Francis Hoppe.

Hoppe was an old time "bank robber." He was not one for wasting words. When offered the coat, he simply reached in his pocket, took out a wad of bills, pealed off two twenties and handed them to Harris. Harris was about to say something, then decided not to. Had he said anything, the old man would probably take his forty bucks back, plus would have kept the coat.

Harris left the scene, and within twenty minutes, an army of cops stormed into Hoppe's apartment with revolvers drawn. They knew that though Hoppe was over seventy years old, he could still be quite cantankerous, and was still considered to be dangerous! The coat was still in the chair where Harris had left it.

This time, the police took the coat, plus Mr. Hoppe! Then they informed him that if he would sign a statement admitting he had received the stolen coat from "Tommy Grey," they would release him. Hoppe looked the cops in the face, and without any hesitation said, "You can go fuck yourselves!"

Within one hour the gray haired Hoppe was standing in front of a Municipal Court Judge trying to explain what the police tried to make him do. Also telling the Judge that it was Paul Harris, and not Tommy Grey who brought the coat to him, must have helped.

The Judge brought Hoppe into his chambers, and asked him what happened. Hoppe, a little calmer now, explained that Harris had brought the coat to his place, and told him that he needed a place to hold the coat for a while, and that he had bought it for his wife. He said he would pick it up later.

The Judge, after hearing what Hoppe had to say, thought for a moment, and then released him on his own recognizance. He told him to come back in a week.

A week later, Francis Hoppe came back to the court. It was the same Judge. Mr. Hoppe pleaded guilty to possession of stolen property, and was given a sentence of one year in jail. He then suspended the year and placed the old man on probation for a year.

Hoppe, was elated over the fact that he did not have to go to jail, but still pissed at what Harris did to him so he spread the word about Harris all over the city of Minneapolis. Harris could go nowhere without someone confronting him.

A week after this all happened, Tommy Grey was arrested on a warrant, charging him with burglary! He was immediately transported to the Douglas County Jail in Alexandria.

Thomas Rief, the prosecuting attorney for Douglas County had received word from the Sheriff's Department that they had received a tip that Thomas Grey had been involved in the burglary of Bartholomew Furriers!

Upon his arrival in Douglas County, Grey immediately called an attorney by the name of Stewart Perry, from Minneapolis. He got the name for the attorney from a cellmate in the jail.

Mr. Perry agreed to represent him immediately, and told him he would be there shortly. It crossed Tommy's mind that attorney Perry seemed to agree to represent him pretty fast, but Tommy did not really think about it very much. Later, it would come to pass that Stewart Perry was working hand in hand with the FBI on the Piper Kidnapping!

Mr. Tommy Grey appeared before the Honorable G. Saetre, for his preliminary hearing. The courtroom sat silent as a witness slowly approached the witness stand. This person was supposed to be able to identify the person which he witnessed leaving the Bartholomew Furrier store.

County Attorney Rief approached his witness, asked him if he could identify the person he saw leaving the fur store. The man turned, looked around, pointed to a person in a "red jacket", and said, "That's him!"

The person he identified was Kenny Callahan! Judge Saetre asked the person in the red jacket to stand up. Kenny obliged him immediately. The judge then asked him what his name was. Kenny quickly replied, "Kenneth Callahan." He then went on to explain that he was the pilot who flew Tommy Grey's attorney to Alexandria from Minneapolis. Needless to say, the judge, and the prosecutor were both quite shaken at this turn of events. Judge Saetre immediately called both lawyers into his chambers.

The only ones who knew what was said in the chambers were the judge, the two attorneys, and the court stenographer; however, those in the courtroom could hear a very loud voice coming from behind the chambers door!

When everyone returned to the

Courtroom, Judge Saetre who was red faced immediately set Tommy's bail at ten thousand dollars. Tommy Grey was immediately released, and told to be back in court in thirty days. His attorney had made a motion for a "speedy trial."

Tommy reappeared a month later, ready for his "day in court." The trial did not last much longer than that! A jury was picked, a few witnesses got on the stand, the jury went out to deliberate, and he was found "guilty as charged." The trial lasted a whole three days! At the request of his attorney, Tommy was allowed to remain on bail until the following Monday morning when he was to report back to the court for sentencing. Later, Tommy received another continuance of two weeks.

Upon their return to Minneapolis, Grey fired Attorney Perry, and notified the court that he needed additional time to hire different representation.

The group arrived back in Minneapolis about four p.m. When Grey and Callahan arrived in Minneapolis they immediately went to Grey's house.

When they walked in the door, there sat Donald Larson. They immediately told him what had happened, and Donald got up, escorted Grey to his car, and brought him to the office of Ronald Meshbesher, famed Minneapolis attorney.

Meshbesher had been involved in some high profile cases that had drawn national attention. He was considered as the best attorney within hundreds of miles of the Twin Cities. He was involved with the T Eugene Thomson murder case, the Marjorie Caldwell, "Millionaire Murder" case, and various other cases, which drew notoriety.

Donald and Tommy sped to Meshbesher's office located on Park Avenue in Minneapolis. They entered the elaborate Suite of offices marked, Meshbesher and Singer & Spence.

Ron Meshbesher interviewed Thomas Grey. Grey, in no uncertain terms, told Meshbesher what a lousy job Perry had done for him.

Meshbesher told Tommy, "There's nothing I can do as long as you have Perry for an attorney." He also told Grey that he would need a retainer fee.

Attorney Perry was immediately called. Few words were spoken. Just, "This is Thomas Grey, you are fired!" Then Thomas Grey reached inside his pocket, pulled out a one dollar bill and said, "This will have do for now!"

Meshbesher's first act as counsel for Tommy was to call and notify the Douglas County Clerk of Courts Office that he was replacing Mr. Perry in the Bartholomew Burglary case. He then ordered that a court transcript of the proceedings against Tommy Grey be sent to him POST HASTE! As luck would have it, the clerk was an old acquaintance of Meshbesher's. She diligently worked all evening transcribing the transcripts. In the morning she sent the finished records to Meshbesher, via Greyhound Bus.

On Saturday morning at ten o'clock, Tommy Grey's phone began to ring. Tommy, in the bathroom, ran to it, and as he got there, it quit ringing! "That really pisses me off," he muttered. He turned to go back to his shaving, and the phone rang again. It was Ron Meshbesher. He instructed Grey, and Larson to come to his office immediately. He seemed to be in a jovial mood, and went on to say that he had some news, which he thought, would brighten their day.

Grey and Larson hastened to Meshbesher's office immediately. When they walked into Ron's private office, he was sitting there in his plush leather chair, laughing uproariously! With smiles from ear to ear, he told the two that there was no worry about Grey's Monday morning sentencing hearing.

Attorney Meshbesher opened the transcripts he had received from his acquaintance at the Douglas County Courthouse. He pointed to a statement that Grey's previous attorney, Perry had made to Judge Saetre, and to County Attorney Rief. It said, "I sure hope Thomas Grey won't get another attorney, because if he does he'll charge me for being incompetent for allowing you two to violate all of his Constitutional rights!"

Unknown to Judge Saetre, the prosecutor, and to Mr. Perry, the Court Reporter had taken down everything that was said in the Judge's Chambers! With this news, Tommy offered to buy breakfast. He said, "I'm taking you two to a place that has some of the best food in the United States!"

They went outside, got in Meshbesher's Deville, and Tommy gave him directions on how to get to the Lowell Inn, located in Stillwater, Minnesota. It is indeed known to be the top eatery in Minnesota.

When they entered, Mrs. Palmer greeted them just inside the door. She said, "Hello Tommy, it's good to see you again." She then introduced herself to Donald Larson, and then approached Ron Meshbesher. "How are you today Ron?"

Both Tommy and Donald were surprised that she knew him. Donald muttered, "Isn't there someone you don't know?"

Meshbesher just smiled as they were led to a large antique table, exquisitely set in antique silver and ornate china plates, cups and saucers.

Two other people were already sitting at the table. One gentleman was Dick Kircher, president of the Cosmopolitan Bank in

Stillwater, and unbelievably, an old acquaintance of Donald's was also seated at the table.

It was Seamus D McGee! Mr. McGee just smiled at Donald, and Donald instantly got the message. *(They had both done time together in the sixties, and Seamus did not think this was the time to bring up "con talk.")*

The discussion around the table was friendly. Introductions were made and small talk mostly prevailed. Donald sat there with his fork ready and an excited look on his face. This was about the fanciest restaurant he had ever been in. He could not wait for the food because he knew it had to be good!

The food came remarkably fast. It seemed there were waitresses for each of the people sitting at the table. One carried a large plate with pork chops; another carried bacon and Canadian bacon, another sausages and ham, another potatoes, French toast, coffee, orange juice. It just did not end. When Donald didn't think there could be anything else, Mrs. Palmer showed up at the table carrying a large bottle of wine. She graciously poured everyone a glass.

The food was the best Donald had ever consumed, and he made a vow to eat here again, again, and again! It was definitely a day he would never forget.

The fine repast took almost two full hours to eat. Before they departed, Mrs. Palmer brought them on a tour of the Inn. During this tour, Seamus gave Donald a telephone number where he could be reached. There was also a $$ sign on the paper the number was written on.

With smiles on their faces, a full, but pleasant feeling in their stomachs, everyone departed.

When the trio got to Meshbesher's office, Meshbesher thanked Tommy Grey for the wonderful breakfast, and said he would meet them on Monday morning in Alexandria.

At nine o'clock sharp Monday morning, Tommy Grey, and Attorney Meshbesher entered the Douglas County Courthouse. They went immediately to the Courtroom of Judge Gaylord Saetre.

There seemed to be a frown on the Judge's face as he entered the courtroom. There was a real look of concern on County Attorney Rief's face.

When the two found out that their conversation had been taken down word for word, it caused both a little consternation. Neither one knew exactly what was going to happen. In fact, they did not remember exactly what they had said!

Along with that problem, there was yet another. None other than Ron Meshbesher had replaced Perry! The Judge looked around and asked everyone involved with the case to report to his chambers

After entering and seating themselves Meshbesher immediately faced Judge Saetre, and confronted him and Rief! They both knew that the proverbial "shit was about to hit the fan!" Sensing what was about to happen, the Judge immediately postponed Thomas Grey's sentencing for another two weeks.

Shortly thereafter, Douglas County Attorney Rief contacted Mr. Meshbesher, and informed him that the FBI's Agent, Peter Neuman had called, and informed him that

Donald Larson and Thomas Grey were involved in the Virginia Piper Kidnapping! He told Meshbesher that this was the reason Tommy Grey was framed for the "fur burglary." Two weeks later Judge Gaylord Saetre sentenced Thomas Grey to twenty years at the maximum security prison in Stillwater, Minnesota!

Ron Meshbesher immediately filed an appeal for "fast relief." The Minnesota Supreme Court ruled that indeed Mr. Grey's Constitutional rights had been violated. They reversed his conviction and he was immediately released from prison!

Of course, this in no way made up for the eighteen months it took for him to get out. Tommy came out a pissed off x-con! The state of Minnesota and the FBI managed to get their pound of flesh, even though they had to frame an innocent man to do it!

While Tommy was in prison, FBI Agents would visit him on a regular basis. Of course, these visits were in regards to the Piper kidnapping. Grey explained that on July 27, 1972, the day of the kidnapping, he was working for the American Fruit Company, located at 4th Street and Chicago Avenue in Minneapolis. Eventually, his "time clock" records and his delivery receipts for that day would prove beyond all doubts that he was indeed not guilty of being involved with the Piper caper.

Upon learning that they were not having any luck with setting Grey up, the FBI soon embarked on a different mode of action. They began pointing fingers at Donald Larson and his partner Kenneth Callahan. They were now in a frenzied state of anxiety. The "statute of limitations" was drawing dangerously near, and they desperately needed to arrest someone for this crime! Their targets were identified, their sights were set, and with trigger fingers tensed, they took aim!

PART II

DONALD LARSON
"HIS TRAVELS"

I
DIRECTIONS

Donald Floyd Larson was born November 6, 1926, in Minneapolis, Minnesota. He and his nine brothers, and sisters grew up on the South side.

Donald attended Clay School until the 8th grade, and then he decided that he had enough schooling, and wanted to go out on his own. There were various other reasons he quit, and we shall go into them later.

When Donald talks about his schooling, a smile comes to his face. He says, "I am not the great criminal genius that the FBI paints me to be." "All I ever wanted out of life was to get along with people, and I have never intentionally set out to harm anyone."

Those who have known Donald for a long time, all say the same things about him. He is easy to get along with, has a good sense of humor, is very hard to get mad, and is good hearted. He tries to help all those in need of help, and has been that way for at least forty years!

As a youngster, he was well behaved and did his chores as he was asked to. He complained very little and often helped the elderly who lived in his neighborhood. He would help with their chores, mowing lawns, shoveling snow and various other tasks. (This trait is still with Donald. At almost eighty years old, he still tries to help others.)

Ole and Sophie, Donald's parents, survived on the pay, which Ole gleaned from his painting business. Ole took pride in his trade, and made every endeavor to do excellent work. He had a thriving business, and was able to support his large family quite well during "hard times."

Around the age of twelve or thirteen, Donald began getting the urge for adventure. He and his boyhood buddies were always on the lookout for new things to do. This was in the years when there were no televisions and or concerts to go to. There were no video games to play. In the thirties and forties, kids had to manufacture their own entertainment.

By the time Donald turned twelve, he and his friends had learned that they could hop or jump freight trains! There was one small problem. It seemed as though it was easier boarding them, than it was getting off! When a person looks down from a moving train, the ground looks as though it is being passed over much faster than it actually is. They learned that the easiest way to get off was to actually wait until the train had come to a complete stop.

The excitement of the whole excursion was the fact that when the train stopped, they did not know where they would be getting off.

Their excursions brought them to South Dakota, North Dakota, Montana, Wyoming, Nebraska, Kansas, Wisconsin, and Iowa.

It seemed the farther they traveled, the farther they wanted to go.

When they would return from these excursions, they'd gather all of their friends together, and tell exciting stories about the adventures they partook of, the dangers they faced, and the various people they met. Their friends would sit, wide eyed, with rapt attention; secretly wishing they too could join in on these trips.

Sometimes the stories would be embellished a little, but most were true. There were many dangers that they actually faced, and colorful, never to be forgotten people they had met.

Their exploits became the talk of the South Side! Even some adults liked hearing about the adventures.

Donald's most regular traveling companions consisted of Kenny Callahan, Tommy Grey, Donald Wise, and Bobby Bundage. Bobby drowned while swimming behind the University of Minnesota in the Mississippi River. This is where the boys would go "skinny dipping," on hot summer days.

Donald states that Bobby was only sixteen years old, and adds that it still bothers him when he thinks about it. One other friend, Richard Covell would go with the boys.

Young though they were, these adventurers had "savvy and skills" which were far beyond their years. Many grown men had never experience nor gained the "life skills," which the boys possessed.

They had traveled thousands of miles, met as many people, lived off the land, learned how to con their way into the hearts of strangers, and above all, learned respect and protection for each other.

Sometimes their skills would cause them to run afoul of the law. Donald recalls that on one such occasion they had gotten off a train in Rapid City, South Dakota. As they were walking along the tracks, still in the "railroad yard," a "bull," (railroad policeman) approached them. The look on his face caused instant fear in the boys. They began running! They had heard many stories from "hobos" about how some "bulls" were mean enough to beat a person with chains and boards!

They departed the railroad property as fast as they could, and were walking down a street, talking over what their next move would be. Suddenly a "squad car" pulled up and stopped!

The officer beckoned them over to his car, and started asking questions. He wanted to know where they were from, where they were going, and how they were living.

He soon ascertained that the boys were not from the area, and that they were not very sure where they were headed, and could not come up with much of an answer when he asked about how they got money to eat on. He invited them to get into the car!

The boys got in the car, knowing it was useless to run. They knew they were going to go to jail for sure. Much to their surprise, the car started traveling southwest out of Rapid City. Donald says they traveled at least twenty or thirty miles. Suddenly the car came to a halt.

The cop told them to "get out," that they were at the Wyoming border, and that they could find a good place to stay, and could get jobs on a ranch!

With a happy wave, the boys started walking down the road. Their heads were filled with pictures of becoming cowboys, riding broncos and wild bulls, of ropin doggies! They were actually "Out West!" Boy, just wait till they got back to the cities after this trip. They'd probably be walking bow-legged by that time! They would tell stories around the ol' campfire, and no doubt would have to carry six shooters! Yes sir, this was gonna be the big trip!

Suddenly a car pulled up. It was a Wyoming County Sheriff's car!

Again, they were asked all kinds of questions. The deputy had a bemused look on his face. He politely listened while the boys told him stories about what their plans were. Finally, looking at his watch, he yawned, and said, "Go back the way you just come from." He added, "I'll be watchin' ya, so don't try to pull nothing fancy."

The boys sadly turned around, and headed the other direction. Kenny looked at Donald and said, "This has not been a very good day!" It suddenly started to rain!

II

A PORT IN THE STORM

The boys walked about a half hour, and to their surprise a driveway appeared. They could barely make out a ranch house at the end of the driveway. All of the boys decided that they definitely wanted out of the cold rain, so they decided that it would be best to investigate this house. They no more than started walking up the driveway when the rain stopped. Kenny said, "Maybe it's not gonna be so bad after all."

The boys, nearing the old house realized that it was in need of repair. The paint was faded, there was loose shingles, and the steps were worn out. It almost looked "not lived in."

Donald knocked on the door, and soon a woman answered it. She looked at the boys sort of warily.

Donald was first to speak. He remembers telling her that he and his friends were really hungry and that they would do anything for some food, and a dry, warm place to sleep for the night.

The lady, whose name turned out to be Marie, looked at the bedraggled boys, and decided that she could let them sleep in the barn, and give them a bite to eat. She needed some wood split, and when she told them, they immediately said they would gladly, chop her some wood.

She led them to the back of the house where a pile of wood was waiting. They took turns chopping, and soon had a good pile stacked up. Marie soon came out and when she saw the amount of wood they had chopped was very surprised. She thanked them, and invited them inside.

The first thing they noticed when they entered was the beautiful interior of the old house. Everything was neat, very old, but in very good shape.

There was something else they could not overlook! The smell of food! It was mouth watering. They looked at each other grinning from ear to ear.

Marie led them to the dining room, where they were then seated at a large table. It was covered with dishes of food!

There was a large bowl of steaming mashed potatoes, a large bowl of browned beef chunks and gravy, a bowl of carrots, homemade bread, butter, and two large pitchers filled with milk.

Marie called out, "Donald, it's time to eat!"

A young boy, about five years old appeared. He had brown hair, and dark shiny brown eyes. After he was seated, Marie bowed her head and said "grace." She then introduced her son to everyone at the table. Then it was time to eat!

The boys ate until they were totally full. The food was great, the meat tender, the gravy rich, and the milk fresh and cold!

When Marie saw that the boys were finished, she hurriedly got up, and went to the kitchen, quickly returning with a large apple pie, covered with real whipped cream. Upon seeing this, the boys somehow made room in their already bulging bellies!

When they had cleaned the last crumb from their plates, Donald insisted that they would do the dishes. When that task was completed, Marie gave each of the boys some soap and a towel. She then led them to the barn.

When they entered, they were surprised to find that part of the barn was made into a sort of a "bunk house!" The inside, like the house, was very neat. There were six bunks, a table, chairs, and a bathroom.

There was also an old radio, a shelf with some books on it, a couple kerosene lamps, and some chairs. In one corner, there was an enclosure made from sheets, and inside was a large copper bathtub! Next to the tub sat a couple of five-gallon pails.

Marie instructed the boys to go to the pump and start carrying in water. She instructed Kenny to start a fire in the big wood stove. When this was done, they started heating water for the tub.

Soon, the water was in the tub, and the boys ended up drawing straws to find out who would be first, after two of them had bathed, they would throw out the water, and replace it with hot, clean water.

After they had all bathed, they sat around and listened to the radio for a while. Kenny was able to pick up a station out of Shreveport Louisiana. The program they listened to was called the "Louisiana Hayride." There was a man singing, by the name of Hank Williams. He had a band called the "Drifting Cowboys." Another man, Jimmy Rogers also sang.

The excitement of the day was too much, and it finally took hold of them, they all lay in their comfortable bunks, the radio still playing, and dozed off.

About seven in the morning Marie and little Donald awakened them. She had slipped in during the evening, taken their clothes, and washed them! She was placing them on the ends of the bunks.

She told the boys, "Now, you wash up, get dressed, and come in for breakfast. It'll be ready in about twenty minutes!"

They got out of bed, washed their faces, dressed, and then went to the house. When they entered, again they were met by the smell of food! Donald of course was already licking his lips!

On the table, there was ham, bacon, eggs, toast, butter, jelly, and milk! The boys ate until they were full, and for Donald that is no small feat! After everyone had finished, Marie gave each of the boys a banana! Again, the boys did the dishes.

After the dishes were done, they went outside and straightened the bunkhouse out. Marie asked them what their plans were. They told her they would go back to Minnesota, go to school, and then maybe make another trip somewhere!

Marie laughed at the boys, and told them that whatever they did, to be careful, that life was short, and that it was best to enjoy it as much as they could. She then went back to the house.

When the boys were done in the barn, they started walking towards the driveway. Out of the house came Marie, and her son. She was carrying bags, and gave each of them one.

Marie told the boys that she wished she had work for them, but was really having a rough go of things. She said that the ranch had been auctioned off after her husband Dewey had died, and she and Donald would be moving out in less than a month. She told them that at one time the ranch had been a thriving business, but her husband and two of her children had come down with the fever, and had died! This had been more than she could bear. She had to get rid of the place, and start a new life.

She did say that there was some guy carving some statues near a place called

Rushmore. She told them how to get there and said there may be some work for them there.

She then said "goodbye," turned, and went back into the house. Donald recalls that he definitely saw a tear stream down her cheek as she turned. The boys hollered their goodbyes, and were on their way.

As they walked down the driveway, they looked inside the paper bags. There was roast beef sandwiches, apples, and each had a jar full of nectar! They all turned, and Marie was standing on the small porch, holding her son's hand. She raised her other to wave a final goodbye. Donald said he became very saddened at that last sight of her.

The boys continued down the driveway, and soon were laughing and teasing each other. Their bellies were full, new adventures were surely just around the corner, but most of all, they were just youngsters, full of "piss-n-vinegar!" To them, life was nothing but a small challenge, one that could be overtaken, and if they failed at a challenge, they would just come back twice as hard next time.

III
HISTORY IN THE MAKING

They no more than reached the road when an old Ford truck came along. The driver stopped and asked the boys if they needed a lift. Two of them jumped in the seat with the driver, and Donald and Kenny jumped in the back. Suddenly, they realized there were pigs in the back with them!

Not knowing a lot about farm life, the two really didn't mind. Now re-calling the experience with a grin, Donald says, "Kenny and me smelled like 'pig shit' for three days!"

After traveling down the bumpy road for about ten miles, the old truck came to a halt, and the boys all got out. The driver gave them directions on how to get to Rushmore, wished them luck, and went on his way. The boys were once again on foot.

They ended up walking about seven miles to the site where "Gutzon Borglum" was carving and blasting his name into history. He was actually memorializing George

Washington, Thomas Jefferson, Abe Lincoln, and Teddy Roosevelt, by carving out their likenesses from a rock mountain!

As the boys neared the site, their eyes widened in disbelief! They got as close as they could when a man approached them. He told them that they would have to move away from the area, that there was going to be blasting going on in about two minutes, and that it would not be safe for them to be as close as they were.

Waiting in anticipation, they had time to look around. There were a couple tents set up, and the one they were standing in had a two-burner gas cooker, an icebox, and a few chairs in front of a bench.

While they were waiting, Donald realized that he had walked a pretty good distance, and had built up a good "hunger" He sat down on one of the chairs, and the others followed suit. Opening his paper sack, he took out a sandwich, and took a bite. It was so good that he wolfed it down, opened the sack again, and ate another one!

The man that escorted them to the tent asked where they were headed. They replied they were on their way back to Minnesota, but would like to find some work so they could earn a few dollars first. They asked if they could work there, and the man said they were not hiring anyone. He did say if they cleaned up around the place, that he could give them a couple dollars and some food. They heartily agreed.

It came time for the blast, and the boys watched, anticipating a huge rumble, roar, and then part of the mountain to disappear.

Soon, there was a small puff of smoke from the mountain, then a small "boom." They waited, expecting to see or hear more, but that was it!

They looked at each other and kind of shrugged their shoulders, as if to say, "What the hell was that?" They then picked up the trash around the "camp."

As they were about to leave, they met a man that was sort of stoop shouldered. He looked very pale. Donald recalls that when he heard the man speak he had some kind of accent. He would soon learn that not long after this encounter, the man, Gutzon

Borglum would shortly pass away. Mr. Borglum gave them each a dollar.

Donald says, "Shoulda saved that dollar! If I'd a known then that the place was gonna become as famous as it has, that dollar would really be worth something!"

IV
BACK HOME

After walking all of the way to Rapid City, the boys were totally tuckered out. They had walked over twenty miles that day!

They found an old abandoned house, and after making sure there were no "bums" or "hoboes" inside, they lay down on the floor and went to sleep.

The next morning they woke at sun-up, walked out back, found an old pump, and surprisingly they were able to get some cold fresh water! They splashed water on their faces, went back inside, ate an apple, the only thing left in their paper bags, and once again started walking.

About a mile from the old house, there was a café. They walked in and sat down at a booth. When a lady came over, and asked what they would like, Donald asked, "What'll a dollar buy?"

The lady smiled, and said, "Honey, fifty cents will get you the best breakfast in the place!"

"That'll suit us just fine Maam, can ya give us each two of your biggest breakfasts, and put one in a bag, and let us eat the other here?"

She looked at the boys, laughed, and answered, "Well, for you handsome young men, I sure will, only if you promise to come back in a couple years and take me out!"

The boys turned red with embarrassment, and everyone in the place, started laughing. Most of the men in there were railroad workers.

The boys ended up with bacon, ham, potatoes, toast, pancakes, orange juice and milk. When they finished with their food, and paid for it, the waitress brought them each a nickel back. They left her nickel apiece tip!

As the boys stepped from the café, the same policeman that had escorted them out of town two days prior suddenly confronted them! He began escorting them to his squad car, when the waitress came outside and hollered. "Hey Ted, leave them young boys alone, they're friends of mine!"

The deputy, red-faced, relented and got on his two-way radio. He called the station, had the station call the Highway Patrol, and had the boys transported, via the Highway Patrol, to the Minnesota border, where they were then transported to Minneapolis, via the Minnesota Highway Patrol.

It took the better part of the day, and about eight different rides to get them there, but Donald was happy. Two of the patrolman actually bought them lunch!

The boys were happy to be back in Minneapolis and gathered up all of their friends immediately. They sat until after midnight, telling them about their big trip! Finally tiredness set in, and the boys headed towards their respective homes, drowsy, but elated. Their elation would soon dissipate!

As they began to walk away, after putting out the bonfire they had started, two Hennepin County squad cars pulled up! With no explaining, they were not told why, but were transported to the county jail.

It came to pass that Donald and Kenny had been involved in some petty thievery. While the boys were gone, Donald's parents were visited by the powers that be, and later, after talking to Donald, it was decided to place him in a foster home.

Everyone realized this was a useless gesture, and Donald took off a week later. He immediately looked Kenny up and once again the two buddies were out adventuring.

Numerous times, Donald was placed in foster homes, all stays ending the same. Sometimes he would not even stay a complete day. He recalls, once walking in the front door, asking where the bathroom was, going to the bathroom, quietly locking the door, closing it, and then walking out the back door. Another time he simply went in a bathroom, crawled out the window and was gone. He said a couple times that he would say he was hungry, try the food and if he liked it, would stay a couple days. If he tried it and didn't like it he would be gone within an hour.

The biggest problem was he would start missing his buddies. He could only take it so long, and then he would leave, look up some of his friends, and they would be gone, riding trains, fishing, swimming, or whatever.

One of the tricks they used to play was "sneaking" into movies. One would buy a ticket, go in the theatre, and go directly to the rear "exit door," open it, let his buddies in, and they would watch the movie, sometimes staying until they would get kicked out. They would do this when it was cold outside. They would break in warehouses, or railroad buildings, just to get out of the cold.

On one of these occasions, Donald recalls it was bitterly cold outside, and he crawled underneath the loading dock of a warehouse. He went to sleep, and during the night the temperature dropped to well below zero. When he woke up, he found that his hands were frozen. He had slept at this same spot many times before and was kept warm by the heat escaping from inside, via a broken window. The only problem this time, the window had been fixed, plus the heat was turned off for the weekend.

Donald was taken to the Hennepin County General Hospital for treatment. They kept him for over two weeks. He was lucky he did not have to have his hands amputated. They were frozen that bad! He wears the scars to this day, and when it is cold out, he has to have gloves on or his hands start hurting.

They would swim in the Mississippi river, Lake Nokomis, or Lake Calhoun. Sometimes they would camp on the shores of the river or in the woods along the beach of the lakes.

He and his friends would steal a couple chickens, some vegetables out of gardens, and cook everything over an open fire. They learned some of their cooking skills from "hoboes" in "hobo jungles." They were adept at using what nature had to offer. They could use empty coffee cans as stoves, tin cans as cups, discarded pots and pans.

Sometimes they would scavenge the neighborhood before the garbage trucks would go through. Donald says, "It is really a shame the good things that people throw away."

As Donald grew older, the "juvenile authorities" became more frustrated with him and his shenanigans. Soon, they began placing him in the State Training School for Wayward Boys. This was located at Red Wing, Minnesota, located about forty miles Southeast of Minneapolis. Most young boys who ended up there, seemed to graduate to a life of crime, and many years later would still be bouncing around in the system. It was like a "junior college," teaching them new tricks on a regular basis.

One such trick was to find a "Boy Scout" shirt, put it on, and go to South Dakota or Wisconsin. Donald and his friends would buy a shirt and neckerchief for about seventy-five cents. They would go to South Dakota and go house to house, asking for donations for a special "Boy Scout" project they were on. Donald said that every house would give them at least fifty cents. After about fifty houses, they would have a minimum of fifty dollars. Then they would buy tickets on the train, instead of hopping it. They would dine in class! He said the cops would never bother them as long as they had their "Boy Scouts shirt on!"

From this point on, Donald's life began to really go down hill. He hated red Wing with a passion, and every time they would put him there he would escape. When he would get caught, they would add another year on to his stay. Pretty soon he had so much time to do that he could not see the end, and started to turn to "serious crime!"

When he would run away, he would usually hang around with his old friends. They would do the things they always did, and would usually stay out of anything serious.

One of his friends, Roy Russ, would end up drinking himself to death by the time he was thirty two years young. He also hung out with Donald Wise, who also drank heavily and subsequently died at a very young age also. There were the Ocasik brothers, two of whom died in a shootout with police in Minneapolis, and the third brother, who committed suicide in the St. Cloud reformatory with a butter knife! He stuck himself in the stomach with it and when he was found, the priest, Father Peter St. Hilaire was summoned. Father Peter saw the knife protruding from Ocasik's stomach, and pulled it out! The youngster died within a few minutes. He bled to death from the knife being taken out.

Many of Donald's friends are still doing time today. "They're mostly dead though," Donald sadly mutters.

Most died from alcohol, gunshots, accidents, beatings, stabbings, or suicides. A couple were put to death in prison by the states they were in!

Donald, who never acquired a taste for alcohol, has remained fairly healthy over the years. Except for his bout with one very serious heart attack, he has managed to keep walking upright, with shoulders back, and a crooked grin on his lips.

He says, "The only weakness I have is food, more food, and much more food!"

He is proud of the fact that he can remember every Dairy Queen, and White Castle in Minneapolis, and the outlying districts.

His fondness for food sometimes got him into trouble. One time he saw a large truck unloading hams at a warehouse. When he saw the driver go into the warehouse, he got in the cab of the truck and drove away! He and Kenny sold the hams to friends, relatives, restaurants, bars, and anyone else they could sell to. It took over a week to get rid of the whole load. There must have been about thirty five thousand pounds!

Another time, he and Kenny nailed a whole load of coffee, and another time a load of whiskey! They were never short of money after they learned how to do this. Many large companies would load their trucks, park them in the back lot, and leave them there until morning. Sometimes they would come out, and the truck would be gone!

Donald began using the alias of Lyle Johnson, a neighbor of his, who never got in any trouble. If he did get stopped and questioned by a cop, he would give the name, they in turn would check on it, and it would come back clean. They would then turn him loose.

V
HOBO JUNGLES

More and more, he and his friends would hang out in the "hobo jungles." It was safe for them there, and the cops would usually leave them alone. It was actually the safest place to be if the cops were looking for them. Cops did not want to enter the "hobo jungles." They did not think they were very safe. There were too many stories of dead, or wounded cops found near them.

Donald would listen with interest about the travels and exploits of the hoboes. They found out how to open locks, and learned to enter buildings from the second story, because the windows were never locked. They were like teachers, giving away information so that those interested could make their way through life in the best way they knew.

One of the stories that Donald liked to tell was about a certain garden, which was planted year after year, about a block away from a "hobo jungle." It was always kept neat, the weeds were always picked, and the vegetables were always very good! The hoboes would sneak into this garden and pick the vegetables they needed. They made it a point to not take more than they needed, and would never make a mess. They would sit around marveling at the freshness of these vegetables. Soon, they noticed a new "hobo" showing up when it came time to eat. His clothes were just a bit too clean, and he would never say much, just sorta nod his head, or grunt a little now and then. One night, as everyone grabbed their favorite sleeping area, one of them noticed that the new hobo sat around for a while, then got up, and started walking away from the camp. One of the others became curious and followed.

He followed for about a block and a half, until the person walked up the sidewalk and entered a big beautiful house!

The next evening, everyone was sitting around when the same person showed up, this time being immediately confronted by the rest.

Well, it turned out that the he was a she, and the owner of the garden where the hoboes were getting the vegetables. She had inherited a large sum of money, and liked sharing her fortune with others, especially with the hoboes!

It turned out she had been visiting the camp for over three years, often changing her disguise. She would bring chickens, ducks, geese and sometimes a roast of pork or beef. When the hoboes got to thinking, they realized that there was always salt, pepper and other herbs and spices mysteriously showing up.

Even after the hoboes found out she was not a real hobo, they would welcome her, and treat her like she was one of them, which in reality she was I guess.

She continued to dress in the same manner as they did.

The hoboes actually took to the boys. She felt protective over them, offering sage advice about everything from love to religion. She would assure them of a place to sleep, a good meal, and some good conversation.

One evening Donald was sitting on an old, but useful padded chair. The lady came over and sat on one of the arm rests. Donald could not help but notice how nice she smelled.

He said, "You smell just like a flower!"

She answered back, "And you are a very sweet boy!"

From that day forward, the lady was called "Daisy!"

One trick they learned while visiting the "jungle," was to walk down the main street of a small town on a Friday. There would be posters placed in the windows of the business places, telling of "barn dances," and where they would be and how to get there.

The boys would wait until dark, walk to the farm where the dance was to be held, hide in a grove, then slowly, but methodically go through the cars parked there.

There would be all kinds of things to be found, flashlights, lots of booze, sometimes food, many times clothing and always blankets. In the trunks, there was usually a gallon can of gas.

The boys would gather up these things and bring them back to the jungles where they would share equally with the hoboes.

Another trick was to hide in grocery store parking lots. When the grocery boy would carry the bags of food out to the car, one or two of the boys would run to the car, grab one or two bags, and escape with many groceries! Usually the customer would get home, carry the groceries in the house, and not realize anything was missing until it was all gone through, and the payment slip was checked. Then, the customer would go back to the store, tell the manager or owner they were missing some groceries. It would be settled by the grocery store replacing the stolen items, and the owner of the store thinking the grocery boy had simply made a mistake.

Sometimes the lads would hang outside the backs of bars, and would listen to the laughter, and music coming from inside. Donald said it was a special treat when a couple drunks would walk out side arguing, and then start to fight. Once in a while the owner would come out back, see them and run them off. The next morning he would usually give them a quarter or fifty cents to help clean the place up.

One such bar was a place called "The Green Parrot." When they went to help clean, the husband was not there. He was home sick.

His wife, much younger than he was, had the boys start cleaning.

She came over to Donald, and said he could help her clean in the basement. They went downstairs. Suddenly the woman, a beautiful blond, came up behind Donald and put her arms around him.

Donald was quite shocked, and said he was immediately paralyzed, so paralyzed that he could not stop the woman from steering him to a small cot in the corner, then taking his clothes off, then taking her own off, and teaching him everything a young boy wanted to learn.

Donald says, "She did things that made me see stars, and then she fed me, and made me see stars again!"

Donald smiled and added, "I think I saw the whole galaxy! For a while I wanted to be an astrologer!"

Donald then smiled again and said, "An astrologer is a person that studies the positions, and aspects of celestial bodies in the belief that they have an influence on the course of natural earthly occurrences, and human affairs. I think that is entirely true!"

(Sometimes Donald can come up with statements that will make a person stare at him in wonder!)

When everyone was done with the cleaning, and it was time to go, the lady gave each of them three dollars, then asked if they could come back the following week. Donald wholeheartedly agreed.

As they were leaving, his head was in the air. He was certain he was not only leaving his last, but also his "one and only true love" of his life. He would visit her on several occasions after that.

This was in Baker, Montana, and the last time he visited there, the woman's husband was really grouchy towards him, so he never went back again. All of this happened in 1940 and 1941. Donald was 14 to15 years of age.

Donald and his friends liked traveling West mostly. He says that, "The farther West you go, the friendlier the people are."

He says now that if he had to do it all over again, he would settle somewhere in the West, probably Montana or Wyoming.

He says, "The reason I really like the West so well is, them folks out there really know how to feed a person. They believe in meat and potatoes!" He grins and adds, "Them Western ladies know exactly how to treat a man too!"

While on the subject of women, the mothers of the boys would always do everything to help their sons. They would always stick up for them, and would always try to look out for them. They knew that they could not stop them from errant ways, but would still try to talk to them and warn them when they were heading into "deep water." In reality, the only thing they could really do was to pray for them, and hope their prayers would be answered.

Whenever Donald would come home from an excursion, his mother would sit and listen while he told of where he had been and what it was like. In addition, whenever he got the urge to leave again, his mother would pack him a bag, with a couple pair of clean underwear, some socks, a couple shirts and a clean pair of jeans. There would also be a bag of food.

Donald remembers with fondness how his mother tried to help him. When he thinks of her, sometimes his eyes get a little watery.

Donald states that the other mothers of his friends were all the same. They would allow their sons and friends to hide whenever they needed to, even when the law was looking for them.

VI
NEW ORLEANS

Donald continued to lead a carefree life, with nothing really bothering him much. He was doing what he wanted to be doing, and there was usually enough excitement to keep him happy. It has to be remembered that it really did not take much to excite him. Food was his big thing. He did not like boozing it up, or chasing women.

Even though some of his friends were starting to get in serious trouble, his life, and minor scrapes with the law did not bother him that much.

Two of his friends, Myron Lawver and Earl Verling burned down the Minnesota Paint Company, which was located on 4th Street and 10th Avenue in Minneapolis. They had been smoking and the fire started accidentally. They were arrested, labeled pyromaniacs and were sent to a mental institution. Larson says he never saw them again until fifteen years later.

He saw Lawver in Stillwater prison in 1979. Varling ended up a "skid row bum" after his mother and father hung themselves.

Even though Donald saw what was happening around him, he continued with the "free and easy" life style that he had so fondly grown accustomed to. At the age of seventeen his behavior would graduate to a more serious level though. It would not be considered simply "play" anymore.

Twenty two year old Victor Lindeman and twenty three year old Roger Sprague came up with an idea. They needed money and they wanted it quick. Donald and his two older friends decided that they would rob the Lake Street Liquor Store in Minneapolis. It was, at that time, the largest Liquor Store in the Twin

Cities area. The daring trio planned this out while driving down Lake Street in a stolen, dark blue Buick.

With guns drawn, the three "desperados" confronted the Liquor Store manager. He quickly told them, "Hey fella's, you're a little late! The money was just taken to the bank!"

The hapless robbers did manage to get twelve hundred dollars though. In 1943 that was considered quite a large sum of money, and even though the daring trio did not get the bulk of the money, they were quite happy with themselves.

After the robbery, Donald and his friends proceeded to the Buckingham Hotel parking lot on 15th and LaSalle in Minneapolis. There, Lindeman had parked his 1941 Ford Sedan. While the three gunmen began switching cars, a woman, looking out her window, became suspicious about what was going on in the parking lot. After she saw the three young men wiping down the Buick door handles, she immediately called the police. She gave them the license plate number off of Lindeman's car, which the police traced immediately. They paid his mother a visit and asked where he was. She replied that she did not know, but did know he was with his friends Larson and Sprague!

After wiping the Buick clean of all prints, Larson and Sprague went to the Nanking Restaurant in downtown Minneapolis. Lindeman went home, where his mother told him that the police were there looking for him about a half hour earlier. Lindeman did not waste any time and went straight to the Nanking and told Larson and Sprague of the "not so good news."

The three "wanted men" quickly bought some new clothing, and a couple suitcases, and then called George Moore, a childhood friend of Larson's. Donald told him that the cops were looking for him and that his friends and he needed a ride out of town. Moore was told that Lindeman's car was "hot" and they need to leave fast.

Moore picked the trio up and proceeded to take them to Des Moines, Iowa. They each handed Moore a hundred dollars for taking them out of the Twin Cities, and then bought train tickets to New Orleans! Donald had heard that New Orleans was known to have some of the finest food in the world. Donald said out loud, "This is gonna be a good day!"

In the meantime, Moore returned back to Minneapolis and began celebrating his pocket full of money. He began running his mouth to everyone who would listen to him about his three buddies and what they had done! Soon, the police caught wind of Moore's antics. They quickly caught up with him, and began with the questions. A few minutes later, the police knew exactly where they were heading.

Upon arriving in New Orleans, the wanted men checked into the Carlton Hotel. Sprague and Lindeman immediately cleaned up, put some new clothes on and went out to sample some of the "New Orleans Night Life."

They had heard that the women were all beautiful, and that they were all hot blooded. They headed straight for Bourbon Street!

Donald however, had bigger dreams. He decided to stay at the hotel. He called room service and ordered steak, lobster, shrimp, a dish called filet gumbo and a large bottle of wine suggested by the hotel staff.

Donald took a bath, and was barely dressed when the food arrived. It was served in silver trays, and plates! When Donald saw the food, he said that his mouth automatically started to water. He quickly reached in his pocket, took out two one hundred dollar bills, and handed it to the waiter. The waiter barely smiled, and left rather hurriedly. Donald took almost two hours to eat. He would eat til he was full, drink some wine, wait a few minutes, and start all over again. When he was finished with the food, and wine, he ate the large piece of warm peach pie with ice cream on it, and the day's excitement finally caught up with him. He went fast asleep! For once in his life his taste buds were totally sated! As he drifted into a deep sleep, he was seriously thinking of moving to New Orleans.

Lindeman and Sprague found Bourbon Street to their liking. The drinks were strong, and the women, all small waisted, dark eyed and hungry for love flocked around the two 'rich men' from Minnesota! The black haired beauties had both of the "big spenders" right where they wanted them. They were playfully rubbing there very visible, and ample breasts on their arms and shoulders. At one "bistro" four stunning Cajun girls escorted the two men upstairs, where the entertainment got much more interesting. They returned about an hour later, had a couple more drinks, began getting a little too rowdy, and when Lindeman insulted one of the girls, they were quickly thrown out. They went to another club, where Lindeman accused a girl of taking his money. The police were called, and both men were escorted out, then straight to jail. Within ten minutes the Parish Police knew who they were, where they were from, and what they were wanted for.

The New Orleans Police notified the Minnesota authorities and the FBI of their arrest.

They then proceeded to the Carlton Hotel where they were admitted to Donald's room. They found Donald sound asleep, with a big grin still on his face.

When they woke him up, and asked who he was, he said, "Lyle Johnson!" Though he acted very sincere, the police didn't buy it for a minute. In addition, they placed him under arrest.

The Police found out where Donald was staying, by the Hotel keys that Donald's partners had with them. He said that at first he thought that one of them may have snitched on him, but that was not the case.

The three robbers somberly sat in the Parrish jail, thinking about what had happened. Two were suffering the beginnings of severe hangovers, and one of them did not know it, but would find out in a couple days, that his, "such a beeg thing," as the girl whispered to him, would be dripping, and that it felt like there was a "beeg fire in it!"

Donald was pretty much the happiest. He stayed sober, had the best food money could buy, and had a memory he could keep forever!

The three robbers sat in the Orleans Parish Jail, somberly thinking about what was happening. They had already told police that they would sign extradition papers to be brought back to Minnesota.

Donald recalls that when he arrived in the jail, and saw Sprague and Lindeman, that they both still had lipstick on their faces! When he jokingly mentioned it to them, Sprague said, "I will never wash my face again!"

With lipstick on their faces, and gravy on Donald's shirt, they all felt pretty good, considering the trouble they were in.

Their cellmates happily listened while the three told of their exploits "up North," in Minnesota.

Two days later "extradition papers" were brought to them. They were promptly signed, and the three were ready to go home! Two detectives from Minnesota would escort them. One's name was Eugene Bernath, and was the Minneapolis Chief of Police.

About fifty miles down the tracks after boarding the train, Donald told Bernath to order food for everybody, and that he would pay for it. He at least wanted another sampling of some Louisiana Cooking before they got home.

Bernath looked at Donald like he was crazy, and answered, "How the hell are you going to pay for anything? Between the three of ya, there's only two dollars!"

It seems that all of the money they had was gone! It had mysteriously disappeared while they were in the Parrish Jail!

Donald said, "This is really horseshit, can't a person even trust the law?"

To this day, Donald still wonders what happened to that money. He doesn't know for sure if the cops in New Orleans got it, or Bernath got it. Either way, the money was gone, and Donald could not order the food. There would be no more fine Louisiana Cuisine on the trip back to Minnesota.

To make matters worse, Donald had to sit handcuffed, on a bouncing train, with his stomach growling, all the way back to Minnesota! The only thing he was given was a baloney sandwich, plus a glass of milk! Today, Donald states that he hates "baloney" but admits that under "emergencies," he can be forced to eat it! Mr. Larson, currently incarcerated at the Correctional facility, located at Faribault, Minnnesota, has proven on a couple occasions that he will eat it, and actually seemed to enjoy it!

VII
DO THE CRIME, DO THE TIME

Sprague, Lindeman, and Larson were all charged with the "armed robbery" of the Lake Street Liquors, plus the theft of the blue Buick used in the robbery.

Donald, because he was the youngest, and because he admitted to the robbery, and of stealing the Buick, thought that they would go easy on him, because of his age. The Judge however, did not take it into consideration. He sentenced Donald Floyd Larson to a period of "10 to 80 years" to the "Youth Conservation Commission!"

Lindeman, who actually took the car, received five years, and Sprague received ten! All three were sent immediately to the Reformatory, located in St. Cloud, Minnesota.

After going through a brief period of "orientation," Donald went to work in the kitchen! This seemed an appropriate place for him under the circumstances.

Donald states that at that period in time, the prison system was "self supporting." They operated their own dairy and beef farm, raised their own hogs, chickens and had hundreds of acres of land they used for the feeding of the animals and for vegetables! All of the food was grown and prepared with "convict labor." They received from twelve cents a day to about twenty-seven cents! This proved good for the taxpayers, the prison system, and also the convicts.

Donald states that the convicts were proud of their work, and of the food they prepared. There were never any arguments about the food. Not many people on the outside ate as well as the convicts were eating! They even had their own "butcher shop" and killed, cut up, and prepared their own food.

There was also a canning factory where inmates canned the vegetables grown on the farm.

This entirely worked fine until some business people got together, with some legislators, and had a law passed that forced "Corrections" to buy the food products from "outside sources!" It seems that people wanted a slice of the pie! The prison system had to shut down one of the top Holstein cowherds in the U.S.A.! They were forced to sell all of them! They had to quit farming, canning, meat cutting, and everything else involved with food!

To this day, the prison system has not recovered. Every year the cost of food for the prisoners in Minnesota costs more, and the taxpayers are suffering for it. Now, outside companies run the food industry in prison. There is no more "pride" for what a person has grown, and or prepared. Now, it is hard to get cons to work in the kitchens!

After serving three years in the Reformatory, Donald was transferred to the maximum-security prison, located in Stillwater, Minnesota. He was only twenty years old, still underage, and with a mountain of time to do!

Actually, Stillwater was a much better place to do time. The population was older, with most of the convicts over thirty years of age. It was more "laid back" and the wages were a little better. A guy could go to work in the "twine factory" and make up to thirty-seven cents a day and an extra twelve cents a day by working in the evenings for three hours!

Cigarettes were only nine cents a pack, twenty four candy bars in a box for eighty seven cents, bags of popcorn for eight cents a bag, or five bags for a quarter.

There were movies shown in the auditorium every weekend, and you would get your popcorn or candy and sit and watch a good movie! There were no televisions. In the cells, there was a box on the wall with a plug-in for your metal headphones with three stations. There was one religious, one country music, and the station WCCC that had soap operas, sports, and news.

When Donald arrived in Stillwater, he was first taken to the laundry where he was given sheets, pillowcases, blankets, and clothing. The boss down there was SGT Murphy, a grouchy, ornery man about fifty years old, five feet eight inches tall, and weighing about a hundred and thirty pounds! Though small, he did not take any shit from anyone, convicts, or other guards! However, he was fair, and protected those who worked for him.

If you complained that your clothes were too big, he would holler, "Grow into the fucking things then!"

If they were too small, he'd yell, "Then lose some weight, you're too fuckin fat!"

There was no winning with Murphy. His bark was worse than his bite though, especially if you worked for him. He was a good man to work for, and if he liked you he would stick up for you all the way. He'd even go to the "Parole Board" with you!

From the laundry, Donald got a pass. *(A permit which allowed you to walk to wherever you were supposed to go)* This one was to go to the hospital. There, you would be thoroughly examined. Sometimes this would take at least five minutes, depending on how many were being examined on that day.

A nurse would take your temperature; a doctor would stick his finger up your ass, and listen to your heartbeat, "both at the same time!" Then, with the same hand, he'd been playing with your ass with, would grab a tongue depressor, stick it in your mouth, tell you to say aaaaaah, then would look into your eyes, say you were ok, and yell, "next," not even taking off the rubber finger!

VIII
"DOC JOHNSON"

The doctor in Stillwater at that time was Doctor Johnson! He had glasses at least a third of an inch thick. He would bump into a stone pillar, say excuse me, and go on his way. He was an extraordinary doctor though. As blind as he was, he could still perform major operations! Of course, a few of his patients died on the table, or shortly thereafter, but he gave his all! He would not let a few failures dissuade him from "cutting" the next time!

One night a convict by the name of Douglas complained about having chest pains. He had just had open-heart surgery at the University of Minnesota. Doc Johnson was called, and told the convict was having problems. Johnson said he would see him in the morning. He was called two more times that night.

Finally, the third time, he said, "Look, just tell him to relax, and I'll see him in a few hours." The guard said he couldn't tell him that, explaining that the convict was dead!

This was finally the end of Doc Johnson. When he showed up for work the next morning, he was not allowed to enter the prison.

All of the convicts, after passing physicals, usually went to work at the "twine factory." If not there, you would go to the kitchen, or the yard crew. Many complained about having bad hearts or being sick, and old Johnson would say, "My God son, you are a perfect specimen of health. You're alive and alert, go to work in the twinery!"

One convict by the name of Larry "Peg" Dahl only had one eye. He would need to have his glass eye taken out about once a month, and have the doctor clean out the socket. Working in the twine shop could get a little dusty. After washing the socket out, he would replace the glass eye, bandage it, and send Larry back to work.

The last time Larry saw him, everything went well, until the doc told Larry to go back to work.

Larry asked, "How? You bandaged my good eye you quack son of a bitch!"

IX
LARRY DAHL

Larry Dahl's nickname was "Peg Eye," due to the fact that he only had one eye. There were probably as many stories about him as there were about Doc Johnson. He was definitely a character, and was always in trouble. He was prone to fighting a lot, whether it was with a guard, guards, or another convict.

When he was in the Reformatory, he made minimum security, and was put to work on the outside carpenter crew. Every day, three or four of the guys would jump in the back of an old green Chevy pick up, go through the gate, and would work on the houses on the highway that ran in back of the wall. The highway had frost bumps, and holes in it, and was quite bumpy.

On the way back one afternoon, Larry was sitting on the "tail gate" of the truck with two other cons. Larry was in the middle.

They were going about thirty miles an hour. Behind them, was a Red Ford convertible with two good looking women in it. The three guys were waving at them, and they were waving back, honking the horn, and laughing. The crotch in Larry's pants was gone, and he had no underwear on! Needless to say, his "privates" were hanging out! Everyone, including the girls thought it was hilarious.

Suddenly the old pickup hit a deep pothole, and the back of the truck was in the air. So was Larry, and when he came back down, the truck was no longer under him. He landed on his ass, skidded a few feet, got up, and began running behind the truck! Everyone laughed about that for weeks!

You had to be careful if you sat with Larry at chow. Everyone had tin cups, and if you had milk, kool-aid, or coffee in it, and Larry was sitting next to you, he would drop his glass eye in your cup when you were not looking. When you'd go to take a drink, you'd see that eye looking back at you!

Peg's friend and crime partner's name was "Easy Eckman," and also known to be about half crazy. One time they stole a Buick in St. Paul, and headed East towards Chicago. Easy was driving. They had made a deal. They would take turns driving, each driving two hours, then they would switch. Larry went to sleep, and when he woke up it was past two hours. Easy wouldn't stop! It seems that Larry was a pretty crazy driver, and with only one eye, nobody really wanted to ride with him.

When Easy refused to pull over and let him drive, Larry simply grabbed the shift, and threw it in reverse! They were doing about ninety miles per hour! They said later that pieces of transmission were scattered for two miles! Easy asked Larry why he did it and Larry matter-of-factly answered, "Because it was my fuckin turn!"

X
PRISON LIFE

Donald ended up going to work in the "twinery," and soon found that he knew most of the guys working there. Almost all of them had been in Red Wing, graduated to the Reformatory, and then to Stillwater. Some of his old friends from the "streets" were there! It was like "old home week."

After his first day of work as a "Twino" Donald returned to his cell quite tired. He had really never worked hard before in his life. Even though he was in good shape, his muscles were not used to work. He could walk at least ten miles without tiring, and lift a ton, but repetitive work, he was not used to.

When he slid the iron barred door open, he was surprised to see a large paper bag on his bunk. He opened it up. There was toothpaste, soap, hair oil, shaving equipment, and best of all, candy bars, popcorn, chips, and even cookies!

It was kind of a "welcome bag," left by some of his buddies. Everybody liked Donald. He was known as a "stand up con," and could be trusted!

Donald's starting wage was not much, but allowed him to buy the few things he needed from the small canteen. He got most of his needs from friends that worked in the kitchen!

He had a steady supply of roast beef, ham, bread, baloney, pork chops, and about anything else he needed. He would get together with his friends, and they would put together some pretty good meals from the ill-gotten supplies.

Tommy Grey, a life time friend, worked in the butcher shop. He was the "head butcher," and Donald did not have to worry about food! Every once in a while, he would even "score" a gallon of ice cream! Tommy had been on many excursions with Donald on the "streets." He would and did take care of Donald's hunger! He got him prime cuts of beef and pork every week.

Tommy was married then, and his wife visited him on a regular basis. One time she brought her sister along. Donald visited with her and they soon became good friends. She then started visiting him on a regular basis. She visited him for years. He said he would have married her if things had been different. He also says, "I woulda actually straightened out!"

What Donald did not know about crime when he arrived at Stillwater, he soon learned. He says he was like a sponge, "just soaking up information."

He said he learned about shop lifting, but never liked it, about burglary, opening safes, and other lucrative "jobs" he could pull to make large amounts of money! After all, he was now living in a world of robbers, burglars, check writers, counterfeiters, safe crackers, car thieves, and on and on!

One of the best teachers was a guy called Leo Campa, who while in Stillwater, counterfeited over a million dollars while working in the "prison print shop!"

He counterfeited driver's licenses, ID cards, title cards for cars, trucks, and motorcycles. Anything that could be printed, he would print. The big thing was his one hundred dollar bills!

Leo's best friend on the streets had no legs. He would pass about ten thousand dollars worth of checks, and hundred dollar bills each weekend. He smuggled the counterfeit hundreds, and Minnesota state checks, out in his fake legs when he got out of Stillwater!

Later, Campa would send out everything he printed in the backs of paintings. Another friend, Frank Pepin drove the prison truck, and would smuggle things out for Campa. (He got killed by Police while pulling a burglary.)

Another friend of Campa's, Donald Haley, also passed some of the money after he escaped from the University of Minnesota Hospital, after being transferred there for cancer treatments. He ended up being shot to death by police also. He was "holed up" inside a "Goodwill Store" at 13th and Franklin Avenue. When he walked out, the Minneapolis Police immediately gunned him down!

Campa himself suffered a very violent death! After he was paroled, he moved to New Mexico where he actually became a Juvenile Parole Officer! Police killed him, while in the middle of a family dispute.

(Larson wonders today, if that is really all that life has to offer.)

When he thinks back over the years, and of all the people he has known who are now dead, crippled or still in prison and mental institutions, he gets very depressed. He says, "A curtain of blackness descends upon your soul and takes a large toll on your life and destiny!"

Donald kept a clean record while in prison. He minded his own business, watched out with whom he hung around with, and tried to keep a very low profile. His actions and behavior were both rewarded when he appeared before the parole board in Stillwater.

Unlike the judge who sentenced Donald to "ten to eighty years" they actually felt a little compassion towards him. Taking into account Donald's record while in prison and his still young age, they granted him parole!

PART III

GOING
STRAIGHT

I
"PAROLE GRANTED!"

Not only did the Parole Board have some faith in Mr. Larson, one of them, Mr. Arthur Stillman, hired him! Mr. Stillman owned 17 Super Markets and a large warehouse at the rock Island Terminal in Minneapolis.

Stillman, not only a Parole Board Officer, was also known as a humanitarian. He believed that everyone deserved a second chance, especially if they were willing to help themselves. He would give Donald Larson the first real job that he ever had. Donald was now twenty-five years old!

After serving over seven years in prison, one would think that the person would want to celebrate. Most would want "booze," "women," and "song!" Not Donald! He looked up his old buddy, Kenny Callahan, and took him and his wife out for a big dinner! After eating his fill, Donald said he had to get some sleep because he had to go to work the next day.

132

Donald's duties at Stillman's were loading and unloading trucks. He also helped unload boxcars. It was a tough job for sure, but Donald did not seem to mind. He was well over six feet tall, weighed two hundred and twenty five pounds, and was in very good shape. He actually thrived on the hard work. He did so well that within a couple of months he got a promotion. Mr. Stillman offered him a job driving truck. To this day, Donald says that Mr. Stillman was a very good boss, and was willing to treat Donald the same as anyone in his employ. The fact that he had been in prison was never mentioned.

Donald never forgot his buddy Tommy Grey, who was still doing time in Stillwater. He talked to Mr. Stillman, and within six months Grey was paroled, and immediately hired by American Produce Company. He went to work as a "driver" also. His recommendation came from none other than Arthur Stillman.

Grey worked for Stillman until 1974, and would have continued to work for him, but was convicted of the "Bartholomew Fur Heist!"

After Tommy's conviction was overturned and he was subsequently released, he went on to live a crime-free life. To this day, he remains a close friend of Donnie Larson's. (Tommy visited Donnie in prison for years, but has not been able to for the last six or seven. He has had a stroke, and is in pretty tough shape.)

While working for Mr. Stillman, Donald met, and fell in love with Marjorie Christensen. They became married and bought a home in Crystal, a fairly new, quiet suburb of Minneapolis.

Marjorie and Donald ended up having four children, one son and three daughters. This marriage would last until Larson, and a friend would become involved in the "burglary" of a liquor store in Cleveland, Minnesota. Donald was arrested, and his wife, divorced him.

II
"DOIN TWENTY"

The mastermind behind the burglary was an old friend of Larson's. His name was Arne Sandberg.

Their haul consisted of a measly, fourteen cases of expensive liquor! Donald said, he knew better, and that he had no intention of ever getting into trouble again, but admits, it was his fault, and cannot blame anyone else. He said it was because, "my errant behavior just got the best of me, and I could not overcome what I had learned during my formative years." (Sometimes Donald can really surprise a person!)

Sandberg was also involved in a "check writing scheme," which involved the use of various young people. When some of the youngsters were arrested for passing the checks, they of course immediately snitched on Sandburg, who was immediately arrested, and who immediately snitched on Larson for his involvement in the liquor store burglary.

He also snitched on everyone else he had anything on. This would put him in good standing with the authorities. They in turn, dropped the "check" charges!

Both Sandburg and Larson ended up receiving twenty years on the burglary charge and were promptly sent to Stillwater. This seems a rather stiff sentence for a thousand dollars worth of booze!

Six months after arriving at Stillwater, Larson went before the "parole board." They too, evidently felt the sentence was a little harsh. They continued him for three years, making a total of three years, six months, and eighteen days, which he ended up doing. That is the same as "expiration" on a five-year sentence.

Mr. Sandburg, after all of his snitching, and whining, did not fare quite so well. His blaming everyone else for his behavior seemed to work against him. He ended up doing a total of five years!

Donald ended up getting out in 1966, and went to work for Arthur Stillman, where he would remain employed until his massive heart attack in 1974.

III
A NEW ENTERPRISE

Besides working for Arthur Stillman, Donald worked part time for his old friend, Kenny Callahan. He worked with Callahan, and Harold Combs. The company was called "Custom Cabinets." Not only did they have a thriving business in "cabinetry," they were thriving in the "fencing" business also! (For those of you who do not know what that means; "fencing" is buying stolen property from people, then re-selling it at a profit.)

This "side line" for the trio was extremely lucrative, and reached throughout Minnesota, all of the U.S. and Canada!

Donald said he had more money than he thought existed! He was living very well. He had a new automobile, money to support his "eating habit," and did not have a worry about anything. He kept a low profile, and minded his own business.

Through business relationships, Donald would meet some pretty interesting people, many of whom were quite wealthy. Some of these people were also known to be a little on the "shady side" when it came to their choice of business.

Donald would be invited to Chicago, New York, Miami, Atlanta, New Orleans, and Las Vegas! He was wined and dined in some of the top "eateries" in the United States! Moreover, the big thing was that, "It was free!"

Everything, including his transportation, was paid for by "his friends." He would stay at the best hotels, ride around in Limos, and be in the company of some of the most gorgeous women in the world. Donald definitely enjoyed their company, and shyly admits that, "Once in a while, I would enjoy their favors also!" However, Donald was not known as a "womanizer!" His big quest in life was "food!"

He said that if a beautiful woman happened to be in his company, while partaking of a beautiful meal, "Sometimes I would have a hunger for a little 'dessert' too!"

IV
SEAMUS

During his lucrative, though illegal business dealings, he again ran into an old friend. While dining at the "Kings Supper Club," Northwest of St. Cloud, Seamus "D" McGee walked in.

It seems that Seamus habituated the Kings on a regular basis.

Seamus and Arnie Schiller, owner of the Kings, knew each other quite well. Seamus managed a bar called the "Woodland Lodge," owned by a friend of Arnie's.

It turned out that some of the "business dealings" Donald was involved with were similarly related to the things that Seamus was doing "as a side business."

This whole "accidental meeting" turned out to be no accident at all. Donald had received word through a mutual acquaintance that he was to go to the "Kings" and have someone by the name of "Mac" paged. He was told it could mean earning some "serious money!" To Donald, serious money, and good food were related. Therefore, when he was told the "meeting place" was to be at the Kings, he was very happy. When he found out that his "meet" was Seamus McGee, he was also happy!

Seamus explained there was some "heavy equipment" buried in a gravel pit, near Little Falls, Minnesota. It was all dismantled, and consisted of three turnapaults, and a "lay down" machine! They were brand new, and valued at over two million dollars!

They were to be transported to the "buyer" who lived in Edmonton, Canada.

While Donald and Seamus were talking over old and new times, and laughing about both, the conversation finally turned to business.

Seamus said that the total payment for the delivery of the equipment would be a half million in cash! He also explained that if Donald wanted to help, he would receive twenty five thousand, before they departed and another twenty five thousand when they reached their destination.

Donald did not have to think long. He did not miss a chew of the delicious filet mignon he was eating. He simply answered "ok" and then asked, "When do we leave?"

Seamus laughed, and said, "We need to be there in four weeks. The delivery date is July 3rd. everyone thinks that would be a good time. There will be heavy traffic, and trucks will not be bothered. The borders to Canada will be very busy, and they'll be pushing trucks, campers, and cars through as fast as they can."

Donald asked, "What's my job? I know I'm not getting paid just to be a passenger!"

Seamus laughed and said, "Your job will be to drive, and, if need be, some 'muscle' on the delivery end. There's supposed to be a guy there that can get a little ornery, and likes to try to hold back on the fees!"

It was Donald's turn to laugh. He said "you know I don't like physical confrontations! I handle my problems in a different way!"

Seamus simply replied, "I know!"

Seamus told Donald that they already had four trucks, but needed one more. Donald said he knew someone at the Peterbilt Dealer, in St. Paul, and would have a truck and trailer available.

The date was set, and the two old friends went to Brainerd, stopped at the "Canteen," a bar outside of "Fort Ripley," and then went to the show at the "Red Carpet." Seamus knew one of the dancers there by the name of Sandy Smith. She had a message for him, and after a drink, they went to St. Cloud, to a place called McNasty's. Bobby Vinton was playing there, and both Donald and Seamus thought it would be nice to take in his act. They were later sorry they did. Vinton was so drunk when he came on the stage, that he had to be escorted off the stage, and actually out of the building! It seemed the "Polish Prince" was not that much of a prince!

Donald went back to Minneapolis, and made arrangements for the "Pete" tractor, and the trailer. The Tractor had a 1693-t Cat engine in it, putting out about five hundred and fifty horsepower, more than adequate for the heavy load it would be hauling.

The big "conventional" had been ordered by a guy that was set to be running to Alaska.

He got crippled in a car accident, and when the truck arrived, he could not buy it. Peterbilt then put it on a lease program. Donald got it for favors that he did for a friend of his who worked in the "finance" department.

He got the "drop deck" trailer from "Brown Trailers" on County Rd. C in Minneapolis. He leased it for thirty days.

Everyone met at the designated time at the truck stop just East of St. Cloud. After having breakfast, they headed for Little Falls.

It only took about three hours to load, and secure the heavy pieces of equipment. After tarping the loads, they were ready to leave. Seamus led the way in a new KW on loan from Koch leasing, Donald followed in his Pete, the "Cherokee" followed in his KW Cabover, the "Racer" in an International Eagle Conventional, and the "Big K" in his Western Star Conventional. It made for an interesting convoy!

All of the cabs were equipped with CBs and a Bi Lateral Linear to insure talking power, plus each radio had a "lower band" switch to insure privacy when conveying messages, so that other unwanted listeners would not be able to copy.

Before they left, Donald asked how long the trip would take, Seamus answered, "A little longer than usual. We don't want to cross any weigh stations, or ICC inspections. That should be easy, seeing that we're traveling so close to the fourth. We should be there in approximately three days, and back in two. It will be a total of about 1,700 miles up there, and about 1,500 back."

Donald thought a moment and said, "Well, we better get started then!"

They got on Highway 10, and headed west. Their first stop was Bismarck, North Dakota. It took them six hours. Everything was going well. As they sat eating lunch each man was thinking that if the rest of the trip went this good it would definitely be worth the danger. They had made about four hundred miles smoothly. Each had hopes for the rest of the way.

Traffic was a little heavy until they reached Fargo. The farther west they traveled, the less traffic.

They pulled into Beach, N. Dakota at a little after six in the afternoon.

Staying on Highway 94, they arrived in Billings, four hundred miles farther, at shortly after midnight. There, they fueled up, ate, and decided to get a little sleep. By six A.M. they were back on the road again!

From Billings to Helena Montana took only four hours. Their next stop was at Missoula, where they stopped and all partook of giant T-bone steaks! The Truck Stop there knew how to treat a trucker for sure! Donald made a mental note to remember that place.

When they left Missoula, they stayed on "90" until they reached "93" headed north towards Kalispell where they pulled into a large parking lot at a motel. There, Seamus went inside and got the keys to four rooms. Each went to his own room and Donald and Seamus went to the one they were sharing. It was a double, and unlike the others, had a hot tub, and a bar!

Seamus mixed a drink, and gave Donald a Michelob. A few minutes later, a short heavy set man knocked, and then came in. His name was Mike Parker, and turned out to be the go-between in the whole operation. He set it up, would make sure everyone would get paid, and formulated the times, dates, and everything else.

Seamus introduced Donald to Mike, and the three sat talking a while. Mike was about to leave, when he stopped, turned, reached inside his coat, and took out a large brown envelope.

Seamus opened the package, and pulled out a wad of hundred dollar bills that would choke an elephant! There was fifty thousand dollars in one big bunch!

Seamus gave Donald ten thousand, then went to the other rooms and gave each driver ten grand. It was "good faith" money, and the rest would be paid upon delivery of the merchandise.

When Seamus had finished his payments he took all of the men out to eat. With the help of Mike Parker, they were steered to a fine dining club, where they had buffalo steaks, wine and everything that went with it.

All of the men had a wonderful sleep, with the fresh air of the Kalispell area wafting through their windows.

At six AM, Seamus woke all of the men and went and had breakfast and again they were on their way.

Leaving Kalispell, they stayed on "93." They were nearing the Canadian border, and Donald was wondering if they would have any problems. They reached a very small town called Eureka, and Seamus pulled over. The rest followed suit.

Seamus walked back to Donald's truck, and told him he would be gone for about five minutes. A car pulled up, Seamus got in, and the car disappeared down the road.

Within ten minutes, the car returned, Seamus got out, waved for the trucks to follow, and started heading north again.

In no more than three miles the small convoy came to a sign that read, "Port Of Entry, 1 Mile." As they neared it, Donald could see that it was closed. There was a large gate blocking the entrance into Canada!

Seamus came to a stop, got out of his truck, and walked up to the phone booth on the outside of the small building which served as the "Port." He reached up, took something from the ledge above the phone, walked over to the gate, unlocked it, and waved the trucks through. He then got in his, drove through, stopped, and relocked the gate, placed the key back where he had found it, and again they were on their way.

They followed "93" until they reached "3" and followed it to Fort McLeod. There they got on highway "2" which took them all the way to Edmonton, Alberta, Canada. They stopped at Calgary and had a quick lunch.

When they arrived in Edmonton, they went to a truck stop, fueled up, and had another small lunch. When they got the bills, Donald mentioned the fact that the meals were quite expensive! He had steak, eggs, fried potatoes, and a big piece of apple pie. It came to $ 7.95! Even though the meal filled him up, he still thought it a little high. When he went to pay for it, he paid with a ten-dollar bill. The cashier gave him back five dollars. The currency exchange between Canadian and American money was that much of a difference! Then Donald felt quite happy, and mentioned that he would like to stop there on the way home.

Seamus made a phone call, and returning to the large table where they all sat and he informed them that they still had a considerable trek ahead of them. They had to deliver the merchandise to a place called "Peace River." This was another 500 miles! It would be midnight before they would get there!

They stopped again when they reached "Slave Lake." The place was beautiful, with everything green, and clean. The air was so clean that it almost hurt to breathe.

As beautiful and as green as it was, it would not stay that way very long. The summers were very short, and in the winter, temperatures were known to dip to "60" below!

When they arrived at Peace River, all of them were quite tired. They stopped at a large motel, parked their rigs, and got rooms for the evening.

They were fortunate enough to get there just as the dining area was getting ready to close. The men managed to get some cold beer, and roast moose sandwiches. Along with a salad, and a couple bottles of Molson, it made for a delicious meal.

Seamus woke at six in the morning, and woke the rest of the men. They all met at the dining area, and had a nice breakfast.

While they were eating, a large, dark complexioned man approached their table. He simply introduced himself as "Brewer," and said that they should stay at the motel while his crew took the trucks to the unloading spot, and then he would meet them afterwards. Seamus and the other men hurriedly finished eating, and then went to Seamus' room.

Seamus was quick to point out, that he would not turn the trucks over to anyone, without the rest of the money owed. Brewer scowled at him, walked out, and returned with a small suitcase.

Seamus opened it, glanced inside, saw American money, lifted out one of the stacks, and found that the money on top was American, while the money underneath was Canadian!

Seamus said, "Look, you big, ugly, SOB, we agreed on 'All, American Money!' If you ain't got 'All American Money,' you ain't gettin any 'All American Machinery!' Make it easy on yourself!"

The big man stared at Seamus with contempt and said, "You bloody yanks are all the same! Ya all think yer money's better, and that you're better than anyone else." He grabbed the suitcase, stomped outside. Within three minutes he was back with a different suitcase. This one had all American money inside.

Seamus said, "Ok Brewer, you already got on the wrong side of things! I notice you got five of your business associates with you. Call one of them inside now!"

Brewer opened the door and stood part way outside waving towards the station wagon that he had driven up. One of the other men with him got out and Brewer hollered at him to come over.

The man came over and Seamus spoke. "You and the rest of ya can take the trucks, go get em unloaded, and return them. You have three hours to do it. Mr. Brewer will be staying with us until you bring the trucks back."

The confused man looked at Brewer, who shrugged his shoulders and said, "Ya Panko go do what he says. I'll stay here!"

The next three hours drug by very slow, but finally the five trucks slowly pulled into the parking lot, trailers empty, tarps folded neatly, and strapped down on the front of each trailer.

The trip home was uneventful. They averaged about seventy miles per hour, stopping only two times to fuel up, and get some sleep, and four times to eat. Donald was a little upset they took a shorter route back home. He wanted to stop at the same place in Edmonton, where they had eaten earlier.

Donald would team up with Seamus on a several more occasions. They had some prosperous dealings together and in fact bought a place together. It was called "The Outpost." It was a three/two Bar which served set ups, and lite lunches.

Surrounded by lakes, and woods, it was sort of a hidden club, or getaway. There were six cabins. They served very good meals, and did a thriving business, and served as a good spot for their "business associates" to meet and relax.

Both Donald and Seamus would agree that neither of them would ever get involved with anything that had any violence involved.

Seamus would disappear sometimes for weeks at a time, and Donald would do the same. Neither questioned the other about where they had been. Then, Seamus disappeared for over two years. The next time they would meet would be in Stillwater prison!

IV
AN OMEN

One day Donald decided to visit his friends at Occie's Bar.

Donald no more than entered the door, when Occie beckoned him to the back room. He told Donald that one of his employees, an off duty policeman, mentioned that Donnie, Kenny, and Harold Combs were buying large quantities of stolen property. He told Occie that the trio was "going down!" In other words, they were going to get "busted!" The off duty cop went on to say that the "Cabinet Shop" was just a front for a "mob" fencing organization!

This was enough for Donald. He immediately got hold of Kenny, and Harold. He told them the disheartening news, and within two hours, all of their "business associates" were also informed that the business was temporarily closed.

This included the Cabinet Shop. The proceeds from both businesses were split between the trios.

Kenny moved to Wisconsin, where he built a beautiful home, Combs started a small construction company in Minneapolis, and Donald bought an eighty-acre farm near Willow River, Minnesota.

Donald's house had four bedrooms. Kenny and Donald completely remodeled it, along with all new wiring, and plumbing. They redid the kitchen, and added a three-car garage. Not quite finished, they planted over three thousand trees throughout the property.

This was Donald's retirement home, where in his "twilight years," he could sit back, with nature abounding all around him, fish when he wanted to, and take long walks throughout his property.

With his "fifty grand" from the Canadian score, his split of the Cabinet shop, and other properties he had stashed throughout the U.S. he could live a comfortable life. Later he could start drawing SSI, and still later, Social Security. Fate however, would later play an important part in his plans for the future.

PART IV

THE RETIREMENT

I
A DEVIL IN DISGUISE "JAMES FALCH"

After being paroled in 1966, Donald met Ruth Powell. It turned out that Ruth's husband had abandoned her and her two children. He ran off with a seventeen-year-old girl, and ended up in Las Vegas. He took all of their money, left Ruth with the two children, with no food, no car, no place to live, nothing!

When Donald met Ruth, he of course felt instantly sorry for her, and the children. Thinking back, this would have had to do with his childhood, and how he grew up. He and his friends "stuck up" for each other, helping when trouble befell one or more of them.

Material things did not mean that much to Donald, so when he found out that Ruth, and her kids were in need, he stepped forward, and offered assistance. He got her a place to stay, furnished it for her, bought her groceries, and when she needed to go someplace he would take her. He treated the kids as his own.

Soon Ruth and Donald began dating. It seemed they were made for each other. Ruth suddenly became pregnant and soon had a son. They named him Mark. Neither Donald nor Ruth was overly eager to rush into marriage. However "six" years later did become "man and wife."

Being married, and having a family seemed to suit Donald fine. Their home, nestled amongst the lakes, and woods was the tranquility that Donald so eagerly longed for throughout his life.

The children enjoyed the surroundings. They had acres of land they could play on, and explore, or just be children.

As soon as Kenny and Donald finished with the remodeling, the Larson family, moved in. They did this in 1974.

On the day that the Larsons moved in, they were unexpectedly visited, by what you might say was a neighbor. The person's name was James Falch! It seems that he had followed Larson's truck from Willow River, all the way to Larson's farm.

When Donald pulled into his driveway, Falch pulled in right behind him. Falch got out of his truck with hand out thrust. With a hardy shake, he introduced himself, and explained that he lived ten miles away from the Larson place.

Falch offered to help Donald, and his family to get moved in.

With a big smile he said, "That's what neighbors are for!"

Had Donald any inkling of what this meeting would bring, he would have immediately kicked Falch off his property with no hesitation!

This encounter would bring ruination to dozens of people, some of whom would die, get divorced, go to prison, turn into snitches, and disappear from the face of the earth, cause hatred, distrust and misery.

While talking with Falch, Donald soon learned that Falch knew more about him, than what he knew about Falch.

For instance, he knew that Donald had, had a heart attack, he knew his name, he knew Kenny Callahan's name, and when Donald thinks back, knew other small things about him that he really had no reason, nor business knowing. This entirely befuddled Larson, but he "let it go" as, not very important.

Donald was glad to have his help. He was strong, and handled moving the heavy things into the house with ease. Donald was still considered to be on "shaky legs." Besides that, Donald had learned early in life, "never look gift horses in the mouth!"

Donald, against most of his teachings, totally accepted the over helpfulness, and friendliness of Mr. Falch! It would not be long until Falch would show how friendly he could really get!

Ruth, Donald, Cye, Scott, and Mark were soon comfortably nestled in their new home. This was a far cry from the "city life" they were all used to. The kids were the ones that were really impressed about the big move. They did not know there could be that much room to play, roam, hunt, nor explore!

A month after the move, Donald decided to have a "moving in" party. It would coincide with the fourth of July, so he figured it would really be nice to have a big barbecue.

They decided to invite Mr. and Mrs. Falch, their children, and some friends from Minneapolis. Donald reasoned that it would only be right to invite the Falchs, if for no other reason than, him being so helpful in moving in. Falch and his family were eager to accept the invitation.

Larson, tending the coals for the barbecue, thought to himself, "This is what life is really about. No worries, good friends, and living amidst nature were the only ways to go!"

He smiled as he could hear the laughter around him, his reverie only interrupted when he heard a car in the driveway.

Donald looked up, and exclaimed, "Paul Harris?!" He thought to himself, "This is a little strange!"

Donald let the feeling of unease pass, and as Harris got out of his car, he said, "I brought a friend to Duluth, and thought as long as I was in the neighborhood, I would stop and say hello!"

To Donald, this seemed perfectly plausible, and was quick to introduce Harris to everyone. When he introduced Harris to Falch, Donald had a distinct feeling that this was not the first time they had met. In the back of his mind, he remembers thinking, "These two already know each other!"

When the beer started to run low, Falch eagerly volunteered to go, and purchase more. He said his friend owned the "Squirrel Cage" Bar in Willow River. His name was William Cooper. *(It would turn out later that along with both Harris and Falch, Cooper was also a Federal snitch! Much too late, Donald would learn that all three were in cahoots with FBI Agent Peter Neuman, who was heading up the Piper kidnapping, and who incidentally had his sights aimed at Donald and Kenny Callahan.)*

Falch invited Harris to go on the trip to get beer, and at the time, Donald did not think this very strange.

II

STRANGE VISITS

Harris began showing a lot of interest in Larson's farm. In fact, he was so impressed that he went to his car, retrieved a Polaroid camera, and asked Donald if he would mind if he snapped some pictures. Donald did not mind, and in fact, was sorta proud that he would ask. Later though, after he took pictures of every building, inside and out, Donald began wondering what the hell was going on. He also took numerous pictures of Donald, and finally, after about ten of them, Donald had to tell him to quit! Both Harris and Falch explored the whole place together, inside and out.

Later, in the afternoon, Donald heard Falch and Harris make plans to go fishing together. This seemed very odd to Donald, as Harris once said, "If there's anything I really hate, it is fishing!" He said it was too boring.

The party lasted until after nine in the evening. Donald was quite pleased with himself. Everyone, including himself, his family, and his guests had plenty to eat, and everyone seemed like they enjoyed themselves. It was a good party.

Shortly after the party, Harris became a regular visitor at the Larson farm. It seemed that every time Donald would turn around, he would look around, and either Harris or Falch would be there, and Harris would always have a "deal" of some kind for him.

Once, Harris showed up with a "Poulan" chainsaw, which was worth over four hundred dollars. He told Donald that he would take fifty bucks for it. When Donald told him the saw was too big for his needs, Harris just gave it to him. Donald traded it for a smaller one, and made a few extra bucks off it!

Another time Harris brought him a new Roto Tiller worth at least two thousand bucks. When Donald asked if it was "hot," Harris said it was not. He did repaint it, and actually gave that to Donald also.

Another time he showed up with a fifteen thousand dollar Ford tractor! It had a loader and a backhoe on it! When Donald said he could not afford it, Harris said, "Don't worry about it, some day maybe you can give me a few bucks for it."

He brought him a Greyhound bus! Donald gave him fifty bucks for it. He used it for a chicken coop! Donald said there was no motor, but that it looked brand new.

On several other occasions Harris brought him rifles, pistols, shotguns various tools, and even clothing! One time he brought him a military issue M-1 with ammunition, along with a box full of live grenades!

Donald, who is quite jovial by nature, told him he had no intention of blowing up the countryside, but did end up buying two "38" caliber pistols, and two 22s. He sold them to Dave McPhillips, a friend of his, who later got killed by police in Columbia, Missouri, during an armed robbery attempt.

Donald also recalls Harris trying to sell him various articles of expensive jewelry, and tires. All of these items were so under priced that Donald became wary, and stopped doing business with him.

He still brought him things but Donald wouldn't buy anything, so Harris would just leave it!

One night Paul Harris was having a party at his house in Minneapolis. Things got a little out of hand, and soon neighbors started complaining about the noise. The police were called, and shortly after their arrival, over "eighty thousand" dollars worth of stolen property was found! Harris immediately proved what a wonderful, stand up con he was. He snitched on his own son Richard! Not only did he snitch on him, he demanded the five thousand dollar reward! His son received "five years" in prison. A short time later, his house was raided once more! This time, police found a large amount of "pot!" Without batting an eye he said it belonged to his sixteen-year-old daughter!

Six months after that incident, ATF Agents arrested Harris for selling stolen firearms to an undercover agent. His son and daughter were doing time, so he didn't have anyone to snitch on.

Because of his life-long criminal career, he was given "forty years!" Five months after he was sentenced, Harris made an emergency phone call to his old buddy, FBI Agent, Peter Neumann! He also made another call to Francis Grady, FBI Agent! *(It would later be ascertained that Harris had been a full time snitch for the FBI and Grady for over fifteen years!)*

Harris dropped a bombshell! He told the Agents that he had important information about the "Piper Kidnapping!" In 1972, he told Agents he knew nothing about the case.

III
FALCH STAKES CLAIM

Meanwhile, back on the farm, James Falch began making himself at home. The problem was, the home he was making it in, was not his own. It belonged to Donald Floyd Larson!

Whenever Donald would leave home for a doctor's visit, or go fishing, or visit friends, Falch would be there within minutes.

The children would tell Donald about Falch snooping around, and going through the buildings, including the house!

On one occasion, while Donald was seeing his doctor, in Minneapolis, the weather turned bad. Not wanting to worry Ruth, he called her, and said he would be staying in Minneapolis, at his sister Shirley's house. He later called again, and said he would be home as soon as the weather cleared. Ruth told Donald to stop on the way home, and to pick up a couple cases of beer. Donald had second thoughts about this. He had noticed that Ruth had started drinking quite heavily at that time;

however, he did buy the beer on the way home.

Donald stayed the night at his sister's place, and returned to his farm the following day. It was about three in the afternoon when he got there. When he pulled into the garage, 14-year-old Cye was sitting in the garage, waiting for him. The first thing Donald noticed was that Cye was crying, and that he looked very upset.

Donald rushed to his side, and asked what was wrong. Cye began telling him about what happened the evening before.

He said that he was awakened around midnight by loud voices, laughter, and other noises. He went on to explain that his mother, and James Falch were in bed together, and had no clothes on! He said he became upset, and told them both to be quiet, and for Falch to get out. The only response was, "Get your ass upstairs, go to bed, and don't come back down here again!"

As soon a Falch finally left, Cye went back downstairs, and entered his mother's bedroom. He confronted her about being in bed with Falch, and a big argument ensued.

He said he called his mother some pretty bad names, and then returned to bed.

When Donald received this information, he quickly rushed into the house, and confronted his wife. He told her to pack her "shit," and get the hell out. He told her that if she wanted James Falch so damned bad, to just leave, and go live with him!

Donald recalls that Ruth was still quite drunk, and smelled like a wino. She began crying loudly, and soon all of the boys were also crying! They were afraid Donald would throw their mother out in the cold weather.

As Ruth sobbed, she said, "It will never happen again. I promise you!"

Donald finally relented, and told her that this was her one and only chance to straighten up. He added that if it happened again she would get kicked out on her ass, and never be allowed to return!

A few days later, Donald was in Willow River, and decided to call James Falch. When Falch answered, he quickly hung up the phone. A week later, Donald again decided to try to call Falch. This time Falch decided to talk to him.

Donald told him in no uncertain terms, "Don't ever go near my wife or children again. Stay clear of my house, and my property, you rotten bastard!"

Falch told Larson that no one could tell him what the hell to do, and then hung the phone up.

IV
THE BREAKUP

On an early March evening, Donald sat down at the dining room table. It was almost suppertime, and he'd had a pretty busy day. He'd been walking around his property making a list of things that needed to be done in the springtime. There were a couple trees needing to be cut up for firewood, some fences needing repair, and a couple other minor tasks.

Donald was getting healthier by the day, and it seems the more exercise he got, the better his appetite became.

He remembers that it was pretty cool out that evening, and was thinking how good supper would be.

Suddenly the phone started ringing. It was Jesse Fencemaker, his neighbor. Jesse told him that one of his ponies was over at his place. Donald quickly assured Jesse that he would be there right away, and would retrieve the errant pony.

Donald grabbed a rope, and walked the mile to Fencemakers. When he got there, it took but a couple minutes to catch the pony. It was quite tame. He put the rope on it, and visited with Jesse for a while, then led the pony back home, and repenned it.

When this task was complete, he went to the house to have supper. To his surprise, Ruth was not in the house. In fact she was gone!

Donald fixed himself a small lunch, and then sat down, watched wrestling on TV, and finally after the ten o'clock news, he went to bed.

Shortly after sunup, his wife awakened Donald. She was just returning home from the previous evening. Donald recalls that she "stunk like a brewery!"

When Donald asked Ruth where she had been, she looked at him through drunken, bloodshot eyes, and said she had received a phone call from Falch, and that his pickup would not start. He said it was stalled along side the road. Moreover, he needed help to get it started. She went on to explain that she went to help him, adding that she pushed it until it started. Donald knew without a doubt that this whole story was a bunch of "bullshit!" Donald did not feel like confronting her at that time, because she was still obviously drunk. She staggered to the bedroom, laid down fully clothed, and was immediately asleep.

Shortly after noon, Ruth woke up. She was fairly sober, and Donald immediately told her he could not take her drunkenness, and whoring around any longer. He added that he was leaving her!

Donald said he would move back to Minneapolis, and added that she could then have all of the whiskey, beer, and John Falch she wanted!

Donald recalls that he really did care for Ruth, but knew it was useless to try to save their marriage. The first time he caught her cheating on him ruined it. There was no repair, and he accepted that, knowing that it was just a matter of time before a showdown.

With the medical problems involving his heart, Donald could not handle it any longer. The torment she was putting him through with her drinking, and her cheating was just too much. Ruth Larson's sickness, as bad as Donald's or worse, had progressed to where Donald no longer could, or would be a help to her. He was helpless to offer aid.

Falch's wife's name was Shirley. Donald describes her as very pleasant, and very attractive. He also says that she was very hard working, and that she was an excellent cook. Donald had eaten there on several occasions, while he helped Falch remodel their house. This was when they were still on good terms with each other.

Shirley had an ear for music, and possessed quite a bit of talent when it came to singing. She had been the "lead singer" in various "country" bands around the area. She was also adept at playing several musical instruments.

She had but one big problem; an abusive husband, a cheating husband, a drunken husband and a trouble-making husband.

When Shirley would get a "gig" that paid pretty good money James would show up and start fights in the club. Pretty soon no one wanted to hire her. He would start problems with the other band members, accusing them of cheating her out of her money, or worse yet, accusing them of trying to "screw" his old lady! Finally, she said "to hell with it," and gave her singing up.

When she found out about her husband's "cheating" with Ruth Larson, it was too much for her to bear. She also said "to hell" with her marriage, and immediately packed up her clothes, and headed North. She put everything she could pack in the family van, and went to Alaska! The farther she could get away from James Falch, the better. She was totally devastated by her husband's treachery. Her brother, living in Alaska welcomed her immediately.

When Ruth Larson found out that Shirley had left her husband, she too decided to leave hers. She packed a few things, loaded the kids into the car, and headed to Falch's house. This was in March of 1975.

V

LETHAL CHAIN OF EVENTS

Not long after Ruth had moved in with Falch, Donald found out that he was really starting to feel relaxation for the first time in a long time. His health was improving, and he was totally at ease with himself. His worries had all but disappeared, plus he could again sleep at night. He said it felt like a giant weight had been removed from his shoulders. Now, it was someone else's turn to worry about Ruth's drinking, and whoring around. It no longer was Donald Floyd Larson's responsibility to try to protect her from herself. He pitied both Falch, and Ruth! With both of them suffering from being "drunks," who would protect them from each other?!

This was not Donald's concern. They would need to figure that out themselves.

After carefully considering his options, Donald decided it was in his best interest to move back to Minneapolis temporarily. Though he loved his small farm, he needed to get away from it for a while, and get rid of the "sour taste" in his mouth left there by the events which had transpired.

At least for the time being, he felt that it was best to move. Slowly, he started bringing personal belongings to his sister Laura's home.

The reason he decided to move in with her, was so he could save up some money. He would also be closer to his friends.

Laura and her son Dale were living in their home by themselves, so they were glad to have Donald move in with them. He got along well with both his sister, and his nephew.

Donald again started having some chest pains, and needed a place where he would feel comfortable, and wanted! Though the burden of caring for, and worrying about his alcoholic wife had been lifted from his mind, there was still his son Mark to worry about, plus his property, his own health, and rumors that the FBI was snooping in his business.

He also had an extensive collection of woodworking tools. They were worth thousands of dollars, and all first grades in quality. He knew that he would have to move all of them, or they would probably be stolen.

On Friday, April 23rd, Donald had an appointment with his doctor in Minneapolis. During that visit, the doctor told him that he was suffering from stress, and that he should take it easy, and not become overly excited about anything. Donald's blood pressure was up, and he was very shaky.

After the visit with his doctor, Donald decided to pick up his nephew, Greg Erickson, Greg's wife Cheryl, one of her girlfriends, and then decided to head up North to his farm. Their main intention was to go "smelting."

On the way to the farm, Donald decided to stop at the "Corral Bar" in Willow River. There, he called Falch's home to tell his wife that he was definitely moving back to Minneapolis. He also mentioned the fact that he, his nephew, and his wife were going "smelting," and that they would be stopping at the farm to pick up some of his personal belongings. He said he would do this periodically until he had his personal property in Minneapolis. He also mentioned that he and his nephew would be smelting the following day also. Had he known what would transpire on that day, he would not have told his wife that he would not be at the farm on the following day! He says that he would have told her that he would be there!

Upon leaving the "Corral," Donald went to Falch's house, and picked up his son Mark, then five years old. They all proceeded to the farm.

Around suppertime, Ruth showed up to visit Greg, and Cheryl. They all ate supper, then sat around, and talked about fishing.

About midnight, Donald began feeling a little dizzy, and decided to rest for a while. He went to the bedroom and lay down. He recalls that about an hour later, his wife, crawling in bed with him awakened him. Donald wanted absolutely nothing to do with her, and immediately rolled over with his back towards her.

Finally he again went to sleep, and when he awoke in the morning she was gone.

During the night, the weather had turned bad. It was cold, rainy and the wind was high. This is typical "smelting" weather in Minnesota.

Donald still felt a little queasy, so they all decided to call off the "smelt run" and re-schedule it at a later time. Donald grabbed a few of his belongings, and they all headed back to Minneapolis.

After arriving, Donald gave his nephew fifty dollars to go rent a U-Haul trailer so they could return later to the farm, and pick up some of his expensive belongings, especially his power tools. He wanted to get these items back to Minneapolis where they would be safe.

Donald went to his sister's garage to make room so they could put his belongings away. As he was moving some of the boxes, which were already in the garage, Donald ran across a box that his dead friend, Dave McPhillips had "hidden" there.

Upon opening the box, "lo and behold," Donald found two police uniforms, and two

38 caliber Police Special handguns! Paul Harris had sold these items to McPhillips.

Donald did not want anything to do with what he found in the box, and quickly decided to get rid of it. He put the box and all of the contents in the back of his station wagon. After having some lunch, he decided to take his son, and head back to Willow River.

They headed North on Highway 35 until Donald came to a "rest area." He pulled in, deciding to get rid of the box of contraband.

He took the box out of the back, and started to carry it to a dumpster, then noticed some people looking in his direction. Deciding there were "too many eyes," he again placed the box in the front seat of his car, and then drove away. He decided he would throw the box away later.

As Donald and his son traveled North, Donald recalls that he had been making faces, and teasing his son. His son was laughing, and so was Donald. They definitely enjoyed being with each other. Donald was very glad that there was no dispute with Ruth over his visiting, and taking their son with him when he wanted to.

The happy pair traveled North at a leisurely pace, enjoying each other's antics, and not worrying about anything.

As they arrived at the driveway leading into the farm both father, and son were still laughing. As Donald made the turn into his farm, the smile disappeared from his face. He was shocked, and surprised to see James Falch's pickup, and a large four-wheel trailer backed up to Donald's kitchen door!

Donald exited his car, and was immediately confronted by James Falch! Donald turned to his son Mark, still in the car, and told him to stay in the car.

When he turned again, this time towards Falch, he was immediately aware of the angered look on the man's face, and realized that he was drunk!

With fists clenched and blood veins sticking out of his neck, Falch screamed, "What the fuck are you doing here?! You're supposed to be smelting!"

Donald retaliated by asking, "What the hell are you doing here, taking things out of my house!?"

When Falch saw that Donald actually had the guts to confront him, the already crazed man became angrier! He swung his arm, hitting Donald in the stomach! In an effort to protect himself, Donald swung back! Falch, younger, and in better shape than Donald, hit him "about" three more times, knocking him against the car! The pain Donald felt was excruciating! He thought for sure he was going to die, and that he was having another heart attack. There was a tremendous weight in his chest, and he could not breathe!

Through glazed eyes Donald saw Falch approaching again. He thought, "This man is trying to kill me!"

The box, on the front seat, only inches away, held the answer to Donald's dilemma! "The guns!"

Donald made a grab, reached a gun, then turned, and fired, the bullet nicking James Falch in the shoulder!

Falch, with sudden shock, and fear on his face, turned, and ran towards the house!

The exploding pistol not only shocked Falch, but Donald too. The only thought in his mind was to "get the hell out of there!" He had to get back to his sister's house!

The next thing he knew, there was someone screaming obscenities at him! He looked around. He was again being attacked! He knew it had to be Falch, and fired at the charging figure. He thought, "I won't let this bastard kill me!" He fired the gun two more times! Later he would find out that both bullets hit their mark. He would also find out the attacker was not James Falch Sr., but James Falch Jr.!

Donald turned towards the car, and realized that his son was not in it. In his dazed mind there was only one thought! He had to find his son! He had to get him away from this nightmare!

He remembers that everything seemed like he was in a tunnel. He was running, could not see left, nor right, just straight ahead. He remembers screaming his son's name! He remembers that it looked like he was looking down on everything, and that everything seemed like it was moving slow. He said he wanted it all to end, but did not have the power to make it stop. He said it was like being in a "nightmare" and not being able to escape back to reality!

Entering the kitchen, Donald saw Falch sitting on the floor.

Falch looked at him with hate, saying, "Now, you son of a bitch, you've really done it! Ruth has got Tom Ryan on the phone!" (At this point Donald did not know who Tom Ryan was. He would later find out that he was the County Attorney for Pine County.)

Donald would also find out that Falch, and Ryan were good friends. This would become known some fourteen years later, when Ryan wrote a letter to the Minnesota Parole Board! He stated that he, and Falch were personal friends, and that Peter Neumann told him that Larson was involved with the "Piper Kidnapping." His friend Falch had told him that!

Thinking back, Donald recalls that his kitchen was sixteen feet long by eleven feet wide. There was a dining room table in the middle of it. Falch was sitting on the floor between the table, and the kitchen cupboards.

When Falch told Donald that Ruth was on the phone with Prosecutor Ryan, Donald turned towards Ruth, and told her to give him the phone. He wanted to talk to Ryan about what was happening at his house!

When Donald reached for the phone, Ruth hit him with it, swinging very hard, in a downward motion. Donald made an effort to block her. The phone hit him on his right hand, causing the gun to discharge! Donald did not know it, but his son Mark was standing near his mother. When the gun went off, the bullet struck Mark in the back of the neck, killed him instantly.

When Donald realized what had happened, he lost all semblance of control or knowledge of what happened or was happening. He heard a gun firing wildly, not even knowing who was firing it. To him he states that it sounded like a group of guns going of simultaneously! Things kept moving slowly, and everything seemed like it had an eerie brightness to it. The shots he heard sounded like echoes.

Later, Donald would find that his son Mark, James Falch Sr., James Falch Jr., and his wife Ruth, along with his stepson Scott, were all dead or dying! (Falch and his son would live for three days before succumbing to their wounds.)

Donald Larson remembers some of what happened. He says it is like in a dream, and in fact is in his dreams to this day. In the dream, his son Mark is smiling, and telling him, "It's ok Daddy, don't cry!!" *(At this point in the telling of the story, Donald abruptly gets up, and leaves the room. He will no longer talk about the deaths, which occurred on that horrendous day. When he spoke of it, the enormity of what happened was etched on his face. He looked at the writer for help, but what could anyone do for him. It is something he has to live and suffer with continuously!)*

Donald does not remember leaving the farm, nor of driving anywhere. He does remember the sudden blast of an "air horn" from a big semi!

The truck was looming directly in front of him. The blast of the horns brought him back to reality. He jerked the wheel of his car, and swerved crazily into the ditch, narrowly missing the big truck. He remembers that when he left the road his speedometer was reading eighty miles per hour! He recalls gaining control of the car, and ending up back on the highway. This was his first conscious memory since the ordeal he went through!

At first, he was totally lost, totally ignorant of where he was. He got out of his car, and looked around. He was near Minneapolis!

At first he could not remember where he had been, where he was going, or why he was going anywhere at all. He had thoughts of a possible heart attack, or of falling, and hitting his head. He had driven a hundred and thirty miles without knowing it.

He got back in his car, and just sat there. Slowly parts and pieces of what had happened started to come back to him. It seemed like he was remembering parts of a novel he read. Nothing fit together.

Donald Floyd Larson's mind was beginning to play tricks on him, probably as a protection because of what had happened. He could remember a gun going off, but could not remember who was shooting, or why. There was a whole bunch of out of focus pictures, wildly circling through his mind.

He drove his car to the Mississippi River, parked it, got out, and then sat down. Pretty soon the pictures, like in a large jigsaw puzzle started fitting into place. Donald did not like the picture, which was beginning to form. He sat there in abject misery, not wanting to believe what was forming in his mind.

When the picture was complete, it proved too much for Donald to handle. He does not know to this day what happened next. He doesn't know if he passed out, went to sleep, fainted, or if his mind just decided to take a break from reality and shut down for a while. Everything went totally blank.

The next thing Donald became aware of was the sound of birds chirping. It was morning, and the sun was up and shinning bright. He had slept for hours!

When he first became conscious of his surroundings, he did not know where he was.

His memory finally started coming back, and he got up, went to his car, and turned the ignition on. The first thing he heard was the announcer on station WCCO. He was giving the "morning news." Soon, Donald was shocked back to total reality!

All law enforcement agencies were searching for Donald Floyd Larson, suspected of shooting five people on a farm near Willow River! There were three dead, and two in the hospital near death! The "all points bulletin" included Minnesota, Wisconsin, North Dakota, South Dakota, Iowa, and Canada!

Now Donald was really confused. He did not know what to do, or where to go. He drove his car into the woods. He found a "park bench" where he sat down trying to sort things out. He stayed there until about seven thirty in the morning.

Finally, Donald got back in his car, and began driving around Minneapolis. He ended up driving around all day long in an effort to come up with a solution. He knew he had to talk to someone, but did not know who he should contact. He knew he had friends, but could not even remember their names! Finally he pulled into a Motel in Oak Grove, where he rented a room.

Donald had a full bottle of Valium, and a fifth of 100 proof Smirnoff, Vodka. He took all of the pills, and then proceeded to gulp down the vodka!

Donald did not wake up until the next morning. When he did, he realized he was in a hospital, securely "cuffed" to a bed and a deputy in the room with him!

As soon as he woke up, he was checked over, and the Sheriff's Department was allowed to transfer him to the Hennepin County Jail. There he was booked, and fingerprinted. He was then brought to the Pine County Jail, in Pine City, again printed and booked, then brought to a cell.

This all occurred on the date of April 26, 1976. On the 27th, Donald was transported to Cambridge, Minnesota where the District Court Judge was presiding. The Judge "bound him over" for trial, and a date was set for October.

After listening to all of the charges against him, he knew he was in more trouble than he ever imagined a human could get into. Knowing something is real, and accepting the realism of it are two different matters. There had to be some sort of a mistake. This could not have happened, nor could it be happening!

Ron Meshbesher, one of the top attorneys in the state of Minnesota represented Donald at his "preliminary hearing."

Donald was transferred from the Pine County Jail, to the St. Louis County Jail, in Duluth. This would make it much easier for Mr. Meshbesher to visit his client, and for the preparation for the upcoming trial.

VI

AFTERMATH

Between April 1976, and October 1976, Donald would have many interviews. Not only did Meshbesher visit him on a regular basis, he was also interviewed on many occasions by various psychiatrists, and psychologists. This was to determine the frame of mind Donald was in at the time of the shootings, and to determine if he was mentally capable of going to trial. There were many episodes when Donald would become despondent to the extent the jail keepers would become very worried.

Doctor Carl Malmquist was the Chief Psychiatrist. He worked at the Hennepin County Hospital, and was appointed by the Court to determine the sanity of Mr. Larson.

At the trial, Doctor Malmquist testified that, "At the particular time of the shootings, Mr. Larson did not know what he was doing!"

Another Psychiatrist, Doctor Schwartz, who at the time was the Chief Psychiatrist at the State Hospital, in St. Peter, Minnesota, testified that, "Mr. Larson, was uncontrollable at the time of the shootings, and was definitely 'mentally ill' at the time."

Thomas Ryan, Chief Prosecutor for Pine County was bitterly in disagreement with the findings of the two noted Psychiatrists. Their testimony and findings did not fit the needs of the zealous prosecutor. This disagreement led to Ryan asking the appointment of yet another Psychiatrist, a Doctor Clarence Row, from the Ramsey County Court system. He just happened to be a close friend of Ryan!

Doctor Row examined Donald Floyd Larson. This examination took place in the Anoka County Jail. It lasted fifteen minutes! After this thorough exam, Mr. Row came to the conclusion that Donald Floyd Larson was indeed "normal" at the time of the shootings, and knew exactly what he was doing, and that he should take responsibility for the crimes he and he alone committed!

(It is a sad state of affairs when the "Court System" is allowed to spend the taxpayer's hard earned money, to "bastardize" the legal system. In reality, the job of the Prosecutor or "County Attorney" is that of being a "fact finder." They are supposed to bring out the truth of a matter, not over zealously strive for convictions! Somewhere along the line, the meaning of justice has been lost and misconstrued. To most prosecutors, the meaning of justice means "guilty as charged." They have, and use, all of the means in which to convict people, many of whom are not guilty of the crimes they have been charged with. Too often, the needs of the "prosecutor" are motivated by political needs rather than of the needs for "justice.")

In the case of Donald Larson, Mr. Ryan, a close, personal friend of Falch's, used every underhanded tactic at his disposal, moral or not, to insure the conviction and that Donald

Larson would receive a life sentence for what happened on that fateful day. Let's face some reality. James Falch was a "low life," probably deserving of what he received. He caused what was done to him, as well as if he would have pulled the trigger on himself. The others, who were terribly unfortunate to have suffered their fates, suffered those fates as a result of the actions of James Falch Senior, and the FBI!

This may sound cold-blooded, but is it? It started with Falch allowing himself to be drug into something he had no business getting into. Everything he did was for personal greed. The FBI was paying him, making him promises, he was getting sex from Donald's wife, and he was stealing Donald's property. In addition, he attacked Donald while he was trying to protect his property! This was a chain of events, not a planned murder! There was no intention of anyone killing anyone. James Falch was committing a "felony" and got caught in the act! The rest was "circumstances," uncontrollable by anyone.

Was Donald guilty of anything? Of course he was. He admits that. He was found guilty of several crimes, some of which he was guilty of. Not one of the crimes added up to be "first degree murder!"

The guiltiest person involved was James Falch! Did he deserve what he got for his greed, and bullying? Probably not. Donald doesn't say he deserved to die. However, he does say the killing of him was brought about by his own actions! He was a bully and a punk, who thought he could take anything he wanted. He was proven wrong!

It is definitely a terrible thing that occurred on the Larson farm. There will never be anything or anyone who can replace what was erased from the face of the earth on that day. Donald Larson knows this more than anyone else. He has suffered more than anyone else. He is the one, now close to eighty years old, who still has nightmares, who wakes up in the middle of the night crying!

Many times Donald has said that he would gladly trade places with those that died that day. However, he cannot do that.

How many people think the FBI has lost sleep over what has happened? That is really laughable!

While Donald Larson was in the Anoka County jail, Pete Neumann, Chief Investigator in the Piper Kidnapping case, visited with him. He informed Donald that he was a suspect in the Piper kidnapping, and that he was going to search his property.

On the "warrant" it was stated that Mr. Larson's farm would be searched for the "one million" dollars paid to secure the freedom of Virginia Piper. Donald said that he had nothing to hide, and that Newman was more than welcome to search his farm or any other place he wanted to.

Neuman proceeded to Larson's farm with a bunch of other agents. They methodically went over the whole place foot by foot! They went so far as to hire an excavator with heavy digging equipment. This machinery was used to dig up the ground around the farm's outbuildings. The agents also tore up the house, looking in the walls, floors, and ceilings for the missing million in twenty dollar bills!

Had Donald witnessed what they did to his place he would have had another heart attack. All of the work, money, time, and love he put into it were ignored, so even after death, Falch was "getting his way!"

Neuman would say later that, "I told him to leave Larson's wife alone, but he wouldn't listen. If he'd have just done what he was supposed to do, he would have been ok, and this would not have happened!"

Those responsible for the "tearing up" of Donald's property had no care at all in what they were doing. They knew the owner was in jail, and their attitude was, "Why be careful?"

After the search, the agent's efforts proved to be fruitless. Not a trace of the money was found, nor anything that could even hint that it had ever been there. They had nothing to point to Donald Larson, nor Kenny Callahan!

The next time Donald would hear from Pete Neumann would be in the Minnesota State Prison in Stillwater.

Donald sat in total misery, and pain, waiting for his trial to commence. Not a moment of wakefulness or sleep went by without Donald's mind dwelling on what had happened. Nothing could interrupt his thoughts of the terrible things, which occurred on his farm. It would take many years before he could wipe some of the thoughts from his mind. Then, it would only be but for a short time before those thoughts would return. To this day he says there is not a day that goes by that he does not think about what happened.

VII
TRIAL

The trial of Donald Floyd Larson began in early October of 1976. It was held in the Pine County Courthouse which is located in Pine City, a small town just South of Duluth, Minnesota, It is a quiet town, where everyone living there knows everyone else. Needless to say, when news of the tragedy on Larson's farm broke, everyone was talking about it. Some of the people were saying, "It was only a matter of time. He's been getting away with his bullying, and stealing all of his life!"

Others said that it was a, "Wife swapping thing that went bad!"

As in any small town, the rumors were abundant! It seems that all had an opinion.

Some were for Donald Larson, others against him. Most of the people that knew Falch, and ever had dealings with him, said, "The bastard had it coming for a long time!"

Thomas Ryan, the Prosecuting Attorney in the case for the state, was a very close friend of James Falch Sr. So close, that one may question the validity of his prosecuting the case. There were many who believed he should have excused himself from it, on the grounds that they were such good friends. They wondered how a person of authority and "power" in a courtroom could act or perform professionally in a case of this magnitude, when one of the people dead was his "good friend!"

When you ask for a "trial by jury," you are supposed to be able to pick from an impartial group of prospective jurors. This sounds really good on paper, but in reality it leaves a lot to be desired, unless it is in a large city! Then you have a chance at a fair trial.

In a small town, in a small County, there is no chance! There are too many favors to be given, too many friends one must not "buck!"

How many people are acquainted with the goings on within a courtroom? Unless directly involved, most people never set foot in a courtroom, let alone know what goes on in it.

People watch "Perry Mason" on TV, and think, "Well, Perry got another free one off!"

In real life, "that ain't what it's like," especially, in small towns! When a person in a small town is brought to court, the people mostly think, "Well, that person was arrested, therefore he or she has to be guilty!"

They also believe that what Perry Mason portrays on TV, happens in all courts. The truth is sure to come out! Bah Humbug!

The courts are run on, "How rich are you?" It matters a great deal who you are also. Unless your name is O.J. Simpson, and you have a battery of top-notch attorneys from all parts of the U. S. of A. you don't have a chance. If you do not have millions in a high profile case, you might as well throw yourself on the mercy of the court.

Donald's prospective jurors consisted of, a secretary who worked in the Pine County Attorney's Office, Paul Razak, the next door neighbor, and very good friend of James

Falch, and others who were friends with the dead man. Razak was a close friend with the prosecutor, and the Sheriff's Department also. He delivered soda to the courthouse and to the jail! A waitress from the Flamingo Bar, who was a girlfriend of Falch's and four who worked at the Federal Prison in Moose Lake.

Mr. Meshbesher had sixteen jury prospects dismissed for cause, but could not get rid of all of them. There is no doubt that the trial should have been held in a different county, however, changes of venue were few and far between in those days.

On the very first day of the trial, Timmy McDonald, a very close friend of Donald's arrived. Donald's sister Shirley accompanied him. McDonald told Shirley to look towards the back of the courtroom. Timmy recognized numerous FBI agents!

Looking back, and thinking about his feelings at the time of his trial, Donald says that he cannot remember a whole lot about the ordeal. He does remember that he really did not care what happened to him. This was the lowest point in his life, and will remain as such. He simply said that what ever happens, will happen. Nothing really mattered anymore. As far as he was concerned, his life, his dreams, his expectations were over.

One of the first people to testify at Donald's trial was Toby Larson, Donald's ex-sister in law. Mrs. Larson was employed at the Lino Lakes Correctional Facility, at Lino Lakes, Minnesota. The facility was a Juvenile Detention Center, used mostly for unmanageable children. She had been employed there for approximately twenty years. She was known to be extremely close friends with Peter Neumann!

In 1972, Toby Larson told Mr. Neumann that she hated the whole Larson family. She said she had not spoken to any of them for over five years. She also told Neumann that if she ever saw Mr. Donald Floyd Larson walking down the street, she would cross to the other side!

Toby Larson testified that on the day of the shootings, Donald Larson had called her. She said that he told her what he had done, and then had asked what he should do. He then told her he wanted to move in with her!

Donald states with fervor that this was a bold face lie. He says, "She is the last person on this earth I would call for any reason. We have hated each other for years!"

There was never any doubt as to who fired the shots on the Larson farm. However, the big question was, did Donald Larson have any idea of what he was doing at the time those shots were fired? Did he realize the consequences of his actions? What actually caused him to shoot? Had he reached the "point of no return" after he himself was attacked?

It had been proven on many occasions that Donald Larson was not a violent person. That includes when the incident happened, as well as the present time. In fact, Donald is quite the opposite. He is a very relaxed, mellow person. Those who have known Mr. Larson for any length of time know without doubt, that he would not intentionally harm anyone. For over thirty years, no one has seen him lose control. If he had such a temper, it surely would have manifested itself by now!

Prison life is not an easy life. There are days when an average person would be capable of snapping. There are "ass-holes" in prison who will push others or try to goad them into a confrontation. Donald has never succumbed to any of the temptations of fighting or causing problems.

Donald's trial lasted for one week. The jury took three days to reach a verdict.

Mr. Larson was found guilty of;

1. One count of first degree murder for the death of James Falch Sr.
2. Two counts of second degree murder for causing the deaths of Ruth Larson, and for the death of James Falch Jr.
3. One count of third degree murder for the death of his son Mark Larson.
4. Acquitted of the death of his stepson, Scott Powell by reason of mental Illness!

This verdict is confusing at best. If one looks at the flow of events, it seems not only ludicrous, but also impossible that there could be such a disparity in the findings of the jury. If Mr. Larson was insane or mentally ill at the time of the shooting death of one of the victims, then why was he not found "not guilty" by the same reason on the others? Is mental illness or insanity something that a person just turns on or off at their own desire?

If Mr. Larson was found guilty of second degree murder on two counts, why not the others?

How could he have been found guilty of first-degree murder in the death of James Falch Sr. when he shot him the second time after he had shot Ruth, and his son?

Did Donald Larson "premeditate" the fact that James Falch was going to be at his house, stealing his property on that day? Did he premeditate the fact that Falch was going to attack him?

Every action of that day was totally un-planned. It could not have been any different. None of what happened on that day could possibly have been planned!

Upon the findings of guilt, to the various charges, Donald was placed in a cell in the Pine County Jail. Approximately three days later he was brought before the Honorable

Judge John Thoreen. This was to be his sentencing.

On first-degree murder he was sentenced to a period of life. On the second-degree verdicts he received two forty-year sentences. On the third degree verdict he was given a twenty-five year sentence. The judge then ordered that these sentences would run concurrently with each other, or together. He would be eligible for parole in about seventeen and a half years, or in the year of 1993.

VIII
PROMISE OF PAROLE

It is now 2007, and Larson is almost eighty. He still sits in prison. In the year of 1990, Donald went before the "parole board." He was given a ten-year continuance. He again appeared before the "parole board" in the year 2000. This time he was given a three-year continuance. He was told to do certain things before he again appeared before them.

He completed "Anger Management, and Critical Thinking." He did exactly what he was told to do. His caseworker told him to start preparing for parole.

During his hearing, he was told, "You are being given a road map to follow." "Follow it!"

Over the next three years, he again and as usual, acted like the gentleman he is. He stayed out of all trouble, prepared for his parole, and could finally see an end to his incarceration.

His son, who built a new home, actually added a special room for Donald in regards to his coming home!

When he returned to the "parole board" after finishing his three-year continuance, the "new" commissioner, Joan Fabian, didn't bat an eye. She simply added another "ten years" to his time! When Donald's son asked her how she could do that, after the previous commissioner gave him three, and he was told to prepare for parole, she simply answered, she did not have to go by what the other commissioner did or said, and that she could do what she wanted to do. She was actually smiling in a vicious sort of way.

Donald remains locked up at the "Senior Unit" in the Prison in Faribault, Minnesota.

Being close to eighty years old, Donald suffers some of the maladies other people of his age suffer. He still has a bad heart, suffers now from diabetes, has started "falling down" lately, with no warning, he suffers from glaucoma, and has numerous aches and pains.

He has reached the eligibility requirements to be paroled twenty-four years ago!

PART V
"DOIN' TIME"

I
STARTING LIFE

Donald Floyd Larson arrived at the maximum Security prison, located at Stillwater, Minnesota, and as he walked up the old, worn front steps, his mind was numb. He was about to start his "life sentence!"

Neither Donald, nor anyone else had any idea how long that "life sentence" would be. Donald had mixed thoughts on that subject. His mind was still spinning with the thoughts of what had "gotten" him to those steps. If he had known then, what he knows now, he might not have been able to handle the situation.

When the cold, steel barred doors "clanged" shut behind him, Donald had feelings of sadness, of being alone, and a deep sense of forlornness. He felt that his life had ceased. He was not alive, nor was he dead!

With his head hung low, he passed through the second gate, and finally the third. With each "clang" his morose feelings became more acute.

Donald was led to the "laundry room," stripped of his civilian clothing, given his "prison issue," his bedding, led to a shower, then to "orientation," where he was placed in a cell.

Orientation consisted of psychological testing, educational testing, a medical examination, and a short program of what the prison was about, and of what would be expected of the prisoner. It was kinda like a "getting to know you" interlude before entering the actual "prison life."

Orientation would also determine where a "convict" was best suited to work. Most times, there would be a choice of the "twine factory," the "kitchen," the "laundry," the "twine factory," or the "twine factory!" If you were physically capable of work, you would be placed in one of these areas. (By "able," it was meant if you could breathe and walk with no great effort!)

Most ended up in the "twinery" and became "twinos!" Everyone complained about the work there, but in reality, it was not that bad of a place to be. The guards, foreman and crew were usually pretty decent people, and as long as you did your job, they would leave you alone.

Many of the jobs were a little dangerous. Many convicts lost fingers, thumbs, even hands. One lost an eye. Most ended up at least having a scar, to remind them later in life of where they had been.

The convicts who worked in the "twinery" had sort of a comradery. They stuck up for each other when the going got tough, and the staff usually listened to their complaints, and tough goings.

Another reason to work in the "twinery" was the wages. A convict could usually work "extra" hours, thereby doubling their income. If they made thirty-two cents a day at their regular job, they could add an extra thirty-five cents by working an evening shift! With the low prices at the canteen, this was well worth the effort.

Donald's attorney, Ron Meshbesher filed an appeal in his case. It went before the Minnesota Appellate Court, and was denied. He then filed with the Minnesota Supreme

Court. They too denied it. By then, Donald ran out of money, and Meshbesher could no longer represent him. Donald wanted to further the appeals process by going into the Federal Appeals Courts, but the State Public Defender's Office also refused to help him.

In all probability, had Donald attained the use of Meshbesher, or the Public Defenders, he would have at least had the "first degree murder" conviction thrown out. He would then have had a "forty" year sentence to do, and would have served that time by now!

Shortly after arriving in Stillwater Prison, Donald was approached by another convict. His name was Donald Hastings. Hastings offered Donald a carton of cigarettes.

Not knowing who Hastings was Donald refused the offer. Donald did not smoke, but could have used the smokes in the "prison barter" system.

Later, Donald became aware that Hastings was a known snitch! Donald was happy that he refused the offer, as Hastings was not to be trusted under any circumstances.

Donald would be given numerous other offers of cigarettes or "goodies" from the canteen. Every day it seems, he was offered cigarettes, candy, popcorn, or other items.

II
OLD WOES RESURFACE

Donald could not figure out the sudden interest by other convicts. True, Donald had many friends in Stillwater, but he was getting offers from people he had never heard of! He could not understand this, but would soon learn the reason why.

One day, Donald picked up the Minneapolis Newspaper. In large print, on the front page, it read; *'$50,000.00 OFFERED FOR INFORMATION LEADING TO THE ARREST, AND OR CONVICTION OF THOSE INVOLVED IN THE "PIPER KIDNAPPING!!"* It was suddenly clear why Donald was a "STAR!"

Eddie Jones, a "con" from Chicago and Donald's long time friend, Tommy Gray, (who had not yet received his reversal for the "Bartholomew" fur heist) contacted him, and told him that a "battery" of FBI Agents had bombarded the Stillwater, Prison inhabitants. They were interviewing anyone, and everyone who was willing to talk to them. There were many who decided that this was a way to get themselves "time cuts," or deals from the "Parole Board."

Pete Neumann, an agent for the FBI, was pulling no punches. He meant to solve the "Piper" case once and for all! He did not care who got convicted. The important thing to him was, "someone" had to be brought to justice!

In Neumann's mind, Donald Larson, and Tommy Grey were the ones that did it, or at least knew who did it. In his frenzy to "beat the clock," he was willing to use every underhanded, trick or ruse at his disposal to get an arrest. He did not care if his inexcusable tactics caused death, broken homes and lives. He would somehow solve this crime. The "statute of limitations" was drawing closer every day. Neumann was more desperate as the days went by. If the crime was not solved, he, as well as the FBI Agency itself would suffer embarrassment. Being a very "vain" individual, Mr. Neumann could not let that happen.

Jones, Grey, and many of Larson's "real friends" told Donald to be extremely careful about who he associated with, and what he said to them. *(Donald was known to say things he actually did not mean. Sometimes he would lead people to believe he knew more about the case than was true. It wasn't as if he would lie, but sometimes failed to tell the whole story.)*

Donald's friends told him that Neumann was offering "big time deals" to anyone that would give information about Larson, and Grey in regards to the Piper case.

Soon, Neumann's suspect list would change abruptly! It seemed that Tommy Grey had an airtight alibi! Grey, never one to waste words, confronted Neumann, and point blank, told him, "Go Fuck Yourself!"

Tommy Grey had made twenty-one deliveries at his job on the day of the Piper Kidnapping. The time-clock records totally backed him up as well as the receipts from his deliveries.

Neumann did not bat an eye. He simply erased Tommy from his list of suspects, and added someone else. Kenny Callahan! It made no difference to Neumann who he nailed, but by God "nail" he would!

III
THE "PRINT"

During his first few weeks in Stillwater, Donald, was visited by Peter Neumann and Francis Grey on several occasions. They tried cajoling him, making promises, offering him deals, but to no avail. On a couple of instances they used the "good cop," "bad cop" routine.

On one occasion, they showed him a small piece of paper. They told him they retrieved it from the "kidnap vehicle," and that it was a part of a piece of paper that had been ripped off a "Piggly Wiggly" grocery bag, and contained the fingerprint of Donald, Floyd Larson!

On three separate occasions, agents of the FBI tested Donald's fingerprints. Callahan's would also be taken. On these instances, there was "not a match!"

The print, which Neumann swore was Larson's, would eventually cause so much controversy amongst various agencies, including between the FBI's own, that it would gain National attention!

It would turn out that "this print" would be the most singular piece of evidence of the whole investigation. It would cause agents to turn on agents, and would cause extreme embarrassment amongst the whole of the FBI!

IV
CASE SOLVED!

Agent Neumann sent telegrams to all of the agents involved in the Piper investigation. In these telegrams, he stated emphatically that that he did not want any of the agents to investigate anyone else. He said the case was "solved," and that "he" had solved it! He listed Donald Floyd Larson and Kenny Callahan as the perpetrators of the "million dollar" ransom and kidnapping of Virginia Piper!

He said, "I have captured the culprits, and now everyone else can finally sit back and relax!"

Donald's fingerprint was submitted to the FBI's Bureau in Washington, D C. This was the fourth time his print/prints were sent to their laboratory. Lo and behold, this time magic happened! The print on the piece of paper from the Piggly Wiggly bag indeed matched the print they took from Donald Larson! Needless to say, Peter Neumann was ecstatic! Almost every evening during "news time" he would be on TV, telling of how "he" solved the case.

Agent Neumann, now a celebrity, really began playing his part. He was a regular visitor of Larson's! He moved between Donald and the "snitches" on an equal basis.

There were plenty of "snitches" to talk to. Many wanted a piece of that "fifty grand!" They would have sold out their mothers for a piece of the action. After a visit with Neumann, the "snitches" would go back to their cells, and dream of money, women, booze, and song! They would dream "happy dreams" every night!

On a visit with Larson, Neumann said, "Don, I've got the sweetest deal in town for you. I know you shouldn't be in Stillwater on a first-degree murder charge. I warned Falch more than once to keep his hands off your wife, and your property! He knew better!"

He added, "Falch acted like a fool, and deserved what he got!"

When Donald heard this, he sat upright! How could this Son-of-a-bitch sit there, and tell him this, when he was the fucking "low life" that was using Falch? He might as well have pulled the trigger himself!

Neumann planned out the whole Falch scenario. From Falch's first visit to his last, fatal one, Neumann knew exactly what was happening, and really didn't give a damned what he did.

Harris was also mixed in it, along with Falch. Neumann admitted that they were working with him, and for him.

Donald wondered to himself about, "How many other snitches and friends were working for this asshole!"

This question would be answered in the future. One thing was for certain; Falch knew Harris and Cooper. Harris knew Fields. They all knew Neumann. They were all part of "one big, happy family!"

Neumann told Donald, "I'm the only friend you have Donald." He then went on to tell Larson how he could help him.

He said, "I've taken the liberty of talking to Tom Ryan, and he's agreed to go along with anything that the FBI has in mind."

He went on to say, "If you'll sign a confession to the Piper case, I'll insure you that all of your charges and sentences will be dropped to manslaughter!"

He went on to say that the maximum Donald would do behind bars would be ten years!

Another part of the "sweet deal" was that if he pled guilty to the Piper Kidnapping, he could fix it so that the Federal Sentence would run concurrent with his state time!

Donald thought the deal over, and concluded that he would tell Neumann that he would agree with it. There was one certain thing that Neumann would have to do before he would make a statement. That was that the deal would have to be in writing, signed by Neumann, Ryan, the Federal Prosecutor, and the Federal Judge!

A few days later, Neumann came back with the confession in his hand, ready to have Larson sign.

When Larson told him of the agreement he had come up with, Neumann's cheery, laid back demeanor changed. He pled with Larson to just sign it, and he would keep his part of the bargain. When Donald told him to, "Put it in writing," Neumann suddenly became very sinister! He became angry, and forceful, telling Donald that he was calling the shots, and unless he signed the agreement immediately, he would spend the rest of his natural life in prison!

Donald ended the conversation and the visit by telling Neumann, "You two bit, lying Son-of-a-bitch, because of you, there are five people dead. I'll never talk to you again, and hope you rot in hell!"

Neumann, red-faced got up, and left the visiting area.

V
RETALIATION

He retaliated in the only way he knew. The next morning at six A.M. "U S Marshals" arrived at Donald Floyd Larson's cell door in Stillwater Prison, formally charged him with the Kidnapping, and holding for ransom, one Virginia Piper. They then placed him under arrest. They cuffed him, led him outside, placed him in a Federal transport, brought him to the Federal Courthouse in St. Paul, and turned him over to one of the most famous "crime-fighters" the FBI had. His name was Raymond Stratton. Stratton made a special trip from the Chicago Office to help in the solving, and prosecution of the Piper case.

Stratton was a large heavily muscled man, who stood over six feet tall and weighed well over two hundred pounds.

Donald recalls that it was plain to see that Stratton was used to getting his way, and was not afraid of using "bullying" tactics to attain his goals.

He told Larson in no uncertain terms, "You have one choice, and one choice only. You better plead guilty if you know what's good for you!"

Donald, also over six feet tall, and over two hundred pounds answered, "You can go to hell you big son-of-a-bitch, I'm pleading not guilty, and I want my attorney right now."

Stratton refused to allow Larson to call an attorney, and the next day started off the same way. This time, however, there were two other agents helping to join in the bullying! The results were identical to the day before, with Donald refusing to talk to anyone other than his attorney!

Finally realizing it was useless to bully any longer, the agents allowed Donald to make a phone call, calling the questioning off.

Donald immediately called Ron Meshbesher, told him what was going on and Meshbesher was immediately ready to come see him.

After Meshbesher visited with Larson, Donald was again cuffed, put in the Federal transport, and hurriedly transported back, to Stillwater Prison.

When he returned to his cellblock, his buddies immediately surrounded him. They all told him that many agents had been at the prison, and had visited with a large number of inmates. They again were offering "early releases" for anyone who would testify against Larson, and Callahan. They had made it very clear that they did not want any information about anyone else. Donald would find out later that many "stand up" convicts would turn into "lay down snitches!"

VI
REHABILITATION

A very strange thing began happening in the Stillwater Penitentiary. "Life long" crooks, criminals, check writers, forgers, armed robbers, rapists, killers, burglars, and car thieves all decided to "go straight!" It did not take "treatment," or any "special tutoring" to work this miracle.

Inmates were tripping over each other to get to the office, which Peter Neumann was using, for interviews. Arguments broke out over who would be first in line. Mr. Neumann could have rented space from the Department Of Corrections to set up a permanent office.

Day after day Neumann would show up to interview, and re-interview those waiting in line.

What bothered Donald mostly was the fact that there were those whom he had known for years, and trusted totally. He had eaten with them, visited with them, was willing to help them if they were sick or in need. To see these very same "friends" turn to "snitches" tore him up.

Donald had always been what one could call an honest con. He was a crook, admitted he was a crook, and did not try to hide that fact. At the same time, he was an honest person, not sticking his nose in others business' nor "snitching" or using others bad luck, to better his own. He liked doing his own time, and nobody else's.

Donald states that during this point in his life, stress, and feelings of deep depression began to take a hold of him. Of course, the fact that he knew he had pulled the trigger, taking five lives, did not help. He was devastated to say the least.

To make matters worse, he could no longer trust anyone. On top of that, the badgering by FBI agents was starting to take its toll. He could no longer get a full night's sleep. The only person he wanted to talk to was Tommy Grey.

All of the problems he was experiencing at that time caused Donald to divorce himself from his surroundings. This was the only thing he could do to keep from "losing it." His life as he knew it had ceased to exist. There was no place to turn, no-one to go to. When he thought he had everything under control, someone would put their nose into his business, and twist things around. He could not figure out why he and Kenny Callahan were singled out for the "Piper Caper!" It made absolutely no sense to him. Many nights he paced back and forth in his cell for hours, as if he were in a daze. He says that it felt like he was walking in a heavy fog, and every time he thought it was lifting and he could again see daylight, the fog would come back thicker than it had ever been.

It would take years for this fog to dissipate, and then, not in totality. Donald says that on the outside, he probably seemed as normal as those around him, but inside he was a raving wreck.

About a week after one of his bouts with the FBI, a convict by the name of Colby Johnson approached him. Colby was doing time for an assault. He told Donald he had been a bartender at the "Squirrel Cage" bar, and that William Cooper, the owner of the bar employed him.

Johnson related to Larson that Cooper, and Falch were very good friends with each other, as well as with Thomas Ryan. He also related to Donald that the two were "snitches" for the FBI! He also stated that the three friends plus FBI agents had many meetings together after closing the bar.

Johnson swore to Larson that after one of these meetings, he heard Peter Neumann tell Falch, and Cooper to "set Larson up" for the Piper deal! At first Donald did not believe him, and thought Johnson was lying and just trying to get on his "good side!" Larson thought that he probably wanted information too. However, shortly after this discussion, everything that Colby had told Larson was verified in an article in a local "News Print."

VII
WILLIAM COOPER

The "Twin Cities Reader" had an article about the Virginia Piper Kidnapping. Ray Chisholm, a very well known St. Paul "Bail Bondsman," wrote this article. He stated that Cooper had informed U S Federal Judge, Miles Lord, U S Prosecuting Attorney Thorvald Anderson, and FBI Agent Peter Neumann that he could solve the Piper Case! He stated that he knew Donald Floyd Larson was involved in it, and in fact, Cooper said he knew where some of the money was hidden!

Suddenly it started to make sense to Donald why Paul Harris and Alan Fields brought the Ford tractor over to Donald's farm. Donald was not supposed to be home on that day. He and his family were supposed to be visiting Donald's mother in law who lived forty miles away. An emergency came up, and the visit was cancelled. This, along with the fact that Peter Neumann showed up at the Anoka County jail with a warrant, and then searched Larson's property, using a back-hoe, brings one to believe that the story about Cooper and the search had something to do with each other.

William Cooper was in jail when he suddenly decided to turn over a new leaf. He had been arrested for the robbery of the Sturgeon Lake State Bank, five miles North of Willow River. He was also facing charges for flying illegal drugs into Minnesota from Mexico. Once again it seemed as though whoever waved the "magic wand," and pointed it towards Donald Larson with regards to the Piper case, would automatically get out of jail free. After Cooper told everyone he would help, he too was bailed out.

Originally, the authorities did not want Mr. Cooper running around on the lose. His bail was set far beyond his means. After Cooper contacted the FBI, his bail was mysteriously lowered to the point where he had no problem getting released. Upon his release, Cooper immediately disappeared from the scene, causing a great amount of consternation between the FBI, and Chisholm Bonding Company. Whether the FBI was actually looking for Cooper or not, leaves a very large question mark. Would they actually give the whereabouts of Cooper to anyone, especially when he was thought to be their star witness? One must remember Larson and Callahan were known to hang around with, and do business with some pretty "connected" individuals. Would the FBI want to protect its witness? Probably! The only problem is that to this day, Mr. Cooper has still not been found, nor heard from.

VIII
LARSON & GREY OUT OF POPULATION

Meanwhile, back in Stillwater, strange things were once again starting to happen. Larson and Tommy Grey had been living in what is called "B" Block. This was considered a "general population" living area, designed for the average convict, who basically held down a job, and got along well with the rest of the population.

The "cell block" Sergeant approached Larson, and Grey and told them, "Pack it up boys we're moving you to 'D' Block!"

"D" Block is where "Insight," a college education program, kitchen workers, and last but not least, "PC" Inmates were housed. "PC" stands for "Protective Custody."

Donald and Tommy did not fit any of the above "criteria" levels for living there. However, they had no choice in the matter, and were promptly moved to their "new housing" unit. They were placed in the "PC" unit, amongst the snitches, punks, and others who had managed to get themselves in debt to other inmates, and could not take care of what they owed. There were also homosexuals held there.

Larson and Grey were placed in cells directly above the Sergeant's Desk, where both were in plain sight at all times!

One of the first to come calling was a guy by the name of Norman Mastrian. He had been convicted of first-degree murder in the "murder for hire" of Mrs. T. Eugene Thompson, a prominent young attorney. Hired by Thompson to kill his wife, Mr. Mastrian chickened out, hired a heroin addict by the name of Anderson to do the job, and when Anderson got caught he snitched on Mastrian, Mastrian snitched on Thompson, and all ended up with life sentences. It would also be learned that Mastrian turned out to be a "snitch" for the FBI!

Mastrian's history of snitching had preceded him to Larson and Grey. They were cordial to him, but knew better than to give him information about anything. Both knew that "no-one" in this unit could be trusted with anything, let alone anything about either of them. Even so, it did not deter the "snitches" from creating "bogus" stories, or at least trying to.

Larson, and Grey had been in "D" Block but a short time when a story came out in the newspapers about the FBI being close to solving the "biggest, for ransom kidnapping" the state of Minnesota had ever witnessed. The story said the FBI was about to have two individuals indicted for the crime. It went on to say that both men were doing time in Stillwater Prison. The story also mentioned the fact that the FBI had to act "quick" because the "statute of limitations" governing the crime was about to expire!

IX
CHARGES FILED

On July 25th, 1977, Donald Floyd Larson was rudely awakened from his sleep. He recalls that it was approximately six AM in the morning. The "goon squad" or high-risk response team, entered his cell, roused him, turned him over to the U S Marshals, who took him from his cell. They had a warrant for his arrest for the "Kidnapping of Virginia Piper," and for the ransom of one million dollars in twenty-dollar bills.

This arrest occurred just two days before the "statute of limitations" would have been exhausted.

A Federal Grand Jury had indicted Donald two weeks earlier. Tommy Grey was cleared of the crime when he proved he was at work at the time. Therefore he was not charged.

The FBI suddenly had changed its attention to Donald's close, life long friend, Kenny Callahan. He was also arrested, and jailed. It was clear that the FBI did not care who they arrested, just so it was someone who they felt could fulfill their greed, and needs.

In the game of "cops, and robbers" the players do not adhere to any stringent set of rules. With the money, and the power that the FBI has, they can usually have anyone they want, indicted, and or arrested. They do not operate under the, "innocent until proven guilty" theory. Instead, it is more, "now I got ya, try to get out of it!"

Needless to say, these arrests caused a "feeding frenzy" amongst the news media. Like sharks, they circled their prey. They were baited by none other than Peter Neumann with tidbits of information about the case. The truth or the falseness of this information made no difference to the hungry reporters. They were only too happy to help convince the public of the guilt of Larson, and Callahan. They were portrayed as criminals, with known "mob connections," and were certainly underground gangsters! Peter Neumann did his job well, spreading the rumors.

PART VI

PIPER TRIAL BEGINS

HARRY PIPER TAKES STAND

The Piper Kidnap Trial began on October 11, 1977 at 9:00 AM. Bruce Hartigan served as Donald Larson's attorney, while Ron Meshbesher served as Kenny Callahan's.

When the court convened, minor preparations were talked about, then "jury selection" began. No one was wasting any time. *(Under the Federal Jurisprudence system, the Judge examines the prospective jurors instead of the attorneys, as in a state case.)*

The selection of the jurors went smoothly, and with methodical expertise. It did not take very long. As soon as they were designated, the prosecution called its first witness.

The crowded courtroom sat in utter silence as Harry C. Piper Jr., husband of Virginia Piper, the kidnap victim, solemnly raised his right hand, and was sworn to "tell the truth, the whole truth, and nothing but the truth!"

Mr. Piper, President and CEO of Piper, Jaffray and Hopwood, Minnesota's largest investment firm, turned his head, and glanced at the jurors as he took his oath. He definitely knew the protocol when it came to impressing people. He had been doing it all of his life.

(So begins one of the most bizarre stories and trials the State of Minnesota would ever see. This trial will show to what depths the FBI is willing to sink to, in order to protect its egotistical image, its mythical reputation, and its greedy passion for power and limelight! This trial drew so much notoriety that Judge Edward J. Devitt's wife sat through the entire proceedings from start to finish. It would be the first time she had visited his courtroom in over thirty years. She told the news media that it was the first trial, which she had attended. Also attending the trial were news agencies from all over Minnesota, as well as Nationwide, and other countries!)

Mr. Piper, clad in a dark blue business suit, with white shirt, and matching tie, had approached the witness stand in a serious, matter of fact manner. He did not exhibit any sign of nervousness or fear.

Harry C. Piper testified as to his being notified of the kidnapping of his wife, and of his obtaining the million dollars in twenty-dollar bills. He told of how it was to be packaged, and as to how it was subsequently delivered.

On cross-examination, Ron Meshbesher asked Piper, "To whom did you deliver the four packages of money?"

Piper, without hesitation, threw up his hands, and answered, "It simply disappeared out of the trunk of the kidnap car!"

Piper also testified that after the delivery of the money, and the dropping off of the kidnap car, he called his brother in law, John Morrison, arranging for him to come, and pick him up. He then stated that he called the FBI.

(This does not coincide with what actually happened. The FBI found Mr. Piper, and John Morrison driving around the Holliday parking lot where Piper had parked the kidnap car. When the FBI found him, they promptly ordered him to leave the area, and go straight home! When asked what he was doing he said he was watching the Monte Carlo with the money in the trunk. He said he and Mr. Morrison were trying to get a look at whoever took the car or the money from its trunk. He

said he would have then followed the kidnappers. Needless to say, no one approached the automobile, no one opened the trunk, and no one was seen retrieving any money from it. The Green Monte Carlo was under scrutiny until the following morning when FBI agents decided to open the trunk. There was no money in it! Like Mr. Piper had said, "It had simply disappeared!")

II
VIRGINIA PIPER
TESTIFIES

The following morning, the courtroom was even more packed than the previous day. News had spread rapidly that none other than Virginia Piper herself would be on the witness stand. Friends, news agencies, and onlookers waited in line to get a glimpse of the well-known wife of Harry C.

The onlooker's wait was well worth it. Virginia Piper, fashionably dressed, platinum blond hair coifed to perfection, approached the witness stand. One had the distinct feeling that the crowd was on the edge of suddenly breaking into applause. Mrs. Piper made a very striking figure. She had a slight smile on her face, and glanced to her right, and left, alternately making eye contact with onlookers, and jurors alike.

Her demeanor was that of someone under complete control of herself, and answered all questions posed to her by the prosecution. She was forthright, spoke with an air of authority, and showed total sincerity in all of her answers. She made eye contact again with all of the jurors when answering the questions.

When the prosecution finished speaking with Mrs. Piper and Bruce Hartigan, Donald Larson's attorney took over.

The first thing he did was to approach the judge, and then beckoned Donald Larson, and Kenny Callahan to approach Mrs. Piper. They ended up standing within a foot and a half of her.

Mr. Hartigan asked, "Mrs. Piper, are these the two men that kidnapped you?"

Mrs. Piper, staring intently at the accused men, emphatically answered, "I have never seen these two individuals in my entire life."

Hartigan again asked, "Are you positive you have never seen them before?"

Mrs. Piper looked at him like she was upset that he would doubt her first answer and answered, "Yes sir, I am quite sure I have never laid eyes on either of them!"

Attorney Ron Meshbesher, defense for Kenny Callahan, asked Mrs. Piper when the FBI Agents had escorted her on the route she thought the kidnappers had taken to get to Jay Cooke State Park.

She answered, "Approximately 'four months' after I was kidnapped."

There are approximately fourteen routes in which the agents or the kidnappers could have used to get to the park. None of these routes left the state of Minnesota. However, the only route the agents took Mrs. Piper on was the singular one that led into Wisconsin! This, of course, made the case a Federal Crime, and would give authorization to the FBI to conduct the investigation. They in turn, barred Minnesota from having anything to do with the investigation or the trial.

Mrs. Piper testified that during a conversation with one of the abductors, she was told emphatically that, "No state lines had been crossed!" She said that her kidnappers reiterated this point many times, leading her to believe they were telling the truth, and had actually taken special care so as "not to have left the state of Minnesota!" She said it was obvious to her that they did not want the case to be a Federal one.

While being cross-examined, Mrs. Piper stated that one of her abductors inadvertently allowed her to see his eyes. She stated that on one of his eyes he had a white circle or partial circle around it. *(In medical terms, this affliction is referred to as "arcus-senilis." It usually occurs in people over fifty years of age, or younger individuals with a very high level of cholesterol.)*

Neither Donald Larson nor Kenny Callahan is afflicted with this trait. However, there is an individual in Stillwater Prison who does have this peculiarity.

(For some reason this Con's name, and mention will come up again in this tale. Supposedly, some of the twenty-dollar bills were found in a grave by two detectives. The grave/graves were marked on a homemade

map. These two detectives had nothing to do with the investigation, but after telling the FBI what they had found, were sworn to secrecy!)

During her testimony, Virginia Piper testified that during a "line up" in which Kenny Callahan was in, she failed to identify him. She did however identify a "police officer" as being one of her abductors!

Mrs. Piper testified that her abductors at all times acted, as gentlemen, and she did not actually feel threatened. She stated that at no time was she harmed or threatened in any manner. She went on to say that while she was chained to the tree in Jay Cooke Park, it had rained all of Thursday night, and into Friday morning. She said she had been given a pair of pants, a sweater, and was covered with a polyethylene tarp to keep her dry, and warm.

During all of her testimony, Mrs. Piper stayed calm, and as she exited the witness stand, she smiled at the jury, the news media, and the rest of the audience.

III
TESTIMONY CONTINUES

The next person to take the witness stand was a person called Murray Miron, a psycholinguist from Syracuse University, located in the state of New York. Mr. Miron was considered to be an expert witness in the art of interpretation of writing, and of determining who wrote certain words. Mr. Mirons's testimony was held at a "side bar" with the jury absent from the courtroom. He testified that Kenny Callahan wrote the "ransom notes!"

Mr. Miron testified that Kenny Callahan had written a letter fifteen years earlier, and had misspelled the word "thorough." In the ransom notes the word "thorough" was also misspelled.

Judge Devitt, after hearing what Mr. Miron was going to testify to, totally disallowed him to take the stand, and testify in front of a jury.

Mike Postle, a deputy sheriff from Hennepin County was called to the stand, and was sworn in. Mr. Postle testified that he and his wife had driven to Jay Cooke Park. They wanted to see where Mrs. Piper was chained to the tree! (*Before we go any further, why would a guy and his wife drive over a hundred miles to see a tree where someone was chained to? Either these people were freaks of some kind, or had ulterior motives. Could it be that they were after a reward of some kind?*)

Mr. Postle stated that they went there about 40 days after the incident took place and Mrs. Piper was freed from her bonds. Mr. Postle magically discovered "eleven Kool cigarette butts" at the location where Mrs. Piper was chained to the tree!

The FBI called this a very important discovery, and said it was crucial evidence in the case. Kenny Callahan was known to smoke Kool cigarettes! Of course, this was definite evidence that Kenny Callahan was one of the abductors.

It had rained a whole night while Mrs. Piper was chained to the tree, probably rained on numerous occasions during the following forty days, and wouldn't they have been found when the area was painstakingly searched inch by inch by FBI agents? Immediately after Mrs. Piper was freed, the place was roped off and a thorough search was made. No Kool cigarette butts were found! Agents had actually crawled on hands and knees looking for the smallest bit of a clue they could use. The only thing they found was a 6-pack of 7/up, a bottle of water, a box of crackers, some Velveeta Cheese, a roll of toilet paper, a pink bottle of Rose wine, a blue St. Olaf sweater, a pair of gray wool pants, thirteen feet of chain, a pair of handcuffs, a brown paper "Piggly Wiggly" bag, a book of matches with the name of a bar in Chicago on it, and some cigarettes with "no brand name on then." These cigarettes were later to have been proven to be "Canadian" cigarettes, and were not sold in the United States. Mrs. Piper did testify that she had been given cigarettes by one of her captors.

It seems ludicrous that immediately after her rescue, there were no Kool cigarettes found, yet forty days later there would be, and by an off duty cop?

This may be a good time to reiterate the fact that there was a $ 50,000 reward in the case. Could it be that, there were fifty thousand reasons why those cigarette butts showed up?

Another witness, William Swanson, manager of "Warner Hardware," located at "Miracle Mile," in Hopkins Minnesota, testified that two young men had entered the store where he worked. They asked him for fifteen feet of chain. Both of these men had black hair, brown eyes and were muscular in build. Mr. Swanson testified that they were "good looking" in appearance and looked like "outdoors" type individuals. The reason he remembered the incident so well was because there were not many "fifteen foot" chain customers.

Swanson told the customers he only had thirteen feet of what they wanted, and both men agreed that what he had would be sufficient. They then purchased the chain and left the store. Swanson also testified that he remembered the incident well because shortly after he sold the chain, it was all over TV that

Mrs. Virginia Piper had been found chained to a tree with "13 feet of chain!"

(Neither Donald Larson nor Kenny Callahan could be described as muscular, outdoors type individuals. Neither has black hair nor brown eyes!)

The next person to testify was a "Sporting Goods" store owner from Duluth Minnesota, just a few miles from where Mrs. Piper was found.

He testified that he had sold the pair of handcuffs used to secure Mrs. Piper to the tree. The only problem was he had absolutely no recollection as to who the person was that he sold them to.

A farmer who lived near Jay Cooke State Park testified that the FBI had set up a road block close to the entrance to the park, and near to the spot where Virginia Piper was found chained to the tree. He stated that he was stopped at the entrance to the park, and then thoroughly questioned by agents. He said he saw four vehicles parked in the vicinity of the entrance to the park. This was on the day that Mrs. Piper was kidnapped! He described the cars as, a red one, a blue Chevy Nova, a

Green Monte Carlo, and another car that was dark in color.

There was a blue Chevy Nova parked outside the Piper residence at the time Mrs. Piper was kidnapped. The man sitting behind the wheel was black haired, outdoorsy, deeply tanned, and handsome looking, and looked muscular. *(Sound familiar?)*

A woman and her fifteen-year-old son saw the car sitting there. They both agreed on the description of the car and its driver. They went on to say it looked like he was reading a newspaper. They were both surprised to see the Nova sitting there, and that there was a man sitting in it looking as if he was just passing the time away reading a newspaper. The boy said it looked like a "look-out man" for something.

A liquor store manager from Minneapolis testified that he positively remembered Donald Floyd Larson as being a customer who entered the store, and purchased the bottle of "White Rose" wine, which was found at the scene of where Mrs. Piper was chained to the tree.

He also testified that he saw Larson on Television, and immediately recognized him as the person who bought the wine.

On cross-examination, defense counsel Meshbesher read aloud the words printed on the label of the bottle of wine. It stated blatantly and clearly; *"Bottled, distributed and distilled" exclusively in Chicago, Illinois.*

When Meshbesher asked the witness what this meant, the liquor storeowner sheepishly lowered his head, and stated that he must have made a mistake. The bottle of wine could not have been bought in his store! *(Did he shamefully desire a $50,000 reward? A red-faced, witness dejectedly left the stand, neither looking left or right. He just made a straight line to the exit.)*

A female bank teller from Rochester, Minnesota took the stand. She testified that Kenneth Callahan had entered the bank where she worked, and that he had passed some of the "twenty dollar ransom money," which was paid out to the kidnappers. This was approximately five years prior to the trial she was testifying at. She testified she had an excellent memory, and that she remembered the incident very vividly!

During this lady's testimony, the judge called a lunch break. During the break, the woman had lunch with FBI Agent Peter Neumann, and another Agent.

After the break, and when court convened, this lady again took the stand. Under cross-examination, Meshbesher asked her whom she had lunch with.

She stated, "With two FBI Agents."

Mr. Meshbesher then asked, "What color were their ties?"

She could not recall.

He then asked her, "What color were their suits?"

Again she could not answer!

Meshbesher then asked, "Now, how good is your memory?"

He quickly withdrew the question, had no further questions, and another red-faced witness left the stand.

The next witness was Frank Hetman, a gas station attendant from Minneapolis. He testified that he had sold Larson a tank full of gas, "five years earlier!" Mr. Hetman stated that Larson was driving a 1972 Green Chevrolet Monte Carlo! *($ 50,000 will help jog anyone's memory after five years!)*

A drugstore clerk recalled that some five years earlier, Donald Floyd Larson entered the store, and had him manufacture a set of keys for a "Green Chevrolet Monte Carlo." When Meshbesher asked, if he had been brought outside by Larson, so he could "see" the car, "his answer was, no!"

Meshbesher then asked the man, "If you didn't go outside to see the car, then how do you know it was green, and how did you know it was a Monte Carlo?"

Another red faced witness walked away from the witness stand with his head hung down, visions of the $ 50,000 dashed from his mind and his dreams!

IV
TOBY LARSON

Next to take the stand was Toby Larson, Donald Larson's ex-sister in law. She testified that on the 27th day of July in 1972, she had called Donald. She remembered this, even though five years had gone by! The reason for this was because she had a message from Donald's daughter who was in the Juvenile Detention Center at Lino Lakes, Minnesota. Toby Larson worked there.

She testified that Donald's daughter wanted Donald to send her some postage stamps.

Debra, Donald's daughter, told Bruce Hartigan it was a blatant lie. She was not even there at that time in her life!

Toby Larson also testified that Donald Larson called her three days after the original phone call, and had said that he and Kenny Callahan had been "up north" fishing for three days. This testimony was heard shortly before the noon break.

During the break, Hartigan got busy. He immediately got hold of a private detective. He had him rush to the Lino Lakes facility. Upon arrival, the private investigator asked for, and received the records in regards to Debra Larson. After the investigator found out that Debra had not been there at that time, he sped back to the courtroom.

As he entered the court, Toby Larson was just sitting down again on the witness stand. The detective rushed to Meshbesher and handed him some papers. Meshbesher quickly scanned them, and suddenly began to smile.

With determination etched on his face, Meshbesher faced Toby Larson. With the sheaf of papers clenched tightly in his hands, he approached.

He reached out, handing the papers to Toby Larson.

Toby read the papers she had been handed. Suddenly the color started to leave her face. Then, she began to shake. All of a sudden she broke down and started to cry! She was sobbing so hysterically that the judge called a recess immediately!

When she again took the stand a half hour later, she did so with reddened eyes. Meshbesher again approached her. This time as he neared, she actually quaked in the chair! Again he handed her some papers.

These were the reports of the Investigator who went to Lino lakes, plus the statements she had made five years prior this. It was in regards to Donald Larson.

These statements were given to various FBI Agents shortly after the Piper Kidnapping. In one of the statements she told how much she hated Donald Larson, and that she had not spoken to him in over five years! She then added that, "Under no circumstances would she talk to any of the Larsons." She went on to say that she hated them all, and that she wanted nothing to do with them. As far as she was concerned, they did not even exist!

After Ron Meshbesher had totally destroyed Toby Larson's testimony with the verification of her lies, and inconsistent statements, Toby Larson stated, "The FBI must have made a mistake." She then denied making any of the statements that Ron Meshbesher had copies of. Finally Meshbesher said he had no more questions from her. The Prosecutor had nothing to say to her, and Toby Larson hurriedly tried to leave the witness stand, again starting to sob. She almost fell, regained her balance, and literally ran to the exit!

Next, there came a long array of informants, rats, snitches, reward hunters, and just plain liars and thrill seekers.

These witnesses were dug up from the bowels of the Stillwater Sewer system, and the Federal system. They consisted of those who had made special deals for early releases, or to have charges dropped and time erased. None of them were what a person could describe as an "honest Joe citizen!"

PAUL HARRIS

Long time stool pigeon Paul Harris was not a very trusted person. He had actually planned a burglary, and then when he got busted with the stolen property, he turned states evidence on his own son, claiming that he did it! He then testified against him in court. He even collected the five thousand dollar reward in the case. When his house was raided, and when marijuana was found, he blamed his daughter and he had her arrested! He got the "pot" back from the cops so he could set someone else up! After smoking half of it he did just that!

When Meshbesher asked Harris if indeed it was true that he collected seven thousand dollars reward money for turning in his own son, he said, "No sir, it was not seven thousand, it was only five."

Harris testified that on numerous occasions, while visiting the Larson farm, Donald had shown him a pair of hand cuffs! He said that Donald told him that he had purchased them in Duluth. Harris also stated that on one of his visits, Donald had asked him if he knew anything about the Piper family! This was supposedly a short time before the Piper Kidnapping in 1972.

Meshbesher reminded Harris under cross-examination that a short time after the Piper Kidnapping, he had stated that he knew nothing about the case or about Donald Larson, Kenny Callahan, or Tommy Grey.

When Meshbesher asked Harris about the forty-five year sentence in the Federal

System, and if it had anything to do with refreshing his memory, Harris replied that there were no deals made. Shortly after Larson's trial, Harris's forty-five year sentence was cut to three years. Then, Mr. Harris was shipped to California and immediately released into society where he was used to ingratiate himself into someone else's life and make a living hell of it!

JOHN DINEEN

Life long criminal, burglar, robber, check writer, rapist, John Dineen was doing time in Stillwater Prison after a "shoot out" with police officers at a bar called "Arones." It was located at Hennepin Avenue and Central in Minneapolis.

(Coincidently, Arones Bar is located directly across the street from Larson Chevrolet, where the 1972 Chevrolet Monte Carlo, used in the Piper Kidnapping was stolen from.)

John Dineen and an un-named accomplice walked into the bar with robbery on their minds. They had guns drawn, shoulders back, and were yelling, "This is a stick up, everyone get on the floor!"

All of a sudden, with no warning, their intentions were embarrassingly thwarted! They were immediately in a gun battle! It seems that Arones Bar was a favorite "cop hangout," and on that particular day, most of its customers were cops! One might say, "The proverbial shit hit the fan!"

John Dineen's crime partner was shot in the shoulder, and the two would-be robbers hastily left the bar a hell of a lot quicker than when they walked in.

After successfully making their getaway, Dineen turned to his partner and said, "You know, we're really lucky, we could've been fucking killed!"

That very same night, Dineen, drinking, and boisterous as usual, was in one of his favorite hangouts. He had quite a few under the belt, and began talking about what had happened that day. A few of his old crone friends sat intently listening. Dineen had a habit of buying drinks for those who would listen to his stories. Meanwhile, someone, sitting at the bar, overheard the crass Dineen bragging about his exploits of the day, and called the police. He told them Dineen was one of the guys that had tried to rob Arones Bar that day. Within a few minutes, John Dineen, for the second time that day was facing guns! The only difference was, this time Mr. Dineen was under arrest!

Dineen was charged with armed robbery, and later pleaded guilty to attempted armed robbery. He was promptly given a sentence of twenty-five years in prison! His six previous arrests, consisting of the aforementioned crimes, enhanced his sentencing. His well known "drug abuse" did not help matters either. The judge was not impressed when Dineen told him that he was an addict.

Sixty-year-old John Dineen limped into the courtroom, having been transported from Stillwater Prison. He approached the witness stand and immediately began talking, "If I were to tell the truth, the whole truth and nothing but the truth, is the court going to release me?"

The judge looked at him incredulously and answered, "No!"

Dineen, nonplussed, answered calmly, "Then I have nothing to say!"

The small wrinkled up Dineen, who had spent over thirty-three years in prison, had been called by the prosecutor Thor Anderson.

Dineen glared at Anderson, and proceeded, "I am here under protest. I don't have anything to say, and I have nothing to testify to."

Upon hearing this, judge Devitt asked the jurors to leave the courtroom. After they had gone, Dineen went on to testify that while he was in prison in Stillwater, he witnessed Donald Floyd Larson wearing a sweater, which matched the one given Mrs. Piper by one of the kidnappers. He further testified that it was a St. Olaf sweater.

His testimony eventually led to Kenny Callahan. He stated that he had instructed Mr. Callahan how to "launder marked money!" Dineen was asked when these conversations took place. His answer was, "I don't remember." With a fierce look on his wrinkled face he angrily stated, "When you've been in prison as long as I have, you don't remember anything, and what you think you remember, might not be real! I don't know if the conversation took place in 1972 or in 1977."

He then insisted that he was incompetent to testify and in fact admitted that he had taken some narcotics shortly before coming to court!

Defense attorney Meshbesher asked Judge Devitt to have Dineen examined by a psychiatrist before allowing him to testify in front of the jury.

Devitt answered, "I do not believe that Mr. Dineen is a normal human being, plus he has been in prison for over thirty years, but I do not believe that he is mentally ill, and because of that reason, I will allow him to testify."

The jury re-entered the courtroom and the questioning of Mr. Dineen resumed.

Dineen said that Larson wore a blue sweater with St. Olaf printed across the front. He said that Larson had worn it on at least one occasion when an ex-con called "Old Nick" Nichols had visited him while he was in Stillwater. At one point in his testimony, he said that it was in the summer of 1972. He added that it was before the Virginia Piper

Kidnapping. Later in his testimony he said he could not remember when he saw the sweater.

He said, "We all used to get visits at the same time. It was sorta like the 'Crime Club of America' and we would sit around talking about crimes we had committed." He added, "Sometimes we would lie a little too!"

When Dineen was shown the sweater that had been given to Mrs. Piper while she was chained to the tree in Jay Cooke Park, Dineen stared intently at it and said, "It sort of looks like it, but I can't be sure if it's the same one or not."

On another occasion, he lost his memory when he could not remember when Kenny Callahan had visited him in prison. Dineen said that they talked about money.

Thor Anderson asked, "Did you talk about laundering money?"

"Well, we talked along those lines." He answered.

"How much did you talk about," asked Anderson?

Dineen answered that he could not remember. He was then asked if it was a million dollars, and he answered emphatically, "No!"

Anderson then started quizzing Dineen further about the laundering of money. "Did you tell him how to launder money?"

Dineen answered, "I told him to go through Toronto, then to Italy, and then back to Toronto, then maybe to Switzerland."

Then, Anderson asked, "Did you understand what money you were both talking about?"

Dineen said, "Mentally I did."

Earlier, Dineen had mentioned that, "when convicts sometimes communicated among themselves, they often used the 'third party' to refer to themselves and thereby saying a lot but leaving much unsaid. When you get to be friends, you know what the other person is talking about and what he is thinking." He also said, "the less verbally said the better."

Prosecutor Anderson asked, "What money did you think that Kenneth Callahan was talking about?"

Dineen answered, "There was no mention of where the money was from, or where it was coming from."

He was then asked, "What was your mental image of where the money was coming from?"

He answered "I figured it was twenty dollar bills, and I didn't figure they was comin from any bank."

When asked if he thought they had come from the Piper Kidnap ransom money, he simply said, "Yes."

(The million dollars paid out in the Piper kidnapping was all in twenty-dollar bills and supposedly, the FBI had taken all of the bill's serial numbers down. Over the years, some of the money has been recovered. However, most is still missing!)

The defense attorneys questioned Dineen on cross-examination about his credibility. When asked if he took narcotics, Dineen answered, that he did. When asked if he got dope or narcotics in prison, he quickly answered that he did not know. When he was asked if he had taken drugs at the prison before he was brought to the courtroom, he answered that he had. He said, "I took some Talwin and Demerol."

Judge Devitt then asked Dineen when the exact time was that he took the dope. His answer was, "Just before they rounded me up, and forced me to come here and testify."

He added, "It must have been about noon."

The judge then dismissed Dineen from further testifying, and called for a recess.

JOHN CARDENAS

Mr. John Cardenas, formerly a "Men's Store" manager, said that in July, 1974, he received one of the twenty dollar bills paid in the Virginia Piper kidnap and ransom. An artist's drawing of the person said to have passed the bill, was entered into evidence. The drawing looked very familiar to a May, 1974 photograph of Kenny Callahan. That picture was also entered into evidence.

The photograph taken in 1974 depicted Mr. Callahan as having a dark beard, and dark hair. Callahan did not have a beard at the time of the trial. Callahan's reddish brown hair is graying at the sides, and temples. The drawing

268

that was described to the artist by Cardenas was that of a dark haired man, with a beard.

The pictures, though possibly damaging to Callahan, lost some of their impact when Cardenas' testimony was discredited by attorneys Hartigan, and Meshbesher during their cross examination.

Cardenas, under cross, admitted that besides identifying Callahan as looking similar to the customer who paid for three T-shirts, and three pairs of shorts, with the twenty dollar bill, he also identified "Gerald 'Runt' Alger," William Cooper and Harvey Kerignan as looking similar to the customer! All three of them were suspects in the Piper kidnapping at one time or another during the investigations. *(It is plain to see that none of these individuals are similar in appearance to Kenny Callahan. In fact, they are not look a-likes to each other! They do know each other though, and one of them, Harvey Kerignan has a white circle around one of his eyes!)*

Virginia Piper described one of her captors as having a white circle around one of his eyes, and as having a "leg problem." "Ol Harve" has both! Moreover, some of the "twenties" paid in the ransom, were purportedly found in a "hand drawn map" of graves, which "Ol Harve" supposedly drew! The chief homicide detective for Hennepin County and his partner found the map, and the burial spot. The detectives name was Archie Sonnestal. He stated that while he and his partner were investigating a "serial killer," they came across a hand drawn map with exes on it. Not only did they locate the remains of some missing girls, they also found some of the twenties!

"Runt" Alger, short, stocky, with a short neck, was described by numerous people, and at one time was suspected to have been the leader of the group thought to have kidnapped Virginia Piper. His description and whereabouts seem to turn up throughout the story, and investigation. Alger, an x-con, did time in the sixties at Stillwater Prison.

Harvey Kerignan is also known as the "Want Ad Killer" in a book written by the famous author, Ann Rule. He was arrested, convicted, and sentenced to numerous "life" sentences in the mid seventies. He remains "wanted" in numerous other states throughout the USA on other murders. He remains to this day in Stillwater Prison. Rumor has it that he has incurable cancer at this time.

As to Mr. Cooper, who disappeared shortly after the Piper kidnapping, no one has heard from him since. His whereabouts remain unknown, or at least secretive!

(Since the beginning of this book, it has been learned that "Gerald 'Runt' Alger" has passed away. His home was near Bena, Minnesota, located on the "Leech Lake Indian Reservation." There is a story that some still laugh about concerning "Runt." It seems that the FBI was at his cabin questioning him about the Piper Case. One of the Agents was leaning on the fireplace, and those in the cabin kept laughing making the Agents nervous because they did not know why they were laughing. The reason they were laughing was because the Agent that was leaning on the fireplace had his hand about five inches from some of the "ransom money!" It was hidden in the fireplace chimney! This is pure speculation and rumor. However this does add some comic brevity and questions to the saga! It is also rumored that the money

hidden in the fireplace was not "ransom money" but was more aptly named, "payoff money" for a job well done! "Runt" and some of his friends started a business together in the Bena Minnesota area and supposedly used this money to open a "wood pulp" enterprise.)

ROBERT NEILL

Robert Neill, FBI Agent and Microscopic Analyst, testified that a reddish brown hair, which a detective found in the kidnapper's vehicle, was almost identical to several hairs found or taken from Kenneth Callahan's head. This was done in June of 1977. Neill admitted that hair couldn't be used as a positive form of identification of an individual.

Neill testified that he found "twenty one" identical characteristics when examining Kenny Callahan's hair, and then comparing it with the hair found in the automobile.

Neill told the jurors that human hair has between fifteen and twenty-five unique, microscopic characteristics. The identical characteristics which he found in Kenny

Callahan's hair, along with the hair located in the vehicle, included; some natural curl, (probably eighty percent of all people have some natural curl) alkaline cuticle, (all or most shampoos, and soap have an alkaline base) no pigment occlusions in the cuticle, (no color dyes) diffuse pigmentation in the cortex, (lack of dye in the interior of the hair follicle) and a narrow medulla (a thin hair shaft.) If you take away the impressive words that no-one knew what the hell was meant by them, you would have a reddish brown hair, which had not been dyed, had no recent dye in it, no old dye in it, and was of a thin shafted nature! My o my Kenny Callahan's hair fit that of probably 99 percent of all America/Irishmen!

Neill went on to testify that he found it very rare that any two individuals would have identical hair characteristics. He went on to state that he had found it in only thirty or forty times out of three hundred thousand times in the thirteen years he had been doing that work. (if one wants to play with numbers, that would mean that Mr. Neill would have to have examined approximately "eighty hair samples" per day, seven days a week, for thirteen years! Let's get real folks!

Neill said that these comparisons were made in June of 1977 when the Minneapolis office of the FBI submitted samples of Callahan's hair to be checked against a "gray" hair that had been dyed brown. This hair had supposedly been found amongst the items found in the Monte Carlo used to abduct Mrs. Piper.

When checking Kenny Callahan's hair against that of the dyed hair, Neill testified that he stumbled onto the matching hair found in the car.

"That's real funny, a fellow just happened to stumble onto a fingerprint just the other day too," said Larson's Attorney Bruce Hartigan.

Mr. Hartigan was referring to testimony given by an FBI agent who was designated an expert in fingerprints. The Agent said that the fingerprint that matched Larson's thumbprint was actually checked three times before a lab technician discovered that it matched!

Neill also testified that he compared the hair found in the kidnap car with hair tested from the head of Virginia Piper. He said they did not match. He went on to say that Mrs. Piper's hair had been cosmetically and chemically treated, for the effect of being "Platinum" instead of its naturally gray color! *(I bet that tid-bit of information didn't set well with Mrs. Piper!)*

Mr. Neill then was brought to the subject of cigarette butts found at the scene where Mrs. Piper was chained to the tree. He testified that the Federal Trade Commission found that one of the filters found, was from a Canadian brand of cigarette. However, a Canadian researcher determined it was from an American brand! "I'm not certain either of these analyses is correct," Neill said. *(Defense attorneys Hartigan, and Meshbesher both suggested that at least one of the kidnappers came from Canada.)*

When attorney Meshbesher cross-examined Neill, he asked him point blank if a person's hair would or could change after a "five year" period of time. Neill replied that a person's hair indeed could change over a period of time. In fact, as a person aged, their hair automatically changed, not only in color, but also in texture, growth and whether it was straight or curly, or vice-a-versa.

JAMES HEANEY

James Heaney an FBI Agent, who worked out of the "West Palm Beach" office in Florida, testified that he, had played five voice tapes to Mrs. Piper at a Florida Condominium. This was March of 1976, approximately four years after her abduction. Mrs. Piper picked a recording, which had Kenny Callahan's voice on it. She said it was the most similar to the voice of one of her kidnappers. The other four voices used in the experiment were of Minneapolis FBI personnel.

(With the numerous number of suspects in the investigation, one wonders whey they did not use some of the voices of the suspects. Was the FBI so engrossed in finding Larson and Callahan guilty that they ignored what was right in front of them? During the whole investigation they ignored "blatant clues," which could have solved a large amount of time, and expenditures, heartache and death!)

JAMES HOWELL

James Howell a fingerprint expert for the FBI stated that tests were conducted in September 1972, January 1973 and November 1976. These tests were in reference to the Piper Kidnap for ransom of Virginia Piper. He stated that all of the tests made, failed to match Donald Floyd Larson's print with the one taken from a piece of paper ripped from a "Piggly Wiggly" store shopping bag, and found in the green Chevrolet Monte Carlo, used in the abduction.

A total of seventy-three palm prints were found in the Monte Carlo. To this day, none have been matched with anyone nor have they been identified. Howell stated that the print from the scrap of paper was found to match Larson's thumbprint in January of 1977.

It was determined that the "all magical" thumbprint was indeed torn from the unidentified Piggly Wiggly shopping bag that certain groceries were believed to have been bought, then brought to the area where Mrs. Piper was tied by chain to the tree!

To illustrate the fingerprint testimony, Agent Howell showed the jurors an enlarged photograph of a print taken from Larson's left little finger. He also showed the print taken from the piece of paper torn from the bag. He then indicated there were identifying characteristics of the two prints, which enabled him to come to the conclusion, that both of the fingerprints were of the same person, namely Donald Floyd Larson! He went on to add that these characteristics were apparently missed in the first three attempts to identify them!

Agent Howell did admit that the print on the scrap of paper was not a "very good" one, but at the same time was legible enough to make identification as to whom it belonged to.

He believed the picture was a little distorted due to the finger being twisted clockwise, therefore making the comparison difficult the first three times!

Howell testified that on January 17th 1977, he had been requested to focus all of his skills, and tests on this single print. This request came from the Chicago office of the FBI. It was the only print given to him, the only one he tested, and therefore the only one it could be!

On January 25, 1977 the lab received another request. This was from the Minneapolis office of the FBI. This request asked the lab to check the prints of a number of people involved in the Piper case, not including Larson or Callahan!

On January 29th, 1977 the lab in Washington notified the Chicago office, and the Minneapolis office that the print found on the small piece of paper did indeed match the print of Donald Floyd Larson! From there, it was requested that the prints of Larson and Callahan be sent from the office in Minneapolis to the office in Washington, with a confirmation of the identification.

Howell testified that eighty-three fingerprints and eleven palm prints were fount to belong to people not suspected in the crime. This included Pipers, FBI Agents, and various others who may have handled the "evidence!"

The remaining sixty fingerprints, eleven palm prints and two prints could have come from a palm or finger, totaling seventy three which were never compared to each other.

On cross examination Meshbesher asked Howell, "So you don't know if those seventy three prints were made by one person, two people, three people or seventy three people!?"

Howell stuttered nervously, "N-n-n-no, we weren't told or asked to do anything about that!"

Attorney Hartigan cross-examined Howell, and got him to admit that the fingerprint on the scrap of paper had been obliterated by a print lifting process used by the technicians.

When asked to explain, Howell stated that there are methods available so as to make prints visible. Two of these methods leave the print, but the third method, in which silver nitrate is used, can cause the print to become erased. The lab used all three methods during its inspection. Although there are photographs of the print, the actual print or "original" does no longer exist. Hartigan intimated that he wished he could have the original print which no longer existed, He stated that he could and would have had the print inspected by a "private" or independent source!

Next, Hartigan read from an FBI manual, which was partially prepared by Agent Howell. The article in the manual indicated that prints lifted with the silver nitrate method can be kept for up to ten years!

Hartigan then asked Howell if he had heard about a California case where a forged fingerprint was used to convict a man of bank robbery.

Howell stated that he had, and Hartigan went on to say that the print was lifted from a "teller's cage" and was identified as the defendant's. A few years later, the print was to be discovered as a forged or manufactured one.

When Hartigan asked Howell if he was aware that the FBI had developed ways in which they could actually "forge" and or manufacture and re-manufacture fingerprints, Howell slowly lowered his head and answered, "Yes I am!"

KENT CHRISTIANSON

Hennepin County Deputy Kent Christianson testified that there were items found in the kidnap vehicle. He witnessed that he was the one that processed the Green Chevrolet Monte Carlo, just two days after Mrs. Virginia Piper was freed by the kidnappers. He stated that he went over the vehicle very carefully, and thoroughly!

Mr. Christianson said that he found a memo pad initialed with, "P, J & H!" He also said that he found a copy of the "ransom note." These items were all together in a packet of material. There were also maps of Hennepin County, the Lake Minnetonka area and other areas including one of Minnesota.

Mr. Christianson also testified that he found a "black, U S Government" pen. Harry C. Piper had testified that he did not take a memo pad with him when he went on the route that the kidnappers told him to follow while delivering the "ransom money." Piper also testified that he suspected someone from his firm might have been involved with the abduction! His reasoning was, "the kidnappers were aware of the fact that he was not normally in his office on Thursdays, the day his wife, Virginia was kidnapped." This coincides with what the maids testified to about the "abductors" asking for "Mr. Piper" rather than "Mrs. Piper" when they entered the Piper residence on the day of the kidnapping.

HAROLD COMBS

Harold Combs a one time friend of Kenneth Callahan, told the Federal Jurors that he saw Callahan with a pair of "handcuffs" and at least two guns shortly before Virginia Piper was kidnapped at "gun point," and was then handcuffed! Combs also refuted Callahan's alibi that he had been fishing during the time Mrs. Piper was kidnapped.

(Another man, Paul Harris, said that he had also seen Larson, and Callahan with handcuffs before the kidnapping, and that he "Harris" was asked if he knew anything about the Pipers!)

Both of these men had very extensive criminal records, and both had reason to give some favors to the FBI! Harris did not tell about the incident when he was supposedly shown the handcuffs. It took him five years to suddenly recall the incident and then, he was doing time in the Federal Penitentiary in Sandstone, Minnesota for "possession of a handgun!"

When Meshbesher asked Harris if he was expecting an early release from his conviction, Harris nonchalantly answered he was. He stated that he was hoping that they would release him early because that is exactly what they told him they would do. He stated with certainty that the, "FBI will get me out!"

Combs admitted to being involved with Larson and Callahan in a "fencing operation" at the time of the kidnapping. Harris admitted that he expects to get out of prison earlier because of his testimony.

(Why would Combs testify against his buddies? If he actually thought that Larson and Callahan did pull off the million-dollar Piper job, he may have been pissed off because they failed to allow him in on the deal. This is the only reason that Larson or Callahan could come up with, to give reason as to why he would testify against them.)

Harold Combs testified that he and Callahan had worked together in the "Cabinet

Shop" from May or June of 1972 until the spring of 1973. He added that they, along with Larson, fenced stolen goods through the "Cabinet Shop!"

Combs testified that the FBI had visited the "Cabinet Shop" in early August of 1972. They asked where he was during the kidnapping of Mrs. Piper. He told them that he did not know where he was at the time. He testified that later, he told Larson about his visit with them, and Larson said, "Don't you remember? That's the day we all went fishing!"

Combs did admit that he had gone fishing with Larson and Callahan, and in fact had told the FBI that he had been with them on the 28th day of July, the day after Mrs. Piper had been kidnapped from her Orono home. This was the day before Mrs. Piper was found, chained to the tree in Jay Cooke State Park.

"I really believed we had been fishing on that day," he testified. The FBI contradicted his testimony however.

FBI Agents showed Combs receipts, and a canceled check for work he had done on a building at 170 Central Avenue on the 26th,

27th, and on the 28th of July in 1972! Combs then said that the fishing trip they went on must have been the week prior to the kidnapping!

In response to questioning by Thor Anderson, Assistant U.S. Attorney, Combs testified that Callahan had shown him a pair of handcuffs while working in the shop in May or June of 1972.

Combs said that Kenny Callahan had reached in his pocket, took the cuffs out, then asked, "What do you think of these?"

This testimony sounded very damaging until Callahan's defense attorney took over. Meshbesher approached Combs, holding some papers in his hand. The papers consisted of testimony by Combs in front of the "Grand Jury" hearing. There, he testified that Callahan had shown him the cuffs while he and Kenny were in Callahan's basement. When confronted with this, Combs stammered, "The only thing that I am certain of is that I saw a pair of handcuffs." He added, "I don't know why, when or where!" Combs also testified that he had witnessed

Callahan as having at least two guns in the shop at various times.

Combs said that at one time, he told Callahan that he was going to take a test that the FBI wanted him to take in regards to the Piper Caper. He said that Callahan asked, "What the hell for?"

Combs then replied, "Because I didn't do it!"

Callahan then said, "Yeah, but you're making it easier for the FBI to find out who did do it!"

Combs went on to say that the FBI came to the shop in 1972, and questioned him about the Piper kidnapping. Both Kenny Callahan and Donald Larson were also there at the time. They all thought that the FBI was there to actually raid the "Shop" in regards to their "fencing operation!" It had grown to such large proportions that it was now "Interstate," and actually reached out of the United States!

When Meshbesher implied that Larson and Callahan were worried about the "fencing business" Combs denied it. He stated that Callahan and Larson were not overly excited, and were not running around like they were scared.

Meshbesher then asked, "Didn't you say that Larson had said, "Oh wow, that was a close one?"

Combs answered, "You're putting words in my mouth."

Meshbesher continued, "Tell me if I'm wrong."

Combs answered, "You're wrong."

Next, Combs testified that Callahan helped Combs's girlfriend move to an apartment in NE Minneapolis at nine AM on July 29th. Mrs. Piper was found in the woods about one PM on the 29th, but she testified that her abductors had left her very late on the night before. Combs testified that Callahan did not look tired as he helped with the move that morning.

LYLE SIMONSON

Lyle Simonson an ex-convict said that he, and Larson committed burglaries together from 1945 until 1952. He stated that sometimes they would wear clothing purchased at a "Goodwill" store or from a "Salvation Army" store, the reason being they did not want to wear their own.

He said that besides wearing old, used clothes, they would purchase some coke or 7/up so they would have something to drink during the burglaries. He said sometimes it took a long time to get the merchandise out, or to open a safe, or a "tough" cash register.

(A blanket given Mrs. Piper while she was secured to the tree in the Park had a "Goodwill" tag on it, and several 7/up cases were found at the area in Jay Cooke Park where Mrs. Piper was found.)

When questioned by attorney Hartigan, Simonson admitted that they were always extremely careful not to leave anything behind and that they always threw the old clothes away or burned them after they finished their "job." Simonson was asked if he was always truthful, and he answered, "Not always, I did lie at another trial not related to this one."

FBI AGENTS

Three FBI Agents testified next. They said that several of the marked "twenties" that were paid out in the ransom of Mrs. Piper, were found in the Philadelphia area. They stated that they were found in "drug related" busts. However, they testified that they did not know if any information was actually received as to how the money got there.

Two "Twin Cities" bank tellers testified that Kenny Callahan bought bank checks with new one hundred dollar bills, issued by the Philadelphia Federal Reserve Bank.

(Wouldn't one be able to hazard a guess that most of the "one hundred dollar" bills in Minnesota probably came from the Philadelphia Federal Reserve Bank?!)

FBI Agent Arthur Sullivan testified that he took Mrs. Piper on a trip along the kidnap route. Mrs. Piper lay on the back seat of the car, and had her eyes covered as the agents drove North on Interstate Highway 35. They drove to highway 210, and turned east to

Highway 23, then south to an access road into a remote area of Jay Cooke State Park.

Agent Sullivan stated that Mrs. Piper remembered a double set of "railroad tracks" on Highway 210, followed by a "stop" at an intersection in Carlton. She also remembered the sounds of a wooden planked bridge about four miles East of Carlton, then a sharp right hand turn into the park. Sullivan added that the "wooden bridge" no longer existed, and that only one set of railroad tracks remained.

Defense counsel Bruce Hartigan questioned the Agent as to why they did not take Mrs. Piper to the Park using the most "direct route," which led to the Ascov turnoff from Highway 35. He stated that there are "double" railroad tracks on Highway 23 via that route, followed closely by a "stop sign!"

Sullivan answered that, "If she would not have remembered the railroad tracks, and the bridge, we would have definitely tried a different route."

Meshbesher pointed out that there is no stop sign at the Carlton Intersection, going east on Highway 23, although there are stop signs at the other three corners. Mrs. Piper testified that she distinctly remembered the kidnap vehicle stopping shortly after she heard, and then felt the railroad tracks.

Sullivan thought for a moment and stated that, "It is a very dangerous intersection," then added, "Most people stop there even though there is no stop sign there." "But, I didn't stop there," Sullivan parried.

"If they were prudent, law abiding citizens?" Meshbesher asked.

"Yes," Answered Sullivan.

After a week of testimony the prosecution rested its case against Donald Floyd Larson, and Kenny Callahan.

Both Larson and Callahan felt that the Prosecution had put up a mediocre case at best. They felt confident in their "Defense team" of Hartigan and Meshbesher. They also felt that they had proven many of the Government witnesses were liars, and that most of them had manufactured stories because they had rewards, and or favors to gain!

Both Hartigan and Meshbesher saw some satisfaction shown on the faces of their clients, and were quick to point out, that the

Feds put on a "pretty good case," and that Larson and Callahan should not be celebrating too fast. They mentioned the fact that they had a steep hill to climb yet, and were confident they would or could change some of the evidence against them, but cautioned them that "there were some damaging things said," and whether they were true or not, the belief or non-belief was, or would be in the hands of the jurors, and jurors did not always go the direction that people thought they were going to go.

PART VII

THE DEFENSE

I
WITNESSES
ERNA CALLAHAN
KAREN WILLEY

Among the first to testify for the defense was Erna Callahan, wife of Kenneth Callahan. Following his wife was Karen Willey, Callahan's daughter.

Both Erna, and Karen testified that Kenny had been home on the two nights that the Federal Bureau of Investigation claimed he had been involved in the process of Kidnapping, then holding Virginia Piper hostage, for a payment of a "cool million dollars" in twenty-dollar bills!

Both, wife and daughter swore that he had arrived home at approximately 5:30 on the afternoon of July 27th, and July 28th, 1972. They stated that they all had dinner, then retired to the "living room," and watched television until around 10 PM.

Kenny's daughter Karen, who was single at the time, said that shortly after the kidnapping of Virginia Piper, she was approached, and thoroughly questioned by the FBI. They were mostly interested in her father's whereabouts on the 27th, and the 28th of July. She recalled that she told them that he was at home on those respective evening, and nights. She also stated that at that time, she did not know that the FBI was investigating the Piper kidnapping, but did find out later that this was what it was all about.

When defense attorneys asked her how she remembered, five years later that her father was home on that night, she replied without hesitation, "Because, the FBI interviewed me about it at that time. Had they not talked to me at that time, there would have been no reason to remember it. In fact, in all probability I would not have remembered my father being home on any night unless there was reason given to me to remember." She added, "I am very thankful to them for talking with me at that time, and cementing my memory in regards to the situation."

Kenny Callahan's wife, Erna Callahan, basically testified to the same thing. When the FBI had questioned them, they were given dates, circumstances, and times which would be forever imbedded in their minds. With the publicity, and notoriety of the Piper kidnapping, it was sort of "hard to forget!"

DEBRA LARSON

Debra Larson, the nineteen-year-old daughter of Donald Larson, testified that she had been living at the Lino Lakes Juvenile Detention Center from May 6th, 1972 to May 31st, 1972. She also testified that she "most definitely 'had not' been there during the kidnapping of Virginia Piper!" She also stated that her father had always visited her on a regular basis for the short time she was in the institution, and that she absolutely had no need for any postage stamps. She could not understand why her aunt and Donald's sister in law would testify earlier that she had asked her to call her father and ask for postage stamps at that time. She went on to testify that her aunt Toby did not even work there at that time!

Toby Larson also testified that Kenny Callahan and Donald Larson had installed a cabinet in her home, and that while they were working she noticed that Kenny had a problem with his leg or legs. She stated that he had been limping.

(It has been proven and never challenged that Kenny Callahan did indeed have leg problems, but they never manifested themselves until at least "five years" after the "Piper kidnapping!" This was totally investigated, and Mr. Callahan's medical records were gone through thoroughly and there were no records of any "leg problems!" At the same time his medical records were checked for "leg problems," they were also checked for any "eye ailments." This also proved to be negative! He did not, nor ever had anything-resembling "Arcus- Senilis!"

Two former waitresses from "Occie's Bar" said that both Larson and Callahan were in the bar on the days before, during and after the kidnapping of Virginia Piper. Annabelle La Tourneau and Doris Lancaster said that neither of the men usually drank anything, usually they had just a soda. They said the reason that they came in there was because they were very good friends with the ladies boss, Occie. They also testified that they seldom missed a day of coming in at least once, and would have been missed had they not come in. When they were questioned about Callahan and Larson, and the Piper Kidnapping, the dates and times were also cemented in their minds forever.

TOMMY GREY

Thomas Grey, life long friend of Donald Larson and Kenny Callahan, had been recently released from Stillwater State Prison. He testified that he had pulled a "prank" on a guy there. This person was rumored to be a "snitch," and that he could not be trusted with anything.

He said that he had whispered to another convict, loud enough so that the "informer" could hear, "I hope they don't dig between the back of the bus and the garage on Larson's farm."

Grey said there was a large slab of concrete between the two, and that he had only wanted to see how quick the FBI would act on the "informer's" information. The "snitch's" name was Mayhew.

Shortly thereafter, Grey said that an FBI Agent came to Stillwater, and questioned him about what he had whispered.

Grey said, "When I told the Agent that it was a trick, he became very unhappy!" The Agent told Grey that he did not think that it was very "funny!" It seems that the Agent had received the information from Mayhew, and immediately hired a contractor, traveled all the way to Larson's farm, and began to dig!

This ended the "defense" for Donald Larson, and Kenny Callahan.

II
THE WAIT

With the end of Thomas Grey's testimony, the trial ended. The Closing arguments were made and the judge gave the jurors their instructions, and they immediately left the courtroom to begin their deliberations.

Donald Larson was transferred back to the Hennepin County jail, and Kenny Callahan was free to leave. He was still on bond, and went straight home. Both were quite nervous, but comfortable with how the trial went, they shook hands, and thanked their attorneys.

(It has been said that the longer a Jury deliberates, the better the chances are for "acquittal" or at least a "hung jury." This seemed to be the case in the Larson, Callahan Trial. After three days of deliberating, THE JURORS SENT A NOTE TO THE JUDGE! It said they were "DEADLOCKED!")

The judge immediately called the jurors to the courtroom where he instructed them to go back and to deliberate some more. Two days later, the jurors were ready to announce their verdict.

Larson, Callahan, Bruce Hartigan, and Ron Meshbesher were all notified that they should report to the courtroom immediately. The jurors had finally arrived on a unanimous verdict!

All of those involved were excited to return to the court, and get the verdict. As they all arrived, and sat down at the "Defense table," they were a little nervous however, all four of them felt that a favorable verdict would be given. They all greeted each other with handshakes, and slaps on the back, each with a big smile. This nightmare would soon be over!

III
THE VERDICT

As the defense team sat silently, each with their thoughts racing wildly, you could hear a pin drop. Someone coughed in the audience, the harsh suddenness of the sound making many in the packed courtroom jump!

Donald said it sounded like a bomb went off. Bruce Hartigan patted him on the shoulder and said, "It's ok Donald, we're just about there!"

The minutes seemed to tick by ever so slowly, but finally the jurors began to file into the courtroom. Larson, Callahan, and their attorneys watched intently, trying to get a sign pointing with favor in their direction, trying to get, even the smallest clue as to what they should expect. There was none! Not one of the jurors looked in their direction.

They seated themselves in the "jury box," and the jury foreman handed the Court Bailiff a piece of paper. Without looking at it, he carried it to the Judge.

Judge Devitt took the piece of paper, and studied it intently. He looked at Larson and Callahan respectively, then to Mr. Meshbesher, and to Mr. Hartigan.

Without a waiver in his voice, he loudly averred, "The Jury has found you both guilty as charged. You will be sentenced immediately!"

As the verdict was read, Larson, Callahan, and their attorneys stared in disbelief!

Ron Meshbesher immediately responded, "Your Honor, we are appealing this!"

As the Jurors left the courtroom, not one of them would even glance at the two men they had just convicted.

Devitt immediately started the "sentencing phase." Without batting an eye or without a breath, he calmly sentenced both Larson and Callahan to a sentence of "Life Imprisonment!"

No matter how well prepared a person is or thinks they are, there isn't any way in hell that they can be prepared for those words. Even if you know that they are going to be said, it is still like getting kicked in the stomach. The words are devastating! The wind is knocked out of you, you cannot breathe, and you are suddenly sick to your stomach. The world and everything around you seems to start spinning. You feel like puking, shitting, laughing, screaming, and crying, all at the same time. It is the most unreal feeling in the world. Kenny Callahan would later say that the feeling had to be like suffering a "sudden death." No matter how prepared you are, you cannot control your feelings at the unexpectedness, and utter trauma it causes your thinking, and your whole being!

These feelings can last for minutes, hours, days, weeks, months and yes, even years. For some they never cease. Those that do not lose these feelings can be spotted in prison easily. They are the ones that walk around as if in a daze, no place to go, no aims, no real wants, nor complaints. They are like zombies.

At first these feelings evoke shock, then anger, and when that wears off you become numb. The only difference between a life sentence, and a death sentence, under a life sentence you are among the living dead.

After Judge Devitt was informed there would be an immediate appeal, Judge Devitt, remarked in a sarcastic voice, "Good Luck!"

IV
DONALD'S RETURN TO PRISON

Donald Larson was immediately transferred back to Stillwater State Prison where he was already participating in a "Life Sentence!"

Kenny Callahan was allowed to stay out on bond pending the outcome of the appeal.

Donald relates that when he was returned to Stillwater, he just walked around in a daze for a long time. He did not know, believe, nor care what was happening. All of Stillwater's "jailhouse lawyers" told him, they couldn't do that to him! This was pretty comical to Donald, because for something they couldn't do, they sure as hell did it!

Donald knows that all of his buddies were trying to help him however their words of comfort and solace did little to ease the ache in his heart, and the thoughts, which were incessantly racing through his beleaguered mind, and body. He could only think of one thing! He was fifty years old, and had two life sentences to do. Life to Donald, at that time seemed pretty bleak to say the least.

Donald knew that to survive the feelings of despair he was experiencing, he would have to do something in a hurry! He decided to embark on a plan to try to figure out exactly how he got to the point in his life that he was now at.

He began to write! He wrote about his life as a child, his friends, skipping school, petty thievery, his friends that had died over the years, and the people that he had killed!

He thought about working for Stillman's Produce for over ten years, and how everything was going so good for him at that time. He recalled how he had rebuilt his "farm" and of going straight, about the first time he did "hard time," about his heart attack, and about Paul Harris, and James

Falch. This part of his life seemed as though it was the beginning of the end!

Donald worked in Cell Block "B." He was employed as a "swamper." He swept, and mopped what is called the "flag" area, or the bottom floor. He was paid twenty-five cents an hour for this duty. It was hardly enough to take care of his personal needs. He needed more income, so he began doing sewing, and leatherwork. He settled into a daily routine, and found that it helped him greatly with his feelings of despair, and his never-ending thoughts of the past. Things actually began going easier, and better for him.

Donald had numerous friends to talk to, and visit with. He got along with everyone, and everyone seemed to like him, including the "screws" as the guards were called back then. Having a good personality, and quick sense of humor, pretty much endeared him to all who knew him.

In prison, most convicts have one problem. That of course is "boredom."
A convict must create diversions. Diversions might consist of gambling, sports, and

writing, making hooch, exercising, hobby craft, or various other ways.

V

"THE MAP"

Many of Donald's friends would tease him about where he had the money hid. Somebody offered him a pint of ice-cream for a map. He started drawing maps, and soon had more ice-cream than he could eat!

It seems that very seldom there would be any two maps alike, and when someone asked, "Why is my map different than his?" Donald simply answered, "You don't think I'd hide that much money in one spot do you?" There was no hesitation in the answer, and soon rumor had it that Donald Floyd Larson had money buried all over the "North Country" of Minnesota.

Not only did the cons want maps, so did the "hacks," "screws," "bulls," "turnkeys," "case workers," and everyone else around the compound.

(Nowadays, all of the above named people take affront at these names, but in reality they are now what they were then!)

Donald says, I bet some of these guys, and women go home at night, and when their kids or spouses meet them, and ask, "How did your day go today honey?" They are answered with, "Pretty good thar 'sweet thang' I really showed them convicts a thing or two. I actually caught one of them using the bathroom during count, and I wrote him up! He asked me if he could go, and I wouldn't let him. He actually had to piss in a 'Folgers' jar HA HA HA!"

"Another one tried to smuggle a piece of bread and a piece of cheese back to his room from the kitchen! I got his ass good. I wrote him up, and when he argued about it, I threw the son of a bitch in Segregation. That'll teach him!"

Then the guard will tip back the "mirrored sun glasses" to his forehead, fart a couple times, say "gimmee a beer," and saunter to the couch where he will spend most of the night!

(They say that the divorce rate and alcoholism rate is very high among guards. I

*can see why. They have to stay drunk to live
with themselves, and after drinking for a
while, start to think they can treat their wives,
and kids the same way they treat the convicts.
I bet this pisses some of em off, especially the
ones with the "mirrored sunglasses!")*

In the "old days," the "convicts," and
"screws" pretty much got along. They would
joke about a "treasure map," and many times
Donald would get a twinkle in his eye and a
growl in his stomach, with the anticipation of
another pint of ice cream, or even sometimes
a giant "Whopper!" "Arby's" were pretty
popular with him also!
He also became addicted to "White Castles!"

When you talk to Donald about his maps,
he admits that it was pretty much a "game"
that kept him occupied. He liked the attention
it got him, and the food, which he enjoyed.

Donald also liked to sew, and soon was
putting maps on "pillow cases" for a few of
the "screws!" As one may imagine, word soon
spread. The "snitches" were performing their
duties as "good citizens" again! The FBI was
told about the "Piper Treasure Maps," which
Donald Larson was selling to "Guards!"

Soon the FBI was once again visiting him. Little did Donald care! What the hell could they do to him now, take away his birthday? They already had him doing two life sentences!

Donald says that he actually enjoyed their visits. He says that some of them were ok guys. They were given orders to come to prison, and talk to them. Most of them knew it was just a bunch of "bullshit" and would sit, and laugh about it with Donald.

A few of them, whom he did not like, took it pretty serious though. For the ones that acted all "serious," Donald would make up some pretty serious looking maps. He was sure that some of them went "treasure hunting," probably the same day they visited him!

When Donald talks about the "ransom money" he gets a half whimsical, half serious look in his eyes. He says, "You know, I don't believe there ever was any "ransom money!" I think it was all a scam, put together by Harry Piper, and his brother in law. They knew someone, who knew someone, who knew some excons from the Bena area, paid them maybe a hundred thousand dollars to set up a phony kidnapping, and then pocketed the other nine hundred thousand, plus collected the million they supposedly lost, in insurance money!"

(When one really gets into the story, and when someone knows who some of those involved were, it is easy to believe that this is exactly what went down!)

Donald says that he wishes those who played the "game" all the luck in the world, and that the money they received gave them a good life. He holds no "ill will" against them, even though today, there are still those who think he did it!

The one big thing that bothers him is the over zealousness of the FBI in trying to "frame" innocent people, and the use of unprofessional tactics in their use of "snitches." Had they, the FBI been professional in their duties and responsibilities, in all likelihood, 5 (FIVE) innocent people would still be alive!

Donald goes on to say that if not for the FBI's inept handling of the case, his family would still be alive, there would be no James

Falch for the FBI to con into playing "snitch" for them, and he would, in all probability be on the streets right now!

The worst part of "prison life" is of course the nights. This is the time that things are quiet. There are only a few things that one can do at night. He can read, do hobby craft, write letters, listen to his radio or watch TV, and dwell on what "may have been."

When you do all of these things, they all soon get boring, and pretty soon the respite of a hectic daily life in prison soon looks good. Pretty soon you start looking forward to the new day.

When you have many years to do, and have no way of knowing if or when you are going to get out, most of the days are all the same. Surprising enough, the time seems to go by at a very rapid rate! When you do not have any certain amount of time to do, you really lose the sense of time, and some mornings wake up and think, wow, I've been here twenty fucking years! It doesn't seem like it until you begin to look in the mirror at your hair, your beard, your face, and your body. Then your mind reverts back to the day you heard that "life sentence" handed down. Again, you get a sick feeling, only this time it is a scared, sick feeling.

You ask yourself, "Will I ever walk on free ground again? Will I die in here? Will I die alone? Will there be someone to hold my hand as I die?"

Then you snap out of it! You start another day, go through the routine you have created and are the master of. No matter how many guards or other convicts are around you, you are the master of your own life in prison! It is up to you how or what you do to control your actions.

VI
TAKING TRIPS

Nighttime is when the "ghosts," "goblins," and all other weird things start to enter your mind. The thoughts sometimes are not very nice. To escape this, a convict goes on what is called "mind trips." When you're on a good "mind trip" some of those around you will think you're starting to "lose it," especially the "screws!"

A mind trip might consist of a plan that you thought out about, what you might have done with your life "IF." You might run or operate a business, or be a successful crook, you might be a playboy, or a farmer or a?

That's the good thing about a "mind trip." You can be what you want to be. You can go to the library, read up on everything about the trip you want to go on. You can figure out how much it will cost for this trip, how much you will make, what you will do with your money. *(Mind trips are really a trip!)* The best thing about a mind trip, is when you get tired of it, you can switch to a different one, and start all over!

(Who knows, you may go on a mind trip some day, get so enamored in it, and taken up by it that you may not be able to escape it, and therefore it becomes, in your mind reality. Then you are on a truly magnificent "mind trip!" You may end up in a "nut ward" somewhere, but who cares? If you're enjoying your trip, fuck the world and enjoy where you're at!

During most "mind trips" there is a "shut off" and you get back into the "real world" again. The old thoughts seem to creep back again, although not with the same terror involved. You now know that you can "escape" any fucking time you want to.)

Donald's thoughts of his old life seemed to creep back every so often. He would have a good grasp on everything, and suddenly a noise, a word, a voice or a TV show would snap him back to something that happened years earlier.

He remembers the "good life" he was leading, and how it all came just tumbling down. When he starts thinking like this, certain faces come into his mind. The faces were Peter Neumann, Paul Harris, and James Falch.

He remembers what Peter Neumann said, "I told Falch to stay away from Ruth, and told him to just work on the case, and quit messing with her!"

Was he trying to lessen the "guilt," which he possibly had over what happened?

Paul Harris, proved to be a "snitch" who was directly involved with Falch, and

Neumann. Other names kept popping into his head. Cooper was another "snitch!" Robert Earl Barnes!

All of the above were considered to be friends of Donald. Was his sense of "knowing" how to judge people so bad, that he let these people drag him down to their level?

Let's face it, all of the people involved in the circumstances surrounding the "Larson, Callahan, Piper" cases were snitches, liars, ex-cons, thieves, con artists, ne-er do wells, or simply, pissed off, ex in-laws! They were all willing to sell their souls, and the souls of their friends to Peter Neumann for extremely small favors!

Many others would falsify facts, they simply made up. Greed played the biggest part in the whole scenario, and in most of the testimony.

VII
MESHBESHER/HARTIGAN
WORK HEATEDLY,
"CASE OVERTURNED"

While Donald was doing time in Stillwater Prison, Bruce Hartigan, and Ron Meshbesher were working feverishly on his and Kenny Callahan's appeal.

Under the rules of the Federal System, a person's appeal from a conviction must go back to the original Judge, and Court where the trial first took place. In reality, this is nothing more than a formality. It is extremely rare that a Federal judge will even think of overturning a conviction that was obtained in his or her courtroom. As was expected, Judge Devitt turned down the Larson, Callahan appeal.

The next step for the attorneys, and convictees was to have the case heard in front of the Eighth Circuit Court of Appeals. It took two years for the individuals to obtain the hearing in the higher court!

On a Friday, near the end of January, in 1979, Donald Larson was relaxing, stretched out on his bunk, in cell # 535, B-Block. Another Convict, Harold Traxel, came running up to Larson's cell. He was panting so hard, and was so overly excited, that he could hardly talk!

Traxel told Donald that he had been watching KSTP, Channel 5 on TV, and that the announcer said that the Station was at the Stillwater State Prison. He said that news people were trying to speak with Donald Floyd Larson!

Donald immediately jumped from his bunk, and started to clean up. He had no idea what it could be about, but knew that it had to be pretty important!

Donald stepped out of his cell, as a guard called his name. He was given a "pass" (Authorization for movement) to the "Attorney/Convict" visiting area. To his utter surprise, a KSTP Reporter immediately started asking questions.

The Reporter asked, "Mr. Larson, how do you feel about your conviction being reversed and set aside?"

(Donald Larson and Kenny Callahan's cases were set aside and "remanded" back to the Federal Court for a re-trial!)

Donald was speechless! He had no idea as to what the reporter was speaking about! He stared at him for a full minute, trying to comprehend the words.

Finally, he stammered, "I-w-w-w-was not aware of that!"

The Reporter said that the news had just come over "United Press International," and was being broadcast all over the United States!

Looking back on it now, Donald states that after, "two years" of waiting, he was totally exhausted, both mentally, and physically! He says that he suddenly felt that a giant boulder had been lifted from his shoulders, and that he actually felt much younger!

Upon returning to Cell Block B, he could not help but tell all of his friends about the news which he had just received. It was not long before a bunch of the "convicts" all got together, and threw a party for him. There were ham sandwiches, soda, and ice cream! Someone even passed around a "jug of hooch!" *(Donald, a non-drinker, grabbed the jug when it was handed to him, and took about four large gulps, before passing it on! He says his doing that even surprised him! He said it tasted really good!*

The Larson/Callahan re-trial would be re-held in approximately "sixty" days after the "reversal" was handed down. During their first trial, the defense team of Meshbesher and Hartigan were "blind-sided" on numerous occasions by the prosecution, and the Court! This time, the underhanded tactics would be thwarted. They would be "primed and ready" with "targets" in their sights, "trigger fingers tensed" ready to fire!

The battle was imminent, but this time, the surprise attacks, and tactics would be delivered by the "Defense" instead of the "Prosecution!")

PART VIII

TRIAL # 2

I
TRIAL #2
10/16/1979

After being found guilty in their first trial, which began on October 11, 1977, Donald Larson, and Kenneth Callahan found themselves, once again sitting in the same U.S. Federal Courthouse in Saint Paul, at an identical table to the one they previously sat at two years ago, almost to the very day! The only difference was this room was down the hall from the one they were found "guilty" in.

As they sat there with their attorneys, Donald said he looked around the room, and suddenly had a very eerie feeling. He said the feeling actually overwhelmed him for a minute!

Kenny and Donald were evidently thinking the same thing, for they suddenly looked at each other, and shrugged their shoulders. They both remembered their thoughts when the last trial started. They were confident they would be found "not guilty" in that trial. Now, they didn't know what to think!

A panel of "ninety" prospective jurors was impaneled to be examined. It was expected to be several days before a jury of fifteen would be chosen, twelve for the jury and three as alternates.

Out of the first thirty-five questioned, only ten had said they had heard of or read about anything relating to the "Piper Kidnapping!"

This second trial was expected to last at least a full month! It was also expected that it would be much more exciting than the first trial.

One obvious, and important difference in this trial, would be the testimony of "Linda Billstrom!" In 1974, she had told the FBI that she had heard her husband, now deceased, plotting to carry out a plan, which would insure a large amount of money to be "paid" to him! The plan was to involve the Pipers, of Piper, Jaffray, Hopwood fame. She said that it was a discussion held with a group of individuals who were friends with her husband. The group did not include Donald Larson or Kenny Callahan!

This was not new news to attorneys Meshbesher, and Hartigan. Federal Judge,

Edward Devitt, refused to allow Ms. Billstrom to testify in the first trial. He used the excuse that the defense had not "called her" until it was too late in the trial. Attorneys Hartigan and Meshbesher appealed that decision, saying that they had not been able to locate Ms. Billstrom in the time allotted for her to be added to the witness list.

The Eighth Circuit Court Of Appeals, in a 2 to 1 ruling handed down, agreed that Judge Devitt's decision to not allow Linda Billstrom to testify, had "substantially prejudiced" the defendants rights to a "fair trial," and therefore, ordered a "new trial."

II
JURY SELECTION COMPLETE
(October 18, 1979)

Eight men and four women were chosen for the second trial of the two men convicted in the 1972 kidnapping of Virginia Piper. U.S. District Court Judge, Donald Alsop set opening arguments in the re-trial for 9:30 A.M.

For the second time, Virginia Piper, beautiful wife of Harry Piper, was called to the stand. She would testify of the ordeal she endured at the hands of her captors who demanded a million dollars in ransom money after her abduction.

Mrs. Piper, now fifty-six years of age, did not show her age. As in the first trial, her "platinum hair" was again coifed to perfection. Her dress and the rest of her attire, as well as her demeanor were impeccable!

Mrs. Piper spent over two hours describing what had happened from the moment she was kidnapped, until the time in which FBI Agents found her chained to the tree in Jay Cooke State Park, in Northern Minnesota. The park is located on the Minnesota, and Wisconsin borders just south of Duluth.

Those who had witnessed the first trial, two years previous to this one, could definitely tell that Mrs. Piper had rehearsed her story more this time. Her testimony was quick, to the point, and without hesitation. She answered all questions posed to her by Thor Anderson who was the Prosecutor for the Government!

Before Virginia Piper took the witness stand, Mr. Anderson spent two hours outlining the Government's case. He explained about the previously mentioned fingerprint, hair fibers found, and the unusual spelling of the word thorough.

"NEWS BREAK"

U.S. DISTRICT ATTORNEY THOR ANDERSON WAS IDENTIFIED LAST EVENING, OCTOBER 18, 1979, LEAVING THE PREMISES OF "MAGGIE'S MASSAGE PARLOR," LOCATED ON LAKE STREET IN MINNEAPOLIS!

Along with six other public figures, THOR ANDERSON is alleged to have paid "prostitutes" for "sexual favors" and or "acts!" Three of the suspected "public officials," along with Mr. Anderson, "admit" that the allegations are true. (As one would imagine, Mr. Thor Anderson was very "red faced" when he walked in the

Federal Court Room the next morning! A few "snickers" could be heard from the audience!)

This story hit all of the local newspapers!

Attorney Ronald Meshbesher, in his opening statement, told the Jury that the case "is full of holes." He also told them that the Defense will show that the case should not even be in Federal Court, because of the fact that there was no evidence that Mrs. Piper was taken across any state lines during her kidnapping. (If indeed the Jury accepts Meshbesher's argument about "state lines," they will have to acquit Larson and Callahan, because there would be no Federal Jurisdiction in the case, and it would have, or should have been a Minnesota Case!

Another interesting fact is that the Minnesota State Statute Of Limitations expired before the Federal Court filed the charges. Therefore, they could not be charged in any state court!

In preparation for a re-trial, Mr. Meshbesher used Private Investigators,

Detectives, Friends, Police Departments, other Attorneys and Retired Judges. He also used his own vast knowledge and experience in court matters.

Ronald Meshbesher had represented a woman by the name of Marjorie Caldwell. It concerned a very well known and publicized murder trial.

Marjorie and her husband Roger were charged with the death of Marjorie's mother, Elizabeth Congdon, multi million dollar heiresses, who lived in her Duluth, Minnesota mansion, along with her night nurse Velma Pietila, who was also murdered.

During the investigation, Meshbesher learned that the only piece of "hard evidence" against the Caldwells was a so-called single, smudged fingerprint on an envelope. Meshbesher contacted Herbert Leon McDonald a noted forensic expert from Corning, New York.

After speaking with Mr. McDonald, Meshbesher sent him a copy of the alleged fingerprint of Roger Caldwell. After careful examination, Mr. McDonald discovered, without any doubt that the fingerprint in question was indeed a "manufactured print," having been made by the FBI. This extraordinary information would eventually prove Roger Caldwell's innocence!

Due to Meshbesher's successful appeal in the Caldwell case, he again decided to contact Herbert McDonald, this time in regards to Donald Larson's alleged fingerprint, supposedly found on a small piece of paper from a "shopping bag!"

Ron Meshbesher worked diligently on the investigation in order to reach a favorable outcome this time in court.

He and Bruce Hartigan worked well into the waning hours on many occasions, drinking many cups of coffee!

Neither of the two was allowed to represent both of their clients. It would have been considered a "conflict of interest."

Meshbesher discussed his suspicions with Hartigan, and Hartigan immediately grabbed the next flight to Corning New York. In his valise, he carried a picture of Donald Larson's fingerprint that the FBI swore they found on the piece of paper from the "Piggly Wiggly" grocery bag.

Upon arrival at the office of Herbert McDonald, Hartigan produced the photo of the fingerprint in question. Mr. McDonald took one look at the photograph and immediately started laughing! At one glance, he surmised that the print was a manufactured one, but that the manufactured print had even been doctored! He stated emphatically that it was not an original photograph.

When Hartigan was informed of this, he wasted no time in calling the Minneapolis office of the FBI. He demanded that they immediately send an original copy of the fingerprint to Mr. McDonald's office. He also wanted a copy of the print from the bottom of the piece of paper that the FBI had supposedly gotten the other print from.

It only stands to reason that if you rip a small piece of paper from a bag, there will undoubtedly be a fingerprint on each side!

The FBI thinking quickly replied that they could not send a copy of the original because it had to stay under the "chain of command" of the FBI.

Hartigan, whose mind worked just as fast, said, "If it must stay under the chain of command of the FBI, then you can simply send it to the office of the FBI in Corning New York!"

The agent Hartigan was speaking to someone and muffled the phone and a few seconds later said, "We do not have an office in Corning New York."

This was a blatant lie, because Herbert McDonald teaches forensics at the Corning, New York Office of the Federal Bureau of Investigation.

McDonald quickly got on the phone and said, "My good friend, the FBI Agents will really be surprised to hear that they do not have an office in which they are employed, and which is located in Corning New York.

The Minneapolis office suddenly had second thoughts and immediately sent the picture. It was identical to the one that they already had. The reverse print was not sent, as there was no reverse print! A copy of a print cannot have a reverse print!

Mr. McDonald explained to Bruce Hartigan how the phony print was manufactured. Hartigan listened intently, making numerous notes and then grabbed the next flight back to Minnesota. Upon his arrival, he sped to the office of Ron Meshbesher he then gave him, and showed him all of the information he had.

Two weeks later, the re-trial of Larson and Callahan would begin.

III
THE RE-TRIAL

Several witnesses testified in the "Larson/Callahan" retrial, they testified that a man believed to have been one of the kidnappers, appeared to be in his early thirties. Kenny Callahan, at the time of the re-trial was fifty-three, and Donald Larson was fifty!

In earlier testimony, the reverend Kenneth B Henderson, pastor of the Apostolic Lutheran Church in Plymouth, said he received a phone call from the kidnappers, telling where Virginia Piper could be found. He stated that the caller was polite, and that his voice sounded like that of a young person, probably thirty to thirty five years of age.

Another witness, Frank W. Hettman, Jr., testified that he worked in a gasoline station in July of 1972. He said that a "green Chevrolet Monte Carlo" the type used in the Piper kidnapping pulled in.

Hettman said he talked to the driver about the car, because he himself owned a Monte Carlo. He stated that the driver told him that he had not had the car very long.

Hettman described the man as between five feet ten inches tall and six feet, with brown hair, parted on the side. He said that he looked young, approximately thirty two to thirty five years old. He added that he had a ruddy complexion.

In summing up Hettman's testimony, Defense Attorney Meshbesher stated, "Therefore, in effect, you did not positively identify Larson."

Another witness, Steve Miller, of Plymouth, related that he had witnessed an unusual scene when he stepped out of the back door of his restaurant, just before he closed at 9 pm on July 28, 1972.

He said that a car drove through the parking lot behind the restaurant, and then proceeded to the corner of Louisiana, and Laurel Avenues, where a package was dropped near a signpost.

He went on to say that he got a very good look at the driver, and described him as looking very determined, as if he had something extremely urgent to do.

Miller said that a few days later, four men came into his restaurant, and ordered lunch. One of them was the same person that he (Miller) had seen in the parking lot. The man had a short neck, as if his head was sitting on top of his shoulders. He was stocky, did not wear glasses, and appeared to be between thirty and thirty five years of age. He kept pointing across the street, and they were all laughing.

John Cardenas, who operated the "Village Squire Men's Shop," located in Brooklyn Park in 1974, testified that a man came into his shop, and paid for some underwear with a "twenty" dollar bill. Cardenas noticed the way the customer looked, and decided to check the numbers on the "twenty." He soon found out the bill was part of the "million" dollars paid out in the Virginia Piper kidnapping for ransom case.

Cardenas described the customer as having brown eyes, dark brown hair, and having no gray in it.

William Swanson, a St. Louis Park hardware store clerk, described two men that entered his store in July of 1972. They wanted to buy fifteen feet of chain. The store only had thirteen feet of the chain which they needed, but they purchased it anyway.

Swanson stated that one of the men had a "red" eye, was six feet tall and had brown hair. He was also sunburned. The other man was shorter, of stocky build, with brown hair, parted on the left side. There is no way that these descriptions fit either Callahan or Larson.

John Dineen, a sixty-year-old convict, was once again brought to Court from Stillwater State Prison, and took the stand. This was his second time to testify in the "Piper trial."

Dineen stated once more, as he had done in the first trial that he had seen Donald Larson wearing a St. Olaf sweater.

Anthony De Gideo, also an inmate at Stillwater, testified that he had been friendly with Dineen, and that Dineen was "putting a story on" for the benefit of the "Feds." He stated that Dineen told him if he testified against Larson, the Feds were going to get him out!

De Gideo testified that Dineen rehearsed the "story" with him prior to coming to court. De Gideo then testified that he had assisted Dineen with the purchase of "illegal drugs" prior to his testifying.

Kenneth Clausen, another inmate, told a similar story. "He said, Dineen, didn't really know anything about the Piper Case. All he wanted was something to deal with the Feds." Clausen also said that Dineen had written out three or four stories, and asked Clausen to tell him which one sounded best. All of the stories were different!

In earlier testimony, an official from the Minnesota "Pardons Board" told the court that a petition on Dineen's behalf had been submitted. In it, Dineen was asking that his sentence be shortened. James B. Bradford, Assistant Attorney General, who acts as Secretary for the "Pardons Board," said that the petition was rejected. He did say, however, that there was an FBI Agent present at the "Pardons board" hearing, and apparently supported Dineen's petition.

The "Prosecutions" last witness was Toby. F. Larson, sister in law of Donald Floyd Larson. She testified in the previous trial and told the FBI that she was unable to reach Larson in regards to his daughter, at the same time Virginia Piper was being kidnapped in 1972.

She said that Larson, and Callahan had installed a cabinet for her, and added that Callahan had "strange" glasses and appeared to have knee problems.

Defense attorneys Meshbesher, and Hartigan both brought out the fact that Toby Larson had become an FBI "informant," and that in fact, had little or no contact with her brother in law since the death of her husband in 1970. It was a known fact that she hated all of the Larson's, and refused talking to any of them many years earlier. She had been known to try to start trouble for the Larson family on numerous occasions.

IV
LINDA BILLSTROM

Ms. Billstrom, the lady the Federal Appeals Court called a "vital witness" for the defense, testified Wednesday, November 14, 1979.

The Courtroom sat hushed as Linda Billstrom said that her "lover," and "common law" husband, Robert Billstrom, was a "key man" in the plot involving Virginia Piper! When these words came out, the only sound in the Courtroom was the intake of breath from the combined audience!

Not only did she implicate her husband, she also testified as to the description of the "other four" men who were involved in the "score!"

She stated that after the "score" was completed, all of those involved, along with her, went to Prescott Wisconsin where they all got rooms in a motel. She testified that they had a party, celebrating "a job well done!" She also stated that she had been present on numerous occasions when the group had meetings to discuss the "plan of action" concerning their involvement in the "plot!"

Billstrom, who was 32 years old at the time of her testimony, was serving a sentence at a Federal Prison in West Virginia, for "armed robbery and escape," told her story in 1977 to U.S. Federal District Judge, Edward Devitt, the presiding Judge in the first "Piper Case Trial."

Devitt, however, ruled that the Jury which eventually convicted Larson, and Callahan, should not hear her testimony! The fact that Linda Billstrom was not allowed to testify, was one of, if not the most mitigating factor that the Federal Appeals Court used to overturn the convictions of the two accused of abducting Virginia Piper. The Appeals Court said that she was a "vital tool," plus a "Defense witness," and that it was improper to exclude her from testifying.

Ms. Billstrom testified that one of the four men involved in the "plot" stated, in one of the planning phases that, "They should take Mrs. Piper, because Mr. Piper has more access to the money, and it would make things go much faster."

She stated that originally they were to take Mr. Piper, but then a phone call was made, and the plans changed. No one ever found out who changed the plan, but whoever it was, was calling the shots!

Linda Lee Billstrom also testified that "Bob" Billstrom took her to Jay Cooke State Park, where they camped out overnight. This camping trip was on July 17th, 1972, just ten days before Mrs. Piper was brought to the Park, and chained to the tree!

On the day of the kidnapping, July 27th, 1972, Linda Billstrom testified she, Robert, and Robert's stepson, Michael, checked into a Prescott, Wisconsin Motel. This was so Robert Billstrom would have an alibi during the transfer of Virginia Piper.

As soon as they checked into the motel, "Bob" called someone he called "Runt," then a couple minutes later, "Runt" called him back. Shortly after that call, Robert Billstrom left the motel. Ms. Billstrom stayed at the motel until the following day.

The following day, Linda Alger picked her up at the motel, and brought her to the Alger residence.

Ms. Billstrom next saw her husband on Saturday, July 29th. That evening, they attended the party with eight or nine others where they all celebrated, "A JOB WELL DONE!"

(Throughout this accounting of the "Piper Ordeal" there has been mention of a person who is short, muscular, with a short neck. "Runt" Alger, now deceased, fit that description.)

Linda Billstrom said that some others besides Robert Billstrom, and Ron "Runt" Alger, someone named or called "Taylor," and another called "Art," who were later identified as Charles Farrell and Charles Van Duesen were there.

(All four of these individuals are now dead! "Runt" Alger passed away in 2003!

Bob Billstrom was shot to death after going to "pick up some sort of payoff" money.

It was to be the final payment of a total of three. He was sitting in a car, parked in a supermarket parking lot, waiting for the "payoff" when two off duty police just happened to drive by, and recognized him as having warrants out for him. One of them "saw Billstrom reach for a gun," then both opened fire, killing Billstrom. Shortly thereafter, both "off duty" cops quit their jobs and became "private detectives."

The government now confirms that they have records of a phone call being made from the Alger residence to a motel in Prescott, Wisconsin on July 28th, 1972.)

Ms. Billstrom characterized the participants of these meetings as being very "protective" when it came to their plans. She vividly recalled observing certain photographs, one of which she subsequently described as similar to a photograph of the front entrance gate to the Piper Residence. The FBI had shown her the photograph in 1974. She also saw hand drawn maps, and testified that, "There were guns all around!" This was nothing new though. Where you would find Bob Billstrom, and Runt Alger, you would find guns.

Part of her testimony also included seeing a "powder blue sweater," with a "St. Olaf" logo or print on it! She remembers seeing the sweater the same day they planned their "camping trip."

There were a total of four meetings. Many topics were discussed, including vehicles that would be used, including which one would be used to transport Mrs. Piper. One of these vehicles was a "red Mustang" owned by Linda, and Bob Billstrom. This was the car that contained tape, gauze, a chain, and a two-way radio. They also used a "blue Vega," as a "stake out" vehicle!

Ms. Billstrom commented that Ron, "Runt" Alger, and Bob Billstrom frequented the "Sportsman's Bar" in North Minneapolis. This was on a regular basis. She also stated that Bob Billstrom had purchased a "Royal" typewriter prior to the "arrangement" from a man whose home was in Chicago. His name was "Alabama!" *(The FBI stated during the 1974 interview with Ms. Billstrom. "The typefaces on the ransom notes were probably made from a "Royal Typewriter!")*

Ms. Billstrom related that during one of the meetings, she saw Ron Alger wearing a pair of "brown slacks," later shown to her by the FBI, and had subsequently been given to Virginia Piper to supposedly keep her warm during a night in the woods chained to the tree!

Ms. Billstrom remarked that, following an FBI's search of Ron Alger's house, after the kidnapping, Ron disposed of numerous articles of clothing, various other things, including a "sawed off" shotgun, which he carried in his car. These articles were gathered together, and "tossed" into the Mississippi River.

Ms. Billstrom testified that there was an artist's conception of a person who passed a few of the bills. This drawing was "identical" to "Runt" Alger, and became quite a joke amongst the "Billstrom Gang!" *(The ones who hung out with Bob Billstrom were known to be members of his "Gang.")*

Linda Lee Billstrom testified that she and Bob Billstrom left Minnesota after July 29th

1972. She stated that they traveled to South Dakota, and then to Utah. During that time, Bob Billstrom spent "large sums" of money. Eventually after her flight from Minnesota, Ms. Billstrom was apprehended and imprisoned for some "previous criminal behavior."

Apparently there was an oral agreement amongst the members of the "Billstrom gang." It was made on July 29th, 1972, which assured Ms. Billstrom that if she was apprehended for her earlier indiscretions, that she would receive money periodically from Linda Alger.

In 1972, Ms. Billstrom told the FBI that Bob Billstrom had not participated in the Piper extravaganza. She refused to discuss the "ransom money," using her Fifth Amendment Right. The only thing she said was, as far as she knew there was no "ransom payoff!"

She did admit she had lied to the FBI about money that she and Bob had received. She further stated that Charles Van Duesen, another participant had died after the culmination of the scheme.

(In explanation of Ms. Billstrom's reluctance to testify, Defense Counsel advised the District Court that the Government had warned Ms. Billstrom that she would be prosecuted to the full extent of the law for any "false testimony" or "statements" she had made during previous interviews. The Government did not deny that explanation. Assuming the truth of the Defense representation, the existence of such a warning to Ms. Billstrom tends to enhance her credibility on matters concerning the Piper case which she has "testified about!"

When Ms. Billstrom left the "witness stand," Donald swears that a couple of the jurors actually smiled at her. He knew she had made quite an impression on them. Everything she said seemed almost like an adventure. During her testimony, there were no sounds from the audience or the rest of the court.

V
RUSS BOSWELL

(Before we get into the testimony of Russ Boswell, let it be said that there is no one in this world like "Russ Boswell."

Russ is so handsome that women almost fall over when he walks down the street. Well over six feet tall, and two hundred and thirty pounds, he keeps in tremendous shape. He has an infectious smile, a saunter when he walks, and carries himself in a manner that makes his wide shoulders look even wider than they actually are. He has a sense of humor that makes everyone laugh.

He has been a professional boxer, but has no scars, nor broken nose, he was a boxing trainer, a burglar, an armed robber, a cook, a bar tender, and just about anything else he has wanted to be.

Russ has dark hair, brown eyes and a dark complexion. He is half Native American. He associates with "Natives" as well as with "Whites," and gets along with both equally.

He has been in and out of prisons most of his life and it never seems to bother him. Wherever he is, he is sure to be known.

Throughout this story there is mention of a dark haired, handsome, outdoors type, and brown-eyed man. This, in all likelihood is Russ Boswell!

Who is "Russ" Boswell? To put it simply, he is a "character" who has the ability to make people "laugh" or to make them "cry!" In all truth, he would rather have those around him laughing rather than crying.

There are numerous stories about Russ and his brother Sonny. "Both of them were extremely adept in the art of "fisticuffs." Russ was a "heavy weight" while Sonny was probably a "welterweight." Both liked to fight, but would not pick fights with others. However, if they had no one else to fight with they would casually "spar" with one another. Sometimes, their casualness would get pretty "hot and heavy."

Both were quite fast, and both were in extreme condition. Who was better at fighting? It was hard to tell. Russ was larger and heavier, while Sonny was smaller and slightly faster. Both of them had knockout punches, as many sadly learned. Because of their happiness, and smiles, they were sometimes thought to be   easily pushed around. To the contrary, they were not to be pushed. They would actually keep on smiling while they "beat the shit" out a person.

Stillwater prison used to have a "boxing" program. People heard about "Sonny Boswell." Soon professional boxers were coming into Stillwater, in an effort to beat him. He did not lose a bout. A couple times, he literally knocked his opponents out of the ring! He took on all who offered to fight him. If they were heavier than he was, they would call it an "exhibition." The outcome would be the same. It was always unanimous, "Winner by Knockout, Sonny Boswell!"

There is no doubt about whether Sonny Boswell could have become a "World Champion." There was one thing that stood in his way, "Dope!" When he would get out of prison, physically in A-1 shape, and clean from dope, he would start boxing, and as soon as he got a few bucks in his pocket, he would be back on the "dope."

Rumor has it that the "dope" finally killed him at quite an early age.

Russ was the "character" of the Boswells. He was always into something, and could not exist unless there was some kind of excitement going on. If there was none to be found, he would create it!

All knew his sense of humor. One time he came back to Prison for a "Parole Violation." As he and his friends were greeting each other, he said that he had gotten married while he was out. He asked if they would like to see a picture of his wife. When they said they would, he reached in his pocket, took out a picture, and handed it to them. It was of a five hundred pound black woman with a big smile on her face. She had no teeth no hair or any clothes on!

As he stood expectantly waiting for a reaction, his friends looked at him warily. They did not know whether to congratulate him or start laughing.

Finally, he would bust out laughing, letting the others know it was just a joke.

One time he came back on a new charge for "attempted burglary." He had just gotten out.

He got an apartment in St. Paul. He had gone walking and ended up getting something to eat. On his way back to his apartment, he was walking by a warehouse. As he walked by, the "burglar alarm" suddenly went off. Soon he heard sirens approaching. He took off running, knowing that if he were found in the area he would be arrested. A St. Paul cop saw him, yelled at him to stop, and when he kept running, shot him in the back, with the bullet lodging close to his kidney.

When he was healed up, he was tried and convicted, and sentenced to Prison once again! A year later, someone was arrested on a "burglary charge" and "cleared" Russ of the burglary he was doing time for.

There are many other stories which could be told about Russ and Sonny but to get back to this story:

Russ had come back to Minnesota after serving time in California. One of the first people he ran into was Tommy Grey, good friend of Donald Larson and of Kenny Callahan.

Russ told Tommy about his "stint" in California. He had been busted for a robbery and while at the California Reception Center, located in Vacaville, he was put to work as a "house" (cell block) painter. The institution found out that he was adept in the manly art of fisticuffs, and put him to work as a trainer in their "boxing program."

During their conversation, the topic ended up on "Piper Kidnapping!" Russ told Tommy that he had just come from a pretty "wild party" held in Wisconsin. He mentioned that it looked like a "Stillwater Prison" homecoming!

He said that all of the "guys" there had done time in Stillwater at one time or another. Some of them included, "Runt" Alger, Bob Billstrom, Charlie Van Duesen, Charlie Farell, and numerous other x-cons.

The party was for a "good score," which "went very well!"

Russ went on to say that he had never seen so much "booze," "money," and "good looking women" in one spot all together at the same time! He also told Tommy that it was in regards to the Piper escapade!

Tommy told Boswell that Donnie Larson was still in prison and that he and Kenny Callahan were going to get a re-trial on their previous conviction.

Upon hearing this, Russ Boswell, the consummate convict, told Tommy Grey that he was willing to testify as to the reason for the celebration and party, held in Wisconsin. He said he would not allow someone else to take the blame for it.

(Russ Boswell and Linda Lee Billstrom were the only two that would come forward and tell the truth, even though the "Statutes of Limitations," both Federal and State, were no longer applicable. No one could be held responsible that had not already been charged!)

Tommy Grey immediately got word to Donald Larson in Stillwater Prison. Donald in turn, contacted his Attorney, Bruce Hartigan. Hartigan, after hearing the startling news, contacted Ronald Meshbesher, Kenny Callahan's attorney.

Both attorneys met, talked things over, interviewed both Russ Boswell, and Linda Lee Billstrom. They found that both of their renditions of the happenings were so close that both of them had to be telling the truth.

The Federal Prosecutor, as well as the Federal Court was notified of the "new witness!"

Russ Boswell, looking "dapper" in a new suit and a fresh haircut, approached the "witness stand." His head held high, his muscular shoulders squared, he made a striking figure. There were audible "oohs and ahhs" from the young as well as the "not so young" females in the audience!

Mr. Boswell answered all questions posed to him. He was forthright, and exuded an air of truthfulness in every answer. He explained why he was at the party, about the money there, the ex-cons there, the women there, and why the party was being held!

On "cross examination," Thor Anderson, the Federal Prosecutor, tried to "browbeat" Mr. Boswell, but Russ' demeanor never faltered, nor did his expressions change. He would quietly but clearly answer all of the questions, not directly to the Prosecutor, but to the Jury, making eye contact, and pleasantly smiling. Thor Anderson actually moved over in his questioning, trying to block Boswell's view of the Jurors, but was unable to do so.

Russ Boswell, at the end of his testimony, stated that, "Bob Billstrom and his wife left the party early." He said that Bob told him that he and Linda were going to take a vacation to South Dakota and then were going to head "West" for a while.

All of Boswell's testimony coincided with Linda Billstrom's.

VI
SELENA JOHNSON

The Green Monte Carlo, used in the so-called Piper Kidnapping was supposed to have been spotted by a mother and her daughter shortly after the news hit the TV's and Newspapers!

Mrs. Selena Johnson and her daughter were gathering "stones" for their aquarium and had driven into a "gravel pit." As they entered the "gravel pit," they saw two "dark complexioned" individuals, with dark hair, standing besides a lady with light colored clothing, and "platinum colored hair!" She stated that the two men were very handsome, and that the lady was very beautiful.

Mrs. Johnson stated that they were standing outside a "Green Chevrolet Monte Carlo!"

When the trio saw the mother and daughter drive into the pit, they got into the Monte Carlo and sped away, with the "platinum blond woman driving the car!" The mother and daughter thought the whole scene was a little strange, but did not think too much about it at the time.

Later, after they had returned to their home, they were watching television. The news came on and there was a story about the "Kidnapping of Virginia Piper!"

Suddenly, the daughter let out a scream! There was a picture of Mrs. Piper on the television screen. She had on the same identical clothing, had her hair fixed in the same manner, and looked the same as she did in the "gravel pit!"

This was definitely the woman they had seen in the "gravel pit" with the two handsome, young men!

Mrs. Johnson immediately called the FBI office, and told them what they had witnessed. The FBI chose to ignore the "first hand account" of the sighting, and in fact insinuated that Mrs. Johnson did not know what she was talking about. (Again, it is abundantly clear, that no-one tells the FBI anything they do not want to hear.)

VII
CALLAHAN FAMILY

Kenneth Callahan's wife and daughter again testified in the "Piper Kidnapping" re-trial. Both the twenty three year old daughter and his wife both testified the same as they had previously testified.

Both said that their husband and father respectively had been at home on the two nights prior to and during the purported kidnapping of Virginia Piper.

The prosecution asked few questions, and their stay on the witness stand was very short.

VIII
KEY PIPER EVIDENCE DISPUTED!

Herbert Leon McDonald famed forensic and fingerprint expert, dropped a "bomb" on the Prosecution's Case against Donald Larson and Kenny Callahan.

McDonald, testifying as a Defense witness, said that the photograph of a fingerprint supposedly belonging to Defendant Donald Larson had been "mechanically altered" from its original state.

He went on to testify that the only reason he could think of for the alteration, was or would be, "to make it (the photograph of the print) more readily identifiable."

McDonald, a college professor and part-time Deputy Sheriff in Corning New York, is the same man whose testimony in 1978, was instrumental in winning an acquittal for Marjorie Caldwell in the murders of her mother and her mother's nurse.

 The current fingerprint under scrutiny, and being questioned by McDonald, was of a fingerprint found on a scrap of paper recovered from the kidnap vehicle used in the purported kidnap of Virginia Piper, wife of Harry C Piper, CEO and Founder of Piper, Jaffray and Hopwood, a very large Minnesota based investment firm.

Fingerprints erode with time therefore; photographs are normally used to protect the longevity of a print. Originally, the FBI concluded that the fingerprint they found on the piece of paper was not that of Donald Floyd Larson.

However, after three unsuccessful attempts to tie him to the case, on the fourth time the print was examined; it turned out to be that of Mr. Larson! That bit of evidence was used to convict him and Kenny Callahan in the first "go around" of the Piper Trial.

During his testimony, Mr. McDonald, who did not testify in the first trial, said that he examined the fingerprint in question and in his laboratory in October he discovered immediately that something was wrong.

He further stated that he noticed the fingerprint ridges and a ruler near by to show the 'scale' of the print in question, were both in focus. He stated that the edges of the paper as shown in the picture were blurred. This cannot happen in any normal photography by any means of which Mr. McDonald knew of. He also stated that the photograph had to be mechanically or physically altered in some way, shape or form!

McDonald said he believed using a pencil to touch up the fingerprint ridgelines in the original FBI picture, which apparently was not in proper focus, did this alteration. He said that the picture was then re-shot, which would explain why the paper was out of focus, while the print and the ruler were in focus.

"I have never seen anything like it," said McDonald, who has testified at hundreds of trials, usually on the side of the prosecution.

Prosecutor Thor Anderson suggested during his cross examination that the blurring may have occurred because the edges of the paper were curled up and thus closer to the lens when the photograph was taken. McDonald answered that he had carefully taken that into consideration, that it could have been a possibility, but then rejected it because the camera that was used had sufficient "depth of field" to avoid that problem. Previous to McDonald's testimony, Prosecutor Thor Anderson had given each member of the jury a blown up copy of the print which was now in question.

Needless to say, this gave the Jury the opportunity to follow along with the testimony of McDonald, thereby negating the Prosecutor's argument.

Anderson tried to re-coup some of the day's losses by recalling a Rochester, Minnesota bank teller, who had testified earlier about receiving some of the ransom money on November 28, 1972.

Esther Dahl, the bank teller, said she was very sure Larson was the man who had entered the bank where she worked on that day. She testified that he exchanged three hundred dollars in twenties, for smaller denominations. She had not identified Larson Wednesday because she had never been asked to!

Under a blistering cross-examination by Attorneys Meshbesher and Hartigan, Mrs. Dahl admitted she could not remember about other people that she had seen that day, including FBI Agents who interviewed her.

Hartigan pointed out that an FBI Agent report taken the next day, quoted Mrs. Dahl as saying her recollection of the man who passed the money, "was not so good."

She did although deny having said that to the FBI Agent and stoutly maintained that Larson was the man she had seen seven years earlier.

IX
TESTIMONY JOLTS DEFENSE

A strong blow was delivered to the defense from a pharmacist who identified one of the defendants, Donald Floyd Larson as the man who entered a Northeast Minneapolis drug store on July 11, 1972, and had a car key made.

Authorities believe that the key was from and for a green Chevy Monte Carlo, used in the Kidnap of Virginia Piper.

The witness, Paul Anderson, had been called by the Defense to show that he could not identify the man who had entered his drug store on that date. However when he was asked if he could identify the person that had the key made, Anderson pointed at Larson and said, "It was either that gentleman who was in the drugstore or it was his 'twin' brother!"

The testimony clearly stunned Defense attorneys Hartigan and Meshbesher. They worked furiously to discredit the druggist's damaging testimony, but Mr. Paul Anderson held fast to his identification.

X
PIPER NEPHEW THROWS CURVE

The re-trial of Larson and Callahan took yet another "strange twist" on Monday, November 26, 1979. The Defense, as well as others, had hinted that in reality, the "kidnapping of Virginia Piper" might have been a "family affair."

Twenty eight year old Thomas Aldrich, a nephew of Mrs. Piper, admitted that he once talked of kidnapping Mrs. Piper. He testified that he was disgusted, with the whole family. He although did not explain why he felt this way. He added that despite his hostility towards the family, and his talk about kidnapping her, he never had any real thoughts or inclination to carry it out. Moreover, Prosecutor Thor Anderson, under cross-examination, established that Aldrich could account for his where a bouts on the day that Mrs. Piper was abducted.

However, this did not deter the Defense from suggesting that a friend or an accomplice could have been involved. In fact, a mysterious figure, named Duane Pederson, may have carried out the kidnapping after getting information from Aldrich. As evidence of this theory, the defense pointed out that one of the twenty-dollar bills did, indeed turn up in a Hopkins Bar, which coincidently was habituated by both Aldrich and Pederson, in 1972.

Defense Attorney Meshbesher, asked Aldrich whether he told the FBI in 1972, that he once talked about kidnapping his aunt.

Aldrich answered, "I don't recall saying that, but if that is what the FBI says, then I must have said it."

Aldrich also testified that he lived with Pederson for a time, and often went drinking with him. He stated that he knew that Pederson was an "ex-con" and admitted he once stole some items from his family and fenced them through Pederson.

Defense Attorney Hartigan, tried to elicit testimony to the effect that Pederson was a "gangster," but was "cut off" by Judge Alsop, who ordered Hartigan's comments strickened from the record.

XI
"RUNT" ALGER

Ronald "Runt" Alger denied having been involved with, and swore that he did not discuss anything with anyone, about the "Piper Kidnapping."

Under questioning by the defense, Alger stated that he had never been involved with Bob Billstrom regarding any "criminal activity," let alone "kidnapping" anyone.

He said, "In fact, I was never asked to perform or join in with any such activities."

Alger said that he met Robert Billstrom when both of them were doing time in the "joint," meaning Stillwater Prison.

Alger was released from Stillwater on June 15th, 1972; Virginia Piper was abducted and held for ransom on July 27th, 1972.

Alger testified that on the day of the kidnapping, he was actually helping to rebuild a roof on a church in south Minneapolis. However, Alger's boss denied that he had shown up for work on that day. In fact, Alger was discharged from his roofing job for failure to show up on July 27th.

Alger did admit that he and his wife had gone to a motel in Prescott, Wisconsin to meet with Billstrom. He stated that the reason he went there was because Billstrom had called him and asked if he could get some money from him. Alger said he gave Billstrom forty of fifty dollars. He also stated that he couldn't remember the date, but that it had been a cold day. The reason he remembered that, was because the "heater" in his car was not working well.

Alger later said that a trip to Wisconsin would have to have been made some time between June 15th, when he was released from prison and October 30th, when Robert Billstrom was shot to death by two "off duty" Golden Valley police.

Alger further testified that he met, through Billstrom, a man called John, who was from Colorado, or someplace else out west. Alger testified that it was rumored that John came to Minnesota to help Billstrom pull some "jobs."

Alger admitted that he and his wife did send some money to Linda Billstrom in regards to the "pact" she stated that everyone agreed upon. She had said that if anything happened to any of the men involved in the "Piper Score," that the rest of the "Gang" would make sure that his "woman" would be well cared for. All of the women were promised that they would receive "money" by the "members" if any of them were ever in need of help financially.

XII
LARSON/CALLAHAN

Defendants, Donald Floyd Larson and Kenneth Callahan took the witness stand on Tuesday. Both of the accused men steadfastly denied any complicity in the abduction of Mrs. Harry C. Piper.

Callahan swore that he had no part or knowledge of anything even remotely related to the "crime of the century." He swore he did not know anything about any "ransom money," where it was, or how it was spent. He stuck to his alibi, insisting that he was fishing on Lake Minnetonka, a very popular lake close to Minneapolis, on the day of the kidnapping.

Prosecutor Thor Anderson grilled Callahan on his "financial matters" in 1973.

Callahan, a carpenter and cabinetmaker, stated matter of factly that his work, mostly paid to him in cash and pretty much paid for everything that he owned. He stated that he built his Cumberland, Wisconsin home with monies he received from the sale of a Minneapolis home, which he had sold to his daughter.

The defense called Donald Floyd Larson to the stand. He was to be their final witness. Like co-defendant Kenneth Callahan, Larson testified that he was not involved with the "Piper Kidnapping" in no way, shape, nor form. I have told everyone a thousand times; I know nothing about the kidnapping. He also testified that he was working at a Cabinet Shop in North Minneapolis on the day that Virginia Piper was kidnapped. He said that he later went to a "tavern" where he met some friends, visited for a while, and then went home.

He added that he followed the same routine that day and the following days, which he normally followed every day. He said that his "whole life" was nothing but a routine!

XIII
VIRGINIA PIPER IDENTIFIES ABDUCTOR!

Virginia Piper took the witness stand once more as she had done in the first trial also. Supposedly, this was to identify Kenny Callahan, which she was unable to do at the first trial.

Under questioning by Prosecutor Anderson, Piper said she saw the left profile of her captor, while in the woods, being held captive.

"It has been implanted in my mind, ever since," She said.

Anderson asked her what she saw when she looked at Callahan, six weeks ago during her previous appearance in the trial.

"I was extremely shaken," she replied, "I observed a familiar look."

Piper said the eyes and the ruddy complexion of Kenny Callahan struck her as familiar.

"Where did you see that familiar look," Anderson asked?

"In the woods," She said.

"At the time of the kidnapping," Anderson asked?

"Yes, Mrs. Piper said."

Piper said that it was a profile of her captor. Under questioning from Callahan's Attorney, Ron Meshbesher, Piper said she had not identified Callahan in a police line-up two years previous, nor did she point him out in the Courtroom when she testified six weeks ago.

Mrs. Piper was supposedly blindfolded during part of her kidnapping ordeal, and her captors wore nylon stockings over their heads.

Mrs. Piper's appearance only lasted about five minutes.

Callahan's appearance was even briefer.

Meshbesher asked Callahan to walk by the Jurors Box so that they could take a good look at his "left" profile and also so they could see his eyes.

Piper had said that one of her abductors had an eye abnormality called Arcus Senilis, meaning a white circle around the eye. Mr. Callahan has never had such an affliction.

XIV
FINAL ARGUMENTS IN PIPER CASE

For nearly six hours members of the Prosecution, and Defense teams worked extremely hard, trying to get their "points" across, concerning the "guilt or innocence" phase of the trial.

Donald Larson and Kenneth Callahan listened intently and watched the Jurors closely as their attorneys, Ronald Meshbesher and Bruce Hartigan worked diligently.

First, the Prosecutor, Thor Anderson outlined their reasons that Donald Larson and Kenneth Callahan should be convicted of the kidnapping of Virginia Piper, and convicted of their demand for the "million" paid out in "twenty" dollar bills.

Prosecutor Thor Anderson told the jury that it must look at the collection of evidence linking Callahan and Larson to the crime. This included a "hair" found in the car used to abduct and to transport Virginia Piper to Jay Cooke State Park, where she was "rudely" chained to a tree, and forced to endure the weather, bugs, and fear of being left alone, not knowing if wild animals would get her or if she would be left there to just perish from lack of water or food.

The "hair," according to Anderson, matched that of Kenny Callahan. The fingerprint, according to the prosecutor, matched that of Donald Larson. He went on to say that Larson and Callahan were identified by various individuals, buying tools for the "caper" and of passing some of the "twenties!" He also stated that their alibis were "no good!"

He pointed to the fact that Virginia Piper testified that Callahan's left "profile" was like that of one of her abductors. At the time of the kidnapping, Piper noted one of the men had "bad knees," a "red eye" condition, and that Mr. Callahan matched that description.

Anderson added that, "Callahan's story that he had been fishing the day of the kidnapping, was truly a 'fish story'!"

"He said he was fishing at Lake Minnetonka that day," Anderson said. If that doesn't fit the bill, his daughter is sure that her father was home all day. His fishing story was contradicted by members of his own family!"

Anderson said the problem with taking Linda Billstrom's testimony seriously, is that the kidnapping, was done by a "gang," and that Linda Billstrom is a liar. When she was first interviewed by the FBI, shortly after the kidnapping, she denied having anything to do with it and no knowledge of, or about it.

She later told the FBI she had lied to "protect" her boyfriend, Robert Billstrom. When it suits her purpose, she tells a lie. Her whole life is a lie, from her name to her story.

Although Linda used the name of her boyfriend, now deceased, they were never actually married. However, they did live together as "man and wife," so in the eyes of most people, they were considered married.

Anderson went on to say that the "case" belonged in the "Federal System" rather than the "State System," the reason being, the abductors took Virginia Piper across the State line into Wisconsin, before chaining her to the tree in Jay Cooke Park. He said Mrs. Piper, even though she had a pillow case over her head, was able to describe the "route" taken by the kidnappers. "She was able to describe by her senses of "hearing" and of "feeling.""

Bruce Hartigan, explained to the Jury why they must find his client "not guilty," pointing out the many inconsistencies in the "prosecution's" case and in the renditions of the prosecution's witnesses.

Hartigan told the Jury that on October 19th, 1972, Larson's name appeared on an official FBI Document, listing people "no longer" being considered as a suspect in the Piper Kidnapping. Those on the list had alibis that had been proven to "exclude" them as suspects. Their whereabouts had been verified.

Mr. Hartigan went over every detail in relation to the fingerprint, which was allegedly found in the kidnap vehicle. The

FBI had even excluded the print as belonging to Larson, not once but on "three" separate occasions.

"If this case would have been tried in 1976, the FBI would have said that it was not Larson's fingerprint!" Hartigan said.

He went on to suggest that it was only when the "statute of limitations" were about to run out, that the FBI determined that the "print" was Donald Larson's!

That fingerprint has been the subject of much testimony in and during the trial. The photograph of the print was not in focus, and three different experts for the Defense raised questions of doubt about it. One of the experts said that the print was enhanced.

Hartigan said the question should have been asked, "Why wasn't a better job done on the 'altered' print?"

"If it was too good, it would have been obvious that it was Larson's, and everyone would have known it," Hartigan said.

He added, "But then, the FBI would have had to explain why it hadn't figured it out right away!"

Hartigan also questioned how two witnesses, who previously had not been able to identify Larson, could possibly do so at this late of time in the trial.

He pointed out that Larson had contacted the FBI a few days after the kidnapping when a friend of his told him that an FBI Agent was looking for him.

"Is that what a guilty guy would do?" He added, "Is that what a guy with the brains to pull off a 'million-dollar caper' would do?"

Next, it was Ronald Meshbesher's turn to give his "final arguments" to the Jurors. His main focal point was that "the evidence was extremely questionable!"

"It is rare when we can show the 'Government' actually 'tampered' with evidence!" I think we can come as close as we can to showing the "fingerprint" was definitely tampered with.

One of the key issues in this re-trial of the Piper Case has been the fingerprint taken from a piece of paper believed to have come from a "Piggly Wiggly" supermarket shopping bag.

The bag was purportedly found in the kidnap vehicle, which was used to transport

Virginia Piper. The FBI insists that the print on that piece of paper matches one of the defendants, Donald Floyd Larson!

Testimony from various witnesses pointed out that the photograph of the fingerprint was not in focus. Meshbesher argued that the FBI's rendition of how that could happen was not believable!

During the trial, Government witnesses said; there were two negatives of the print.

"Something is rotten in this case," Meshbesher, said, "That fingerprint stinks!"

Mr. Meshbesher questioned how Virginia Piper could identify Callahan during this trial, when she had not been able to identify him previously. "Could it be that she and others were afraid that the 'real truth' would come out?"

Mrs. Piper, this poor woman, who had this terrible thing happen to her, was "rooting" for the FBI. "Why" Meshbesher asked? "Does she really see the FBI as her savior? How could she see them as her savior when they left her tied to the tree for hours when they knew where she was? The supposed kidnappers had to call two times to say where she was. They were worried that no one was coming to pick her up. What was the FBI interested in? They were interested in their 'publicity'!"

(Do you remember what the FBI did and how long it took to rescue her after they knew where she was at?)

Meshbesher said that Mrs. Piper could recognize Kenny Callahan and even say she saw a "white circle" or aura around his eye, which she identified as matching that of her kidnapper, because of only one reason, and that reason was because she wanted to. All she wanted was this trial to be over! At what cost? Any cost!

Meshbesher detailed to the jurors why they must consider "jurisdiction!" The case was in a Federal Court because the Government claimed that a Federal Crime had been committed. That reason being, Mrs. Piper was taken out of Minnesota, into Wisconsin, then back into Minnesota, thereby making it a Federal Offense because "State" lines had been crossed!

If the abductors did not take her into Wisconsin, and not cross any other state lines, then the so-called crime would have been within Minnesota's jurisdiction and the defendants should not have been charged by the Federal Court System.

It seems strange, to say the least, that the FBI, when they went to "Rescue" Mrs. Piper, did not even take the route which went into Wisconsin!

Meshbesher showed the Jury a written chart which he said was evidence linking the so-called Billstrom gang to the kidnapping and or involvement in the "case."

"I don't have to convince you that Linda Billstrom was telling the truth in her testimony. I don't have to because the evidence she gave has been corroborated!" he said.

In all, Meshbesher's "closing argument" took over five hours. The strange part of it was, he was so animated and held such a presence in the Court room that the audience, did not get bored, but sat there in "rapt" attention as to what he was saying!

At the end, Thor Anderson again pointed out that the "positive identification" of Larson by two witnesses, and Mrs. Piper's identification of Kenny Callahan was enough to convict both defendants.

"She remembers a profile, and said it was implanted in her mind and that it will be there until the day she dies," Anderson said. "She knows that the 'profile' of Callahan is the one that she saw in the woods."

(This is how the re-trial of Donald Floyd Larson and Kenny Callahan ended. The rest was up to the Jury.)

XV
JURY
REACHES VERDICT!

After weeks of testimony, numerous hours of "closing arguments," and literally "years" of frustration, there was finally a "verdict!"

Even after all of these painstaking plans, hundreds of hours of preparations and again hundreds of hours of testimony, the jury had reached a decision in only THREE HOURS!

Some whispers in the Courtroom suggested that this was much too short of a time for a "favorable" verdict in regards to the defendants.

Both Donald Floyd Larson and Kenny Callahan were found "guilty" in their first trial two years earlier. Was this going to be "just another letdown?" Donald had just about lost all trust in the "legal system." Would it let him down again?

As the jurors solemnly entered the Courtroom, you could literally hear your own breath. The silence was so "loud" it was mind shattering!

As the ballot was read, the audience, stilled by the moment, again sat silent, except for one person.

Gloria LeMieux, Kenny Callahan's daughter, screamed, "The verdict was NOT GUILTY!"

POST VERDICT

The first words out of Kenny Callahan's mouth were, "I'm a little pleased. I felt fairly confident all along. I've been living day by day for the past two and a half years, I'm going home now, but there will be little celebration. I just wish my friend Donald could be going home with me!" There were tears in his eyes as he glanced at Donald Larson, his "life long" friend.

(Donald Larson would not be going home. This victory was "bitter sweet" to him. It had already cost him more than any human can imagine. He was doing a "life sentence," which would not have been, had it not been for the "Piper Ordeal!" The so-called "Piper Kidnapping" caused the deaths of at least "six" individuals. There were those who disappeared, never to be heard from again. Families were torn apart, lifelong enemies made. It is believed that within the state of Minnesota, no other crime has caused or created the consequences that the "Piper Crime" created. No matter how you look at it, it was and shall remain a "crime!" Whether it was a true "kidnap for ransom," or a "scam" perpetrated by the "Pipers," it shall remain a "vicious crime!" The repercussions were horrendous!

The "crime of the century" as it was called, created many questions. How could a

U. S. Entity, such as the FBI, allow its "soldiers" to operate in such a "half-hazard" manner? How could it be so "under-managed" as to condone the ineptness of its operative's actions in and concerning the "Piper Case?" Is the FBI so far above the "law and morals" of our land that it can just "snub its nose," and say, "Fuck the public?" It certainly looks that way.

Agent Peter Neumann had "balls enough" to offer Donald Larson a deal that would insure that he would get out. Now that he had been found "Not Guilty" of the "crime" which cost the deaths of his family and the "reason" for his being in prison, shouldn't his "offer" work just the opposite? Shouldn't the "deal" now be, "Well, Mr. Larson, we're sorry about the "life sentence" you have, and the loss of your family, by the way, we are actually partially responsible for that, through our "ineptness" and our "rush" to find a "patsy" for the crime, so that we could gain the notoriety and fame which we, the FBI are so well known for! Would not that be fair?)

The "cabinet maker," formerly of Minneapolis, and currently living in Cumberland, Wisconsin, said he had no firm plans for the future. He had been free on bond since the FBI's "fiasco" had started.

Every penny that he had managed to save, everything he built and worked for was now so mortgaged that he would never get out of debt, but at least, he was "going home!"

Donald Floyd Larson was told to "stand up" by deputies. He was then handcuffed and brought back to the prison in Stillwater Minnesota, where he would serve another "fourteen years." He would then be transferred to the "Medium Security" Prison, located in Faribault, Minnesota, and would be housed in the senior's Unit, designed for the aged, incompetent, and physically handicapped.

It is now 2007, eighteen, (18) years later. At this time Donald is close to eighty years old. He has a total of over "thirty one" years in prison now.

Through the mis-deeds of the FBI, its snitches, and informants, Mr. Larson is plagued, basically by what all of "them" caused. (Let's not forget, Donald Larson does not say that he is "without guilt." He still has dreams, every time he goes to sleep, about what he has done. He cannot forget it. He does insist that, he never "intentionally" killed anyone. He did not have any "notion" to go to his farm, catch someone stealing from him, nor of having this person attack him.

Had it not been for the "greedy bastards" and the "agents" looking for fame, and for the "snitches" looking for deals, Mr. Larson's story would never have been, nor would it ever be told. Why? "BECAUSE THERE NEVER WOULD HAVE BEEN A STORY TO TELL!

Larson's Attorney, Bruce Hartigan, and Callahan's Attorney, Ronald Meshbesher, said they were pleased with the outcome of the trial.

Meshbesher stated, "I thought we had it in the bag when the Jury came back so quickly. I suspect the case was decided by lunch." He was playing with a "good luck penny" that his daughter had given him that morning. He added, "The first case should have been an acquittal, but we had a 'fluky jury'. It is unfortunate that everyone had to go through it again."

The eight women and four men began deliberating on the evidence about 11 AM. They discussed the case for one hour, took a short lunch, and then voted. It was unclear in talking to the jurors, if the votes were for "guilty" or for "undecided." One juror said there were two who did not understand the case, as they should have.

The jury discussed the case for another two hours, and shortly after two PM, the second vote was taken. This time it was unanimous for "acquittal."

"We just figured there was a lack of evidence," one juror stated.

Another Juror, Henry Wills of Farmington said, "All the way through the trial we just didn't have the kind of evidence that we could have decided any other way."

Carol Larkey, a juror from St. Paul, said they discussed all of the evidence during the relatively short deliberation. "We all agreed there was not enough to convict them," She said.

Neither Hartigan nor Meshbesher could pinpoint any one piece of evidence that they thought made the difference in this trial, although they did say they took greater pains preparing the cases, and also to the fact that they called more witnesses.

"To speculate, I think the jurors thought the whole case was lousy," Hartigan said.

Several of the jurors who were contacted, refused to discuss the details with the press. They would not say that Billstrom's evidence was an important factor or not in their decision to acquit.

District Court Judge Donald Alsop told the jurors after the verdict, they could talk to reporters about the case, but that anything they say could be used in legal motions brought to later, "test" the verdict.

With the verdict through, there appeared to be no further steps available to or for the Government to pursue in the "case against Larson and Callahan."

Thor Anderson stated these words after the verdict was read, "I feel the trial was a fair one." He added "that's the price we pay for the jury system is some acquittals, but the jury system is worth it. It's important the system be preserved. I have no resentment."

Anderson said he did not know on what the jury based its decision, but it may have been a disadvantage for the FBI to have said twice that, "a fingerprint found in the kidnap car wasn't Larson's" and then later say "it was."

That fingerprint was the center of much testimony and controversy during the eight week trial.

Many allegations of misdeeds surrounded the "print" on whether the print was manufactured, or altered. It was revealed that there were at least two negatives of the print, not one as was originally believed.

Meshbesher said the question of the print is one that he would want investigated further, with the FBI.

Whether the fingerprint had been altered was not discussed during the first trial, and the print was viewed as key evidence in linking Larson to the crime.

Piper had not previously been able to identify Callahan in a lineup or court. However, she said on the witness stand that she had recognized Callahan by his left profile when she had testified six weeks earlier.

Callahan said that he couldn't explain why she decided to identify him. "Mrs. Piper had many occasions before, to look at my eyes and my profile in better lighting and didn't identify me. I don't know how to explain it!"

Larson was identified by a woman during the trial who was working in a Rochester bank when some of the "ransom money" was passed in 1974, and by the owner of drugstore where keys for the "Monte Carlo" used in the kidnapping were made, or duplicated. Neither one had made these identifications before.

"The last minute attempt by Mrs. Piper showed that the Government was stretching," said Meshbesher. "This case shows that 'eyewitness identification' is worthless. A lot of innocent people have gone to jail by the use of 'eyewitness identification'."

Callahan and the two Defense Attorneys said they were uncertain what impact the Billstrom testimony may have had on the outcome of the trial, Meshbesher said the demolished fingerprint evidence, plus the

Billstrom testimony of Russ Boswell, definitely weakened the Government's case.

Do the defendants and the Lawyers think that the Billstrom gang did the kidnapping? They all agreed that they did not know who the kidnappers were.

The verdict leaves many questions yet to be answered. Where in the hell did all of that money go?! Was there actually a "million" paid out? Was it all a hoax? Besides the supposedly "million paid out," was there actually an insurance claim paid to the Pipers for a million? Did the death of Bob Billstrom have anything to do with the "Piper Mystery?" What "Payoff" was he waiting for? After the two "off duty" cops shot Billstrom, is it true they opened up their own "private detective" agency? What happened to the two maids? Is it true that a few of the "twenties" turned up in Germany? If the money was ever put in the trunk, and the only person to have driven it was Harry Piper, and the car was under scrutiny at all times by either Piper, his brother in law, or by FBI Agents, just where the fuck did the money go? Come on, give us a break! There are just a few things that just do not add up.

Within the last few years, there has been a "renewed" interest form Harry Piper the 3rd, concerning the Kidnapping of his mother, Virginia Piper. He states he wishes to write a book. The FBI has refused to help get him any information, even though a Judge has ordered them to disclose the information. The paperwork and records which they turned over to him were "all blacked out!" First, they said "the million in twenties just disappeared" and now so did all of their records!

Does Mr. Piper the 3rd, really want to write a book? Maybe it is better to let "sleeping dogs lie." Who knows? Sometimes curiosity furnishes us with answers we really do not want to hear!

Does Donald Larson have the answers to the mystery of the Kidnapping of Virginia Piper? Does he have any idea how the magical disappearance of the "disappearing twenties" occurred? Does he know where the money went after it disappeared? The answer is an emphatic, "No!"

DONALD FLOYD LARSON TO PRESENT

Donald left the Federal Court Building in handcuffs. He was satisfied with the outcome of the trial and very happy for Kenny Callahan. He was elated that Kenny was going home and could carry on a "normal life."

Nevertheless, Donald thought he would be much happier over the fact that he had been found "not guilty" than he really was.

"Don't get me wrong." He said. "I was happy to be cleared of the kidnapping, but could not, and can never 'shake' the feeling that that damned 'Piper' mess totally ruined my life, and the lives of so many other people. Complete families were ruined, torn apart by what happened. Nothing can ever change that, but I wish people would take into consideration what really happened!"

He stops talking for a few seconds, and then gets a faraway look in his eyes. "You know, I deserved to be charged for what I did.

I know that I'm guilty. The fact that I killed five people never leaves me for ten minutes."

Donald reflects some more. "What really upsets me is that I had no intention of ever killing anyone. There was no plan to do it, and I sure did not want to."

He adds, "If I wanted to kill Falch, I sure as hell would not have done it that way. I didn't care that Ruth was moving away with him. In fact, I was relieved! I couldn't handle her drinking and running around. When it became clear she was gone, it took a lot off my mind."

Donald takes another drink of his Pepsi, then says, "Ya know, the part that bothers me is the fact that when I caught him stealing my tools, he attacked me. I actually thought he was going to kill me. I've never had anyone that mad at me before in my life. The look on his face scared the hell out of me. His eyes were crazed!

After taking another sip of his Pepsi he says, "Then he hit me! From that point on it was a 'living nightmare'. Now it's over, there's nothing left. Why the hell did he have to hit me?"

"I'm going to sleep now he says." And after taking another sip of his Pepsi, he laid down, curled up, facing the wall. He looked like a real tall, skinny kid.

Donald Floyd Larson used to weigh well over three hundred pounds. In Stillwater, he was always well over two hundred. He would eat at least five, six or maybe even more meals a day, with many bowls of ice cream in between.

In Stillwater Donald worked in the Infirmary. He worked in a large "Dorm" where most of the men were dying of one thing or another. Some had AIDS, others cancer, some bad hearts, some, just old age and yet others whose livers or kidneys gave out.

Donald's duties were to take care of them as best as he could, with what the Institution would furnish him with. (What the "joint" did not furnish him he would somehow "find" on his own with the help of a friend, and when it came to friends, he had an endless supply!)

Donald's patients were never wanting. He kept them well fed, clean, and smiling. He would sit with many, actually holding their hands and talking to them as they passed on to a better place.

In health services, they had their own kitchen. The food would come from the main kitchen, but there were diets, and "special" meals. There were refrigerators, freezers, and milk coolers in the Infirmary kitchen.

Donald had friends that worked in the main kitchen. He also had a couple "guard" friends that worked in the Infirmary, along with all of the nurses.

He had an endless supply of food, he had roast beef for sandwiches late at night, rolls and donuts, cake, bacon-n-eggs, ham, pork chops, pie, and one more thing, ice-cream!

Donald had an endless supply of ice-cream! He and his "cronies" as they were called would sit past midnight, watching TV and eating quart after quart of ice cream. His friends may have been "terminal" but he kept them smiling! After some of them died, he would receive letters from their families and loved ones, thanking him for the wonderful care he bestowed upon them.

Donald worked at this job until 1993. He was told one evening to "pack up!" He was headed for Faribault, a prison of "medium security!"

When Donald got to Faribault, he was placed in a Unit for "old timers," "handicapped," "sick," "diseased," and some "mentally ill."

One nice thing was that he knew almost everyone there. He says that he knew some of the guys from the "Redwing Boys Training School, from back in the 40's"!

The big thing about Faribault was the fact that you could cook all of your meals yourself. You could buy hams, roast beef, roast pork, bacon, bread, chicken, ribs, and just about anything else you wanted. Donald was in "hog heaven!"

He weighed over two hundred pounds when he got here. Within a few months, he was knocking on the three hundred pound door.

Even at that size, he stayed healthy. He did a lot of walking, and for work, he took care of a quadriplegic we call "Darb." He would help him in and out of bed, in and out of his "electric wheel chair," in and out of the handicapped shower, and whatever else he needed to do to keep "Darb" happy.

On his "off time," he would eat! He could handle numerous meals a day.

In June of 1997, he was really surprised when, who walked in the door, but Seamus D. McGee, his old buddy from past years.

Though they were good friends, and had known each other from back in the "fifties," there was another reason Mr. Donald Floyd Larson was so happy. Seamus was known to be a "pretty good cook," and within a week, Donald, Seamus, a guy by the name of Bubba, and Steve Anderson, Kenny Bliss, and Boyd Smith were eating like kings! There was a full meal every night, with dessert! There were barbeques, ice cream, and watermelons. Everyone was doing great. Most of the guys had their own refrigerators, and a ready supply of foods. What the "State" did not furnish, you could buy yourself.

Then things started to change. An outfit by the name of "Mincor" took over. Pretty soon you could no longer order any of the foods that needed refrigeration, because they took the refrigerators. Then they took the barbeques, then all coolers, then quit furnishing the "food staples," such as milk, potatoes, fruit, vegetables, flour, and on and on. The only food you got was at mealtime, and if you got caught taking food out of the "chow hall" they would "write you up" and charge you $10.00 for food that was yours. That meant bread, apples, oranges, crackers, or whatever.

The only thing you can buy at the canteen now is "junk food so to say!" No real quality anymore. You can buy single slices of "spam," and "peanut butter," but there is no bread, so what's the sense of the other things?

Other than that, you have two "soda" machines, a "candy" machine, and a "frozen food" machine. You can buy a "tasteless" small pizza, or a "bar" of ice cream, or a $3.00 burger. Or you can buy two "White Castles" for a buck and a half!

Donald, doing a life sentence was given a "ten year" continuance in 1990. He completed that in the year 2000. He was given a 3 year continuance at that time. Attorneys Ron Meshbesher and now Judge, Bruce Hartigan gave their support and also attended the hearing. The "Commissioner of Corrections and Head of the Parole Board," told Donald to take an "anger management class," and to keep a clear record, and to prepare for parole. He was told he was "given a road map," and that if he followed it, he would be paroled.

Donald did everything he was told to do. His son actually built a new house and built a "special addition" for Donald to live in so he could be "independent," yet have his family close.

In the meantime, Minnesota got a new Governor, who appointed a new Commissioner of Corrections. Both the Governor and Commissioner said on TV that there would be no more parole for those convicted of "first degree murder!"

The day that Donald walked up to the office where they hold the "Parole Hearings" at, he walked with shoulders squared and back. He had a smile on his face. This was the day that he had waited all of these years for.

Fifteen minutes later, Donald Floyd Larson came walking back, with head bowed, shoulders slumped! The new Commissioner, Joan Fabian, continued his case another TEN

YEARS!! When Donald's son, who was present, asked, "How and why did you do that?" She replied, because I am the new Commissioner and I can do what I want to. She said she did not have to follow what the old Commissioner said or did!

This was like a death sentence to Donald. At that time, he weighed well over 200 or more. Since then, he has dropped to about 135 or 140 lbs. He is skin and bones. He fell down not long ago, went to the "outside" hospital for x-rays and observation. He had bruises all over his head, neck, and body. It is a wonder he did not die! He went to sleep "standing up!"

Donald no longer talks to people. He used to "talk to anyone who would listen!"

Now, he works his five hours a day, making wooden toys for underprivileged children, eats his sparse three meals a day, and then sleeps! He must sleep at least sixteen hours a day!

There is no "spring" left in his walk! In fact, since he fell, he is now in a "wheel chair!" There is no "ready smile" left on his face, just a sort of "blank look" like someone just waiting for it to end! It is the same look as those in a crowded, understaffed nursing home have. He has that lost, alone, no one who cares kinda look. Just waiting!

Kenny Callahan is dead now. He used to visit Donald faithfully for all the time he has been locked up. Kenny died while shoveling snow a couple years ago. Tommy Grey is in tough shape now as well and cannot get here to see him either.

Another person, Steve Anderson, who was a millionaire, died a few years ago. He also promised Donald a home and a free place to live on a farm, where he would have a garden for him to putts around in. Steve's death also hurt Donald.

Donald has also lost his interest in sewing. He used to make bed covers. In fact he won a "Blue Ribbon" at the Minnesota State Fair for one that he entered in a contest. There aren't any more "treasure maps" sold for ice cream. Now, if someone gives him an ice cream, he'll simply say "thanks" walk back to his room, eat the ice cream, lay down and go back to sleep again.

Every evening, Donald and Seamus have "soup and a sandwich." The little bit of food that they can bring back from the kitchen, plus some they can buy from the canteen. Together this has to suffice for their needs.

Recently, Donald seems to be doing a little better. Seamus seems to think it's from his "cooking of the soup!" However, in reality, it is probably because he, Donald, does not seem so lonely, now that Seamus is his "room-mate."

Donald's complexion is now "white." This is from lack of the "outside." He has lost all desire to sit outside and visit.

Seamus says, "A couple days ago, I asked Donald how he was doing."

Donald answered matter of factly, "I'm ok, but I'm old, and I'm dying!" These words are very real but harsh words and just about left Seamus speechless. He said it sounded "so real" that it actually scared him!

For the last couple of years, Donald has been trying to get into the "Courts," but so far he has had no luck. His reason for filing a "Writ" is because the "Department of Corrections" in reality has promised him an "out date," which was in the early nineties! This date is of course long passed.

Every "Convict" gets a printout from the "records department." It gives your name, your charges, the time or sentence that you received, and when you came in. It also gives an out date.

The Department says that the "out date" on paper, which they gave Donald, is a "mistake!" They say that they did not have the proper "form," and put it on the one they gave him because it was all they had!

It seems ludicrous that this can happen; lead a man, for years, to believe that he is getting out on a certain date, allow him to make plans, allow his family to make plans, only to "dash" those hopes with utter disregard for their behavior. If this is not "total disregard" of "moral" and "equal" treatment, what then is?

Why should a "Commissioner" be allowed to make what should be a "moral and rightful" decision, and instead, make one for the benefit of "political greed?" The "deliberate indifference" to Donald's needs and rights surpasses all that is "morally correct!"

Where does this story go from here? No one knows! Will Donald end up just another "forgotten soul," left to perish in prison? Donald really does not want much out of the rest of his life, he just wants to go fishing a couple of times, and sit down to some "real food." And lastly, "but certainly not the least on his wish list" (It's more like his first!) Donald wishes that his last few years could be spent with his loved ones closely surrounding him up until his dying day and not spent in a cold lonely cell!

THE
END?

DEDICATION

   This book is dedicated to the late Kenny Callahan, a true friend throughout a lifetime, and to all the other friends who have passed, along the way.

   It is also for those who remain; those who have known all along, the truth!

   It is for those who languish in prison throughout all of the USA, for crimes they are not guilty of.

   This is for all of my friends, in and out of prison, who have steadfastly remained so for the last "thirty-odd" years! (*D. F. Larson*)

By; *Seamus 'D' McGee*

Post Script: Recently, October, 2007, two Student attorneys from Hamlin University Law School visited Donald. They are trying to get Mr. Larson Paroled because of medical conditions. In the last couple of months he has been taken to the local Faribault hospital twice. One was for a "heart attack" and it is believed the other time was for pneumonia. His health is not very good and he is slowly wasting away. In addition, his memory seems to be slipping a little, but once in a while a "twinkle" will show, and he'll prove that his sense of humor is still there. Needless to say, there is no reason on this "good green earth" for Donald Floyd Larson to stay in prison any longer. He spends most of his time in a wheelchair, and gets pushed to wherever he needs to go to.

About a month ago, two Hennepin County Detectives paid Donald a visit. They told him that Harvey Kerignan, aka "Harve the Hammer," who is serving time in Stillwater Prison, told them that Mr. Larson did indeed pull off the Piper Kidnapping!

As was stated in the contents of this on-going saga, it is quite obvious who was involved in the kidnapping of Virginia Piper, Mr. Kerignan, himself being one of the main players. It is felt that there must be a reason for this untruth. No doubt there is money involved. Mr. Kerignan will never breathe a breath of freedom. Wanted in various states in the US of A, there are a couple states that would like to put him to death. It has been stated that he quite possibly is the most prolific "Serial Killer" in the USA, having killed as many as 112 young girls and women.

One individual has stated that "The Hammer" has incurable cancer, and is making a bid to be allowed to be paroled to a hospice.

The FBI knows who did the "caper," yet refuse to come forward and admit their blundering acts. *(This furthers the belief that the FBI cannot be wrong, even when they are.)*

Hopefully, Donald will soon be allowed to live out the time he has left, and be allowed to enjoy a few more fishing trips with his son Harold.

 *Seamus 'D' McGee*

UPDATE

(Today, Jan. 3rd, 2008 Donald Larson and Seamus 'D' McGee (AKA) were called to visit with two Hennepin County Detectives. (Or were they?) Could it be they were under the "hire" of the Pipers, who have been trying to write a book?)

The detectives seemed very vague about what their names were, and as of yet Mr. Larson and Mr. McGee have not been able to identify them.

It seems that they want to know about Donald's involvement in the Piper Case. A person mentioned in this book, Harvey Kerignan has evidently "owned up to" his part in the Piper Kidnapping. He said that Kenny Callahan and Donald Larson were involved in it also. Why he would make this up, only Harvey knows. Everyone who knows Harve also knows that he is prone to prevarication. Is he writing a book? It is possible. Someone said he is almost dead. Could he be telling his life story? He has nothing to lose

Donald is shocked, and does not know why he would make something up like that. He has asked, "When is this all going to end?" He said he's tired of being hounded for over thirty years.

Does this mean that there will need to be a sequel to "The Piper Pays?" Is there yet more intrigue?

(New news! The names of the two detectives that were here are: McKayne and Gullickson.) (Both of these gentlemen said they were not here to work on any "Cold Case Files." If that is not the reason they are investigating, then why are they investigating? Are they "moonlighting" for someone, such as one of the PIPERS? Could be huh?! When they were here visiting, they were adamant that the "senior" Pipers had nothing to do with the so called kidnapping. Why would they try to stress that belief? There is no reason to convince me, or Donald Larson. I really do not want to write another "part" to this book, although, if I could find out where the missing money is, it would make an interesting ending.)

(Donald Floyd Larson has been transferred to a hospital. He suffers from what the institution calls a "pressure sore" on one of his feet. It started as what looked to be a blister, and within two days turned into an infected sore. Nurses would come in his room every other day and change the bandage on it. He also received a couple pills each day to fight the infection).

(Finally it got so bad that his foot and ankle began to swell, and he could no longer stand on it. It also had a rancid odor to it.)

Is this how it ends? Are there no more chapters? Will Donald Floyd Larson simply fade into the past as so many others before him have? Will he be remembered? By those who know him? He will! We certainly shall miss him. We already do! He always had a story to tell, about places he'd been, and things he'd done. The best part was you never knew if they were entirely true or not. You never cared though, because you knew he believed them.

Final Chapter

Regretfully, Donald Floyd Larson has gone to a much better world. We, his friends, shall certainly miss his wit, his smiles, and his ways. He was truly a "character!"

Donald Floyd Larson 11/5/26 to 6/21/08

Your earthly days are over.
All trials and pains are past.
And in the arms of our Savior,
You are finally free at last!

Accept His hand, let Him guide you.
Don't worry nor have a fear.
You are finally freed from your troubled past.
So please don't shed a tear.

Don't worry about the scars of earth.
Your new home is surely blessed.
With all the things you've dreamt of,
Are yours for the very quest.

And as you wend down that golden path,
And glance from side to side,
There with arms out reaching,
Are your friends with smiles of pride,

There's Kenny Callahan and Tommy Gray,
And the others who went before.
They quickly join and walk with you,
As you enter the golden door!

We on earth have a last request,
We're sure will be no fuss.
Please ask the Lord as he greets you,
To save a place for us!

> "God Bless You Dear Friend"
> From,
> All of your old friends

www.ingramcontent.com/pod-product-compliance
Lightning Source LLC
Chambersburg PA
CBHW020251030726
47499CB00001B/149